Capture of the *Defiance*

Breaking Free series

By S.E. Smith

Acknowledgments
I would like to thank my husband Steve for believing in me and being proud enough of me to give me the courage to follow my dream. I would also like to give a special thank you to my sister and best friend, Linda, who not only encouraged me to write, but who also read the manuscript. Also to my other friends who believe in me: Julie, Jackie, Christel, Sally, Jolanda, Lisa and Jake (who loved Voyage), Laurelle, and Narelle. The girls that keep me going!

I would also like to say a very special thank you to Hsu Lee. Her kindness and consideration in supplying me with Author Survival Packs at the conventions the past few years has been wonderful. Thank you, Hsu!

—S.E. Smith

Montana Publishing
New Adult\Action\Adventure\Fiction
Capture of the *Defiance*: Breaking Free series

First E-Book\print Published January 2017
Cover Design by Melody Simmons

Summary: A young woman's trip to join her grandfather on his sailboat turns into a deadly race when he and the *Defiance* are taken, forcing her to seek help from old friends to discover what happened to him before time runs out.

ISBN 978-1-942562-85-6 (paperback)
ISBN 978-1-944125-01-1 (eBook)

Published in the United States by Montana Publishing.

{1. New Adult – Fiction. 2. Thriller – Fiction. 3. Action/Adventure – Fiction. 4. Suspense – Fiction. 5. Romance – Fiction.}

www.montanapublishinghouse.com

Synopsis

New York Times and USA TODAY Bestselling Author S.E. Smith returns with an emotionally charged action adventure thriller filled with suspense.

Makayla Summerlin is excited to join her grandfather, Henry, in Hong Kong during a college break. She plans to help him sail the next leg of his journey around the world on the *Defiance,* but events take a frightening turn when her grandfather is kidnapped and the *Defiance* disappears! Unsure of what to do, Makayla reaches out to an old friend for help.

Brian Jacobs' work at the Consulate General in Hong Kong is just a stepping-stone for his political career. His life for the foreseeable future is carefully optimized for success, but everything is turned upside down when he receives a frantic call for help from a friend. Their meeting quickly turns into a race for survival when Makayla is almost kidnapped in front of him. Seeing Makayla again awakens old feelings inside Brian and he knows he will do everything he can to help her, no matter the cost.

When the situation turns deadly, both Brian and Makayla find unexpected help from another old friend and a Hong Kong detective. Together, the four race to find Henry and protect Makayla. Their efforts to unravel the mystery of why a wealthy crime lord would target Henry and Makayla; and to find the *Defiance* will take them further than they ever expected to go, but will they be able to discover the truth before time runs out for Henry?

HONG
KONG
HONG KONG ILLUSTRATION

Table of Contents

Chapter 1

Hong Kong

The figure of a man pushed through the crowds gathered along the Graham Street Market, uncaring of the curses he was drawing. Sweat beaded on his brow despite the cool breeze and temperate weather. His gaze swept the collage of faces. Almost immediately, his eyes locked with the intense, dark gaze of a man searching the crowd – for him.

Gabriel Harrington swallowed and backed away. He stumbled when he ran into an older woman who turned and began admonishing him. Pushing past her, he ignored her tirade when she continued to yell after him. His frantic flight that had started earlier that morning was now one that meant life or death.

Turning sharply, he cut between two of the merchants' booths, pushing the colorful material hanging down on display out of his field of vision as he rushed through. He had already past the irritated merchants before the men could say anything. He made another sharp turn along the sidewalk toward the busy intersection, urgently glancing behind him.

If he could just get across it, he could lose himself in the crowd of pedestrians.

The skin on the back of his neck tingled and he could feel the sweat sliding down between his shoulder blades under his shirt. He slipped his hand into his pocket for the small box. It was still there.

He breathed a sigh of relief and glanced over his shoulder again. Slowing to a fast walk, he relaxed a little. He didn't see the man who had been following him. Reaching into his pocket, he pulled out his cell phone and quickly dialed the number he had memorized.

"Do you have it?" The voice on the other end asked in a terse tone.

"Yes, but I'm being followed," Gabriel muttered, glancing both ways before entering the intersection.

"Where are you?" The voice on the other end demanded in a brisk tone. "I'll send backup."

"I'm leaving the market near Shelter Cove. I'll… Shit!" Gabriel hissed, pausing about three-quarters of the way across the intersection.

"What is it?"

"There are two of them," Gabriel said hoarsely. "I'll try to get the package to you."

"I have a team en route," the man said.

"It's too late," Gabriel replied with resignation, turning and seeing the other man he thought he'd lost standing not more than fifty feet from him. "I'll hide the package and notify you of the location as soon as I can."

"Negative," the man hissed, but Gabriel was already turning to cross the intersection at a diagonal angle.

He had only taken a few steps when he saw a third man appear on the corner in the direction he had been about to go. Twisting, he bumped into an older man carrying several canvas shopping bags. Gabriel muttered an automatic apology under his breath, even as his hand slipped the package from his pocket and into one of the bags. His gaze swept over the old man's face, trying to memorize it before he backed away.

He darted across the intersection. He was almost to the curb when a van, trying to beat the red light, turned the corner. Gabriel registered the impending impact just seconds before his body hit the windshield. He rolled several feet before coming to a stop. In the distance, he could barely make out the old man turning to see what had happened before everything went black.

* * *

Makayla looked around the Customs area of the airport from her place in line. There was a sea of people arriving from all over the world. Her lips curved upward when she saw a harried mother trying to grab a wayward toddler in front of her. The smile turned to a sympathetic grimace when the little boy started crying when his mother picked him up.

Several people standing behind her gave the woman an annoyed glance.

Makayla started to turn away when she noticed that the woman had dropped her passport on the ground when she had bent to pick up the little boy. With a murmur, she motioned for the two people behind her to go ahead. With a tired sigh, she waited until they had passed her before she stooped to retrieve the fallen documents.

"You dropped this," she murmured, glancing at the woman's name on the open passport. "Would you like some help, Hsu?"

"Oh, yes, please," the woman stuttered, startled, before she breathed out a tired sigh. "It has been a long trip."

"Where are you traveling from?" Makayla asked politely, adjusting the diaper bag that had fallen off the handle of the stroller before she pushed the baby carriage forward along with her own carry-on.

"Seattle," Hsu replied with a grateful smile. "Thank you so much for your help."

"You're welcome," Makayla replied with a sympathetic grin. "My name is Makayla, by the way."

"That is a beautiful name," Hsu responded, moving forward with the line. She gave a relieved groan when she saw they were next and awkwardly adjusted the little boy who had finally fallen asleep on her shoulder. "I think I can put him in the stroller now."

"Oh, yes," Makayla said, quickly moving the diaper bag so that Hsu could carefully place the sleeping boy in the stroller.

"Where are you from, Makayla?" Hsu asked politely, straightening and placing a hand on her lower back before she took the diaper bag Makayla was holding. "He is getting heavy."

"I'm from Florida," Makayla said, adjusting her backpack on her right shoulder. "He looks it. How old is he?"

"He will be three next month," Hsu replied before she turned to the Customs agent. "Thank you again for your help, Makayla. I hope you have a pleasant visit in Hong Kong."

"You too, and good luck!" Makayla replied, watching as Hsu push the stroller up to the window.

A moment later, it was Makayla's turn. She walked up and presented her passport. The agent behind the window briefly glanced up at her and then down at her passport.

"What is the purpose of your visit?" The agent asked in a cool, disinterested voice.

"Vacation," Makayla replied with a polite smile.

"Are you traveling alone?" The man asked, suddenly more focused on her when he looked up from her photo to her face.

"No, I'm joining my grandfather who is already here," she replied, keeping the smile on her face, even though the man's sudden assessing gaze was making her uncomfortable.

"How long will you be staying?" The agent asked with a smile.

"A week," Makayla answered.

She quietly answered several more questions before she breathed a sigh of relief when he stamped her passport and handed it back to her. She quickly passed through the gate and into the main section of the airport. She was relieved to get out of the crush of people. Fortunately, she was able to bypass the wait for baggage claim. Twenty minutes later, she was in a taxi heading for the marina where her grandfather was docked at the Royal Hong Kong Yacht Club in Shelter Bay.

Sinking back into the seat, she stared at the tall buildings and crowded streets. She didn't even want to think about how the taxi driver was able to navigate through the streets without hitting either a pedestrian or another car. All the sights, sounds, and colorful assortment of people were overwhelming for her exhausted brain.

"Is this your first visit to Hong Kong?" The driver asked, glancing up in the mirror before returning his gaze to the road in front of him.

"Yes," Makayla answered, staring out the window.

"You have friends here? I can tell you the best places to go for young people," he said, laying his hand on the horn when a car cut in front of him. "There are lots of young people here."

Makayla shook her head. She knew he would think she was strange if she told him she preferred to be in places where there weren't that many people, or buildings. That was one reason she had gone into the field of study that she had chosen in college. As a marine biologist, she could escape from the mad rush of urban life and spend most of her time either in a lab or on a research ship.

"No, thank you," Makayla finally replied when she realized that the driver was waiting for her response. "I'm meeting up with someone."

"Okay," the driver replied.

He finally took the hint that she wasn't a very talkative passenger and refocused his attention on the traffic instead of her. She knew she was attractive and was used to drawing men's attention. It wasn't that she was a beauty. She wasn't delusional enough about her looks to think that. It wasn't until she had overheard a couple of guys talking about her in one of her classes that she finally realized what it was about her that drew attention.

It wasn't her looks, but her attitude and appearance of aloofness that was like a red flag to guys. They liked the challenge of trying to get her to open up for them. She had never been very social and really didn't care to be around a lot of people. It had taken a while to finally figure out it was a defense mechanism – a wall between her and the world. Deep down, she knew it was probably because of the way she had been raised. Oh, she didn't blame her mom. Her mom had enough baggage without Makayla adding to the load. Makayla had learned at an early age that life could suck, and she didn't want to fall into the same dark hole that her mom had.

Her gaze softened when she thought of her mother. Her mom had been doing so much better since she married Arnie Hanover three years ago. Makayla liked Arnie. He had been there for her mom, supporting her, encouraging her, and calmly waiting until her mom was ready to take control of her own life. It was something that Makayla had secretly wished for through the years, but had doubted would ever happen.

Pushing the memories back into the box that she kept them in, she refocused on the landscape. It took her a moment to realize they were already traveling outside of the city. It would take almost an hour to get to the yacht club. Henry, her grandfather, had offered to pick her up, but Makayla had told him it didn't make sense for both of them to spend the money to take a taxi to and from the airport. It would give her time to unwind as well.

Makayla leaned her head back and closed her eyes. At twenty-two, she was fortunate enough to be in a better position than most girls her age. Her father had died before she was born, but he had left a trust fund that she had inherited when she turned twenty-one. The fund had grown over the last twenty plus years, and while she wasn't wealthy by most standards, she had a nice nest egg that had allowed her to focus on her education without having to worry about how she would pay for it. Between the trust fund income and the summer internships that she had worked, she had never had to touch the principal to live on. It also helped that she didn't need much. When living in a small dorm room or on a research ship, there wasn't a lot of room for material things.

Makayla opened her eyes when she felt the taxi slow down and turn. She blinked her eyes to clear the gritty tiredness from them. She sat forward when she realized that they were turning into the yacht club.

She quickly fumbled for the information her grandfather had sent her and her passport to show identification to the security guard at the gate. She pressed the button on the window when the guard leaned down to talk to the cab driver.

"I'm here to see Henry Summerlin," she stated, holding out the documents showing Henry's membership card and her ID. "He should have notified you that I was coming."

"Good afternoon, Ms. Summerlin. Welcome to the Royal Hong Kong Yacht Club," the security guard greeted in a polite professional tone. He glanced at the documents before returning them to her. "Mr. Summerlin is located in E40. Please go down to the turning circle. It will be located on the third turn. Have a nice day."

"Thank you," Makayla murmured, impressed with the efficiency of the guard.

Her gaze swept over the man's immaculate uniform of dark bluish-gray pressed slacks and white short-sleeved shirt with the emblem of the yacht club on the shoulders. The man's black hair was cut close to his head, and his dark brown eyes were as warm as his greeting. A small, relaxed smile curved Makayla's lips. The journey from the airport had been less stressful than she had feared.

Within minutes, the red and white taxi drew to a stop at the beginning of a long dock. She could see the numbers depicting the dock slips in several different languages. She quickly leaned forward and paid the driver before grabbing her carry-on and backpack. She drew in a deep breath, relieved to have finally having arrived from Florida, pushed open the door, and stiffly slid out of the taxi.

Chapter 2

Makayla rolled onto her toes and stretched the soreness out of her muscles as the taxi pulled away. She glanced around and lifted her face to the fading sunlight. It felt good to be out of the cramped confines of the airplane and taxi, and to be out in the wide open spaces again.

She shielded her eyes and gazed around her. In the distance, she could see low mountains behind the tall high rises of the city overlooking the sapphire blue waters of the bay. Excitement filled her when she stared out at the variety of sailboats, powerboats, and multi-million dollar yachts either berthed or anchored in the surrounding waters. She couldn't help but shake her head at the thought of how out of place Henry's small sailboat must look there among the larger vessels.

Adjusting her backpack strap on her shoulder, Makayla bent and pulled up the handle of her carry-on and headed down the long dock. She gazed across the long line of boats to the coastline, enjoying the gentle, cool breeze against her face. The temperature was a nice seventy degrees Fahrenheit, but she knew it was expected to drop after sunset.

Her steps slowed as she came closer to the slip where she could see the *Defiance* moored. A slight movement and a tuft of gray hair peeking out near the back of the sailboat told her that Henry was there and probably working on one of a probably endless list of repairs. A rueful smile curved Makayla's lips. She had once heard that the acronym for the word 'boat' was 'bring on another thousand'. She imagined that was true, especially if you owned a sailboat and were sailing it around the world.

"You know, old man, I heard tell that the two happiest days in a man's life are the day he buys a boat and the day he sells it," Makayla called out in greeting.

Henry turned in a quick circle, surprisingly fast for a man in his late sixties and grinned up at her. He wiped his hand across his cheek, leaving a dark smear of grease above the silver whiskers that coated the lower half of his face. The smile on her lips grew when he realized what he had done. He muttered a soft curse and pulled the rag out of the back of his pocket and scrubbed at his cheek while staring up at her.

"Well, seeing that I'm not of a mind to do either one at the moment, I guess you'll have to wait to find out," he replied with a huge grin. "You made it."

Makayla nodded and looked over the deck of the sailboat. "Yeah, I made it. It's good to see you, Henry," she said, pushing the handle of her carry-on down and handing it to him when he reached up for it.

"You, too, girl," Henry murmured, setting her bag down and reaching up to help her onto the sailboat. "I'm glad you're here," he added, pulling her into a tight bear-hug the moment she was on board.

***

Makayla finished stowing her clothes in the cabinet that Henry had emptied for her. It didn't take long. She glanced up through the companionway and saw that the sun was about to set. Quickly pulling out some lunch meat, cheeses, and condiments, she prepared two turkey and cheese sandwiches on whole wheat with a side of potato chips. She grabbed two bottles of water out of the small refrigerator, carefully balanced them with the stacked plates, and slowly climbed the steps.

"Perfect timing," Henry said with a grin. "I just finished cleaning up. Let me go wash my hands. Mm, that looks delicious. I haven't eaten since this morning. I wanted to have the blasted engine maintenance done before you got here, but had to wait on a part."

"No problem," Makayla replied, placing the plates and bottled waters down on a teak table that Henry had cleared and uncovered. "Take your time. I'm going to enjoy this beautiful sunset."

Henry chuckled and looked over at the mountains. "It is a beauty, isn't it? I'll be right back. I might take a quick shower as well," he muttered with a wrinkle of his nose. "I stink."

"I wasn't going to say anything about that, old man, but since you brought it up, you smell like a diesel engine," Makayla laughed, relaxing against the seat and laying her arm along the back of it.

She affectionately watched Henry head down the steps muttering about ungrateful passengers. She chuckled and tilted her head back to look up at the sky when he disappeared from sight. She took in a deep breath, and held it for a few seconds before releasing it. She gazed upward, staring at the faint dots of light beginning to appear. Against the darker backdrop, she could just make out the first few stars that were beginning to shine through the twilight hues.

Her mind drifted in a kaleidoscope of thoughts and images. She turned and tiredly rested her chin on her arm. The last six years of her life had been a blur of activity. It was hard to believe so much had happened in such a short span of time. Most of it had been good, but some of it had been sad as well, she thought.

"Why the sad face? You aren't having second thoughts, are you?" Henry asked, emerging from the galley.

Makayla turned and smiled. It was a good thing Henry was practically bald on top, otherwise his hair would be sticking up everywhere from the way he was rubbing it dry. As it was, it looked like he could use a haircut for the sides. She'd have to see if he had any electric clippers on board.

"I'm sorry about Breaker," she murmured, twisting back around. "He was a good dog."

Henry grunted and hung the towel over the side of the opening to dry. He grabbed two beers out of the refrigerator while Makayla watched him in silence. He twisted the tops off and held one out for her.

"I think we can celebrate your arrival and Breaker's long life with a beer instead of water," he said, picking up one of the plates and sitting down. "He was a damn good dog. It'd be hard to find one like him again, so I didn't bother trying."

"Kind of like Grandma?" Makayla asked with a raised eyebrow.

Henry's hand paused as he raised the bottle of beer to his lips and he shook his head. He took a long swig of it before he set it down on the table. Makayla could see the amused twitch to his lips and in his eyes.

"Anyone ever tell you that you are a lot like your Grandpa?" Henry asked, picking up his sandwich and taking a bite.

"Only everyone who knows you," she retorted, picking up her own sandwich and biting into it. "So, tell me about your trip so far. How was the trip from Australia?"

They spent the next three hours eating, drinking, and talking. Makayla slowly felt her body relax from a combination of exhaustion and contentment. It felt good after the exhausting flight. Being back on the water aboard the *Defiance* soothed her soul. She raised her hand to smother a yawn. She should have stuck to the bottled water, she thought, lowering her second bottle of beer.

"So, are you seeing anyone?" Henry suddenly asked.

Makayla blinked and dropped her hand to her lap. Her lips pressed together and she rolled her eyes, a habit that she thought she had given up when she was sixteen. Leave it to Henry to bring up her love life on the first night.

"That is none of your business," she replied, lifting the bottle of beer and finishing it. "You know most grandfathers wouldn't give their grandkids a beer, don't you?"

Henry shrugged and grinned. "You're over twenty-one and won't be driving. Plus, I hoped between the jet lag, exhaustion, and the slight buzz that you might let me know if you've found someone," he said.

"Well, you've got those three things right, but I'm not talking," Makayla retorted, pushing up off the seat and lifting a hand to her head. "I'm done for the day."

"You get some sleep. You can have the front bunk and I'll take the one in the galley. Don't worry about this stuff, I'll clean up," Henry instructed, rising to his feet.

"Thanks. I'll be more coherent tomorrow," she replied, holding onto the side of the companionway to keep from stumbling.

"Makayla…," Henry called quietly.

Makayla glanced over her shoulder, her foot on the first step leading down into the galley. She could see the love and concern in his eyes. A part of her wanted to look away, while another part wanted to reassure him that everything was fine. In the end, it was the need to reassure him that won.

"I'm okay, Henry. You don't have to worry about me. I'm not broken. I've just been a little busy with school. I haven't exactly been out of touch with the world, either," she murmured. "I'll see you in the morning."

"Have a good night, sweetheart," Henry said after searching her face to make sure she was telling him the truth. He seemed satisfied with what he saw there. "I'll see you in the morning."

Makayla nodded and made her way down the steps. She passed through the galley, grabbed her small toiletry bag from off the shelf, and made her way to the head. It didn't take her long to brush her teeth, hair, and wash her face. She didn't bother with a shower. She was too exhausted and would probably fall asleep in it. Instead, she changed into a pair of pajama pants and an oversized T-shirt.

She barely made it to the bed before she collapsed. Rolling, she pulled the covers over her and wrapped her arms around the pillow. For a fleeting second, the image of a face from her past flashed through her mind before it was gone. Makayla didn't even bother trying to hold onto it. The memory was gone before she knew it, lost in the fog of her exhaustion. She was too tired to think about anything but sleep at the moment.

Chapter 3

Two days later, Makayla sat back and gazed out over the water. She could already feel the itch to leave. She refocused on where she was polishing the safety railing. Henry had made some modifications to the *Defiance* over the last few years to make it more of an ocean-going vessel. She was still amazed that he had made it over halfway around the world already. This would be her fifth time joining him en route and the longest distance since he had started.

"What do you think?" Henry asked, standing near the mast.

Makayla glanced over her shoulder and raised an eyebrow. "I try not to," she joked, watching an expression of exasperation cross his face at her snarky response. She laughed and turned to face him. "I was just thinking how impressed I am that you have made it this far. It is an incredible feat. You know, Mom still thinks that you've totally lost your mind."

Henry bent and sat down next to her. She could see the thoughtful expression on his face while he gazed out across the harbor. His fingers played with the wire he was holding, rolling it back and forth between them.

"I've been smart about it," he commented, turning back to face her. "I watch the weather and stay in the major shipping lanes. I've made some of the longer legs along with other boats. I've been planning this trip my whole life and I have to admit – I don't have a single regret. I've seen places and met people that otherwise would have been impossible."

"You've also had a few close calls," Makayla reminded him. "The Philippines…."

Henry waved his hand. "I know, but that's life. There are never any guarantees. One thing your grandmother made sure I never forgot was that there are never any guarantees in life. Her death was a huge blow not only to your mom, but to me, Makayla. When Mary Rose was dying, she made me promise that I wouldn't let fear stop me from living my dreams. She reminded me every day to grasp life with both hands and live it, because as she pointed out, you never knew when your last day might be. I raised your mom and uncle as best I could. I wasn't perfect, but I can say I did my best. Having you back in my life made me realize just how fortunate I am."

Makayla sat in silence for a brief moment before she shook her head. "I think that's the longest thing I've ever heard you speak," she reflected with a grin before it faded and she grew serious. "You did good, Henry. Mom doesn't blame you for what happened in her life. And as for me – well, I'll be the first to admit you changed mine," she said in a quiet tone, glancing away to look at the water again.

"You already had a good head on your shoulders, girl. You just needed to know what you had inside you," Henry replied in a gruff tone. With a grunt, he stood up. "I'd better get the wiring completed if we are going to leave the day after tomorrow. We'll be following a couple of cargo ships down to Guam, then over to Honolulu."

Makayla nodded. "I saw the charts. It's good to know we won't be alone. The Pacific Ocean is a mighty big place to get lost in," she said, picking up the polish and pouring more onto the rag she was using.

"There's a market about a mile or so from here. I've got a couple of bikes and thought we could stock up on some supplies later," Henry commented. "I went there the day before you arrived. They have a nice selection of items."

"That sounds like fun," Makayla said. "I could use some exercise."

Henry nodded. "Looks like a good day to go, tomorrow it's supposed to rain," he reflected. "I'd better get the new wire run for the lights if we want to be able to see where we are going."

Makayla turned back to her task. Henry turned on some music and all around them other boat owners talking could be heard. She glanced up when she saw a helicopter flying over the marina. Shielding her eyes, she saw it land on a yacht anchored offshore.

"That must be nice," she muttered under her breath before a familiar song caught her attention and she became lost in it while she worked.

* * *

Makayla brushed her hair out and twisted it up into a messy bun. Several strands of dark brown hair fell and she impatiently tucked them up into the mass of twisted hair. Her gaze flashed to the clock on the microwave.

"Henry, if we are going to go shopping, we need to do it before it gets much later," Makayla said, grabbing a pile of canvas shopping bags from off the table. She frowned when she heard Henry's muffled reply. "What?"

"I've got at least another hour or two of work," Henry said, glancing up at the sky. "I need to get this done now, especially since the front is expected to move through starting tonight instead of tomorrow."

Makayla could see the frustration and regret on his face. She could also see the dirt and grease. Shaking her head, she glanced up at the sky before looking at him again.

"I can go," she said. "It isn't far. I saw it the other day when the taxi brought me here. I'll go get what we need and be back before the weather turns bad. If you need my help here, we can wait and go tomorrow."

Henry gave her an appreciative smile and shook his head. "If you can go today, it would be better. I'm not that wild about shopping, if you remember. At least if you go, I know we'll have something worth eating," he said.

Makayla nodded her head in agreement. They had been living on turkey and cheese sandwiches for the past two days. She had quickly discovered that was all Henry had in his refrigerator. At least he had also purchased some bread.

"If you're sure you've got this, I'll handle the food," Makayla promised, stepping up onto the back of the sailboat before jumping down onto the dock.

"Coffee!" Henry called out behind her. "Don't forget the coffee."

"I won't," Makayla responded, placing the canvas bags in one of the baskets attached to the bike Henry had placed on the dock. "Anything else?"

"Just whatever you want," Henry said, already focusing back on the wiring. "Don't talk to strangers."

Makayla didn't even reply to Henry's last comment. Instead, she adjusted the small purse she had draped across her chest and slid the straps of her empty backpack on. Grabbing the handlebars of the bike, she turned it and pushed it up the dock. Once at the end, she slid her leg over and kicked off.

She enjoyed the exercise of riding the bike. She followed the road around to the front entrance. Raising her hand in greeting to the security guard, she rode down the short drive before turning right onto the bicycle path.

* * *

"What did you discover?" The man standing in the elegant office overlooking the bay asked.

Sun Yung-Wing poured himself a cup of tea from the small, antique silver teapot. The steam rose from the delicate white china teacup. He lifted the fragrant brew to his nose and inhaled with appreciation. The tall, slender, elegantly dressed man that had entered the room politely waited until his employer turned before he answered.

"Mr. Harrington is still in a coma," the man stated.

Yung turned to look at the new man in charge of his security. The last one was now at the bottom of the ocean. He carefully studied Ren Lu. The man's slender frame, perfectly cut black hair, and calm face were very deceptive. There was an air of something dark and barely controlled under his polished exterior. Ren Lu had dispatched with his previous boss without hesitation when Yung gave the order after the man screwed up with dealing with Harrington.

"He is still alive?" Yung asked with mild surprise.

"Yes, Mr. Sun. Until we can locate the information that was stolen, I thought it best not to kill him. There is no guarantee that he will survive. If he wakes, I have personnel in position to extract the information before eliminating Mr. Harrington," Ren Lu explained in a quiet tone.

"And what are you doing about locating the information that was stolen from me?" Yung asked in a deceptively pleasant voice before he took a sip of his tea.

Ren Lu stared back at his employer with a cool confidence. "I have accessed the security cameras situated around the marketplace. I was able to narrow in on an encounter Mr. Harrington had with another individual shortly before he was struck by the van. The video was inconclusive, but I believe Mr. Harrington may have given the information to the man. There is a section of the video where it looks like he pulled something out of his pocket. It is unclear if the American was a contact of his or not."

Yung walked silently over to his desk and placed the teacup down on it before he pulled out the chair behind the desk and sat down. Sitting back, he once again studied the man in front of him. The recent discovery of Harrington's double cross had stung. He had prided himself on his ability to recognize someone who was being deceptive.

"Have you located this individual?" Yung asked.

"Yes, sir. The American has a vessel berthed at the Royal Hong Kong Yacht club," Ren Lu replied.

"Bring him to me," Yung ordered. "I have business offshore. I want no mistakes this time. I want the information that was stolen returned to me and anyone involved eliminated."

"Yes, sir," Ren Lu replied with a slight bow.

"Mr. Lu," Yung said, stopping Ren Lu when he started to turn.

"Yes, sir?" Ren Lu responded.

"Remember what happens to those who fail," Yung stated in a cold voice.

"Yes, Mr. Sun," Ren Lu replied, bowing his head once again.

Yung watched his new security chief exit his office. He sat in silence for several long minutes before he reached for his cell phone. Pushing his chair back, he rose and walked over to the floor-to-ceiling, tinted glass windows and stared across the bay. In the distance, he could see the marina in question.

"Send for the helicopter," he ordered his assistant on the other end.

With a press of the button, he disconnected the call. This was one situation where he would need to be personally involved. There was too much at risk. If his clients were to discover that their identities and locations had been compromised because of him, the United States and British governments would be the least of his concerns.

Chapter 4

Henry grumbled a curse under his breath before it changed to a grunt of satisfaction when he finally threaded the wire through the narrow opening. The blasted wire that had taken almost an hour to run only took two minutes to hook up to the back of the last light. Of course, it had been the last one, which made it even more frustrating.

He quickly sealed the end of the wires in shrink wrap to prevent corrosion from the salt water and sealed the area around the light before tightening the stainless steel screws. With a quiet groan, he straightened and tilted his head to listen when he heard the sound of footsteps on the ceiling above him. A sigh of relief escaped him that Makayla had made it back safely and before the rain started.

A grimace crossed his face when he realized that he would need to clean up the galley before they could stow the groceries. He bent to pick up the Philips screwdriver and extra wire. A rueful grin curved his lips and he started to turn around when he saw a shadow pass between him and the entrance to the companionway. Turning, he froze in confusion when instead of Makayla, a tall, slender man wearing black stood in the opening.

"Hey, what are you doing on my boat?" Henry demanded in a gruff tone. "This is a private vessel."

The man's face remained eerily immobile. Henry could feel his gut twist in warning. His hand automatically tightened on the screwdriver in his hand. The marina was guarded with security personnel and cameras, but that didn't mean that crime couldn't still happen.

His gaze swept over the man silently watching him. There was something off about him. This wasn't some ordinary punk looking for a few dollars. Hell, the man's shoes alone would probably pay for his dock rental for a month. No, this man exuded power – danger – and he was here for a different reason. Henry would bet the *Defiance* on that.

He drew in a deep breath and slowly raised his gaze back to the man's face. Henry's fingers flexed on the items he was holding in his hand. If he was going to make it out of this situation alive, something told him he needed to be smart about it.

"I don't have much money if that is what you are after. Kidnapping me wouldn't even buy you another pair of those fancy shoes you've got on," Henry said with a nod. "If that's not what you're here for, state your business."

"You were given an item the other day, Mr. Summerlin. It belongs to my employer. He has requested that it be returned," the man stated, taking a step closer.

"An item…? How the hell do you know my name? Who's your employer?" Henry demanded in confusion before he drew in another deep breath. "Listen, I don't know what in the hell you are talking about. I'm an American. I'm sailing around the world – period. I don't have any item that I haven't brought or purchased. If you're with the police, show me your credentials, otherwise get the hell off my boat."

Henry's eyes widened when he saw the shadows of two more men through the opening. He backed up, but knew he was trapped. There wasn't much room below deck and definitely nowhere to hide, except maybe the head. The idea of locking himself in it was beginning to look very appealing.

"I am not with the police, Mr. Summerlin," the man stated in a cold, steely tone. "The other day in the marketplace, a man bumped into you. He gave you a package. Where is it?"

Henry took another step backwards when the man advanced while he spoke. A confused frown creased his brow. What the hell was going on?

"You mean the guy who got hit by the van?" Henry muttered, shaking his head. "He didn't give me anything."

"He slipped something into one of the bags you were carrying. I want it back," the man continued, taking another step closer until he was within arm's reach of Henry. "My employer has requested your presence, Mr. Summerlin. It would go much easier for you if I were to present both you and the item that was stolen from him."

Henry knew it would be futile to deny that he had whatever in the hell the man was talking about. It was clear that the man planned on taking him whether he had the item or not. Swallowing, Henry could feel the fight or flight adrenaline surge through him. Since he couldn't flee, that left fighting.

Henry threw the wire he was holding in his left hand at the man's face and swung out with the screwdriver in his right. The man countered and Henry grunted, a shaft of pain sucking the breath out of his lungs.

As if in slow motion, Henry saw the man dodge the wire, bring his left hand up, and grab his wrist. He felt the bones in it snap when the man savagely twisted it at an odd angle. The pain sent him to his knees. He gasped, holding his arm against his chest and blinked back the tears of pain clouding his vision. Henry lifted his head and stared back into the man's eyes when his attacker knelt down in front of him.

"I am prepared to break every bone in your body if it becomes necessary, Mr. Summerlin," the man said in a cold, calm voice. "Make no mistake, my employer is more than willing to do much worse to retrieve the information that was taken from him. If you resist again, I will break your other wrist. Do you understand?"

"Yes," Henry hissed out between clenched teeth. "But, for the record, I don't know what the hell you are talking about, and if I had been thirty years younger, I'd be the one calling the shots."

The man tilted his head and studied Henry for several long seconds before a hint of a smile curved his lips. It wasn't a pleasant smile, but it was at least a reflection of emotion which his face had been devoid of up until now. Unfortunately, it didn't make Henry feel any better.

"Perhaps, but you will never be thirty again," the man finally remarked in a quiet tone before he rose to his feet and spoke in a dialect unfamiliar to Henry. "Transfer him to the boat."

That was the last thing Henry heard. He had started to struggle to his feet, but the man had swung back around and struck him on the side of the head with what felt like the butt of a gun. He could feel his body falling over.

Instinctively, he cradled his broken wrist against his chest to prevent it from hitting the floor. His body rolled to the side and Henry foggily registered the trickle of warmth sliding down past his ear. He could add a head wound to his broken bone.

Before darkness washed over him, the fleeting image of Makayla's smiling face flashed through his mind. If there was one shining light to all of this, it was the thought that at least she wasn't here. He could only hope that she was safe.

Chapter 5

Makayla bent and wrapped the bike lock around the metal bars of the bike rack in the small area reserved for bikes near the market. She grabbed the canvas bags that she had brought to carry her purchases out of the front basket, pausing when she felt something in the bottom of the outside bag when she ran her hand over them to flatten them out. Reaching in, she pulled out a small, narrow box. She blinked in surprise before she deduced that Henry must have forgotten it in the bag the last time he had gone shopping.

She slid the box into her pocketbook at her waist. After a quick check to make sure there was nothing else in any of the other bags, she gripped the handles and started across the street toward the market. Her eyes lit up with delight at the wide assortment of stands and shops.

An hour and a half later, the delight had faded and she was grimacing as she adjusted the weight of all the bags in her hands. Still, she couldn't resist stopping to look at the beautiful assortment of straw hats. She already had several but justified her interest because on a sailboat you could never have too many hats.

"Makayla?" A voice asked in shock behind her.

Makayla turned in surprise, her eyes widening in astonishment. The faint image in her mind from the other night was now standing in front of her. Her lips parted and she drew in a startled gasp before her expression clouded with confusion.

"Brian?" Makayla whispered in disbelief.

"It is you! I thought I was dreaming," Brian said, stepping closer.

"I'm surprised you recognized me," Makayla answered without thinking.

A warm blush heated her cheeks when she saw his eyes narrow and he took a step closer to her. She started to move back a step when she saw his hand lift and he tenderly touched a strand of her long, dark brown hair that had come loose.

"I could never forget you," he admitted before clearing his throat and dropping his hand back to his side. "What are you doing here?"

Makayla glanced around before raising an eyebrow. "Shopping," she said.

Brian chuckled and shook his head. "I should have asked 'What are you doing in Hong Kong'," he said with a grin.

Makayla started to lift a hand to push the strand of hair back, but grimaced when she realized her hands were full and she couldn't without setting them down. She started to protest when Brian reached out to take several of the bags from her, but stopped when he gave her a sharp glance.

"These are heavy," he said, weighing them in his hand.

"Yes," Makayla said, pushing the strand of hair behind her ear now that she had a free hand. "I met up with Henry. What are you doing here?"

Brian looked surprised. He glanced around before nodding to a small café across the street. A part of Makayla wanted to grab the bags and run while another part couldn't help but be interested in what he had been up to since she had last seen him almost three years ago.

"Would you like to go get something to drink?" He asked.

Makayla glanced around the market, then up at the sky. She should be getting back to the *Defiance*. She surprised herself when instead of shaking her head, she found herself agreeing. It didn't help that at that moment, her stomach decided to grumble, protesting the fact that she hadn't eaten since early this morning.

"Does the offer come with food?" She asked with a rueful smile. "If it does, then yes."

Brian laughed and nodded. "The offer can definitely include food," he promised, placing a hand on the small of her back and guiding her quickly across the street.

Makayla stepped into the café when Brian opened the door and glanced around the crowded sitting area. Her gaze narrowed on a high top table near the front windows. She automatically moved toward it and placed the bags she was carrying under the window before shrugging off her backpack and sliding it under the table so she could slip her foot through the strap to keep it from being stolen.

Brian followed her and placed the bags he was carrying under the window on the other side of the table before sitting down. Almost immediately, a friendly waitress who looked like she was too young to be serving appeared and asked what they would like to drink.

"Milk Tea, please," Makayla murmured.

"Coffee," Brian replied. "We'll also take two Wonton soups, an order of Sweet and Sour pork and rice, and an order of fish balls, please. Oh, add an order of Pineapple bread, too."

"Thank you," the waitress replied with a friendly smile.

Makayla gazed across the table at Brian with a raised eyebrow. An amused smile tugged at her lips. She hoped he was hungry as well considering the order he had just placed. He grinned back at her before his smile died and a curious light came into his eyes that made her look away.

"So, you are here with Henry? Don't tell me that he is actually sailing around the world," Brian said, briefly sitting back when the waitress placed their drinks down on the table in front of them.

Makayla leaned forward and rested her arms on the table after the waitress left. She ran her fingers along the water droplets on the outside of the cup where it had spilled over the edge. Picking it up, she took a drink before she answered him.

"Yes, he took off a little over a year ago. He's made it about half way so far," she replied. "I've joined him a few times during breaks at school."

"Oh, that's good – a bit dangerous, but good," he muttered, looking down at his coffee. "How is school going?"

Makayla's lips curved in a sheepish smile. "I'm working on my doctorate," she admitted with a wry sigh. "In the field I chose, it makes the most sense and I've been fortunate to have some really great support from my professors."

Brian's eyes lit up with pride. "I could tell you had fallen in love with the ocean after your crazy trip," he confessed. "I'm not surprised. You have an affinity for it."

Makayla swallowed and nodded. Memories of her own teenage defiance flooded her. She fingered her glass, thinking about the voyage that had changed her life. She had been confused, hurting, and angry with life when she had come to live with Henry.

"Nothing like a little teenage rebellion and frustration to make you grow up," she acknowledged. "You have to admit it was pretty awesome as well."

"Awesome," Brian laughed with a shake of his head. "I would have said something more along the lines of insane."

"I would do it again if it meant things working out the way they did," Makayla murmured, staring intently at him. "There is nothing like almost dying to make you appreciate what you have, and what you could have lost."

Brian reached for her hand and squeezed it. "Or being stupid and throwing it away because you are too blind to realize that what you want is right in front of you," he replied in a quiet voice.

He released her hand and sat back when the waitress brought their food. Makayla could feel the warmth of his touch even after he had released her hand. Sitting back in her seat, she remained silent, lost in thought as Brian reassured the waitress that everything looked fine.

Her gaze moved to the crowded market, but her mind was on what Brian and she had been discussing – that autumn six years ago when the anger she had been feeling had overflowed. She had made a decision that would change not only her life, but the life of another boy.

She had been sixteen, a difficult age if everything is going right in your life – an excruciating age when it wasn't. It was the year her mother had finally hit rock bottom and Makayla's life had been changed forever. Her mother had been in an abusive relationship with a loser that had been so bad that Makayla had refused to even think of him by any other name.

Makayla would never forget the day she had been called out of class and told that her mom had overdosed on the prescription pain medication she'd been addicted to. It was the day she had met Henry – and it had been the beginning of a series of events that would propel her and an unsuspecting boy named Tyrell Richards into the International spotlight. It was also the summer she had met Brian.

"Breaker died," she murmured, pulling her thoughts back to the present.

"I know. My folks told me," Brian said, spooning some of the sweet and sour pork and rice onto a plate for her. "Mom tries to keep me posted with what is going on back home. She forgot to tell me about Henry, though."

Makayla picked up her spoon and began eating her soup. "How are your folks doing?" She asked politely.

"Good," Brian replied with a shrug. "They aren't home much. They are having fun exploring at the moment."

"Oh," Makayla muttered. "So, what are you doing here?" She asked, picking up one of the fish balls on her chopsticks and eyeing it with suspicion.

"Enjoying lunch with a beautiful woman," Brian teased, grinning when Makayla rolled her eyes at him. "I work at the US Consulate General as a political advisor among other things."

Makayla knew her eyes were wide with surprise before she remembered that he had been studying Political Science in college. She took a bite of the fish ball and was surprised by the delicious flavors. She quickly added two more to her plate of food.

"Wow, you've done pretty well for yourself," she reflected. "Most Political Science majors end up teaching history at the high school."

Brian's chopsticks paused in midair, and he glanced at her before releasing a chuckle and taking a bite of his own food. Makayla wiggled her eyebrows at him and popped a fish ball into her mouth. He just shook his head at her.

They spent the next hour talking about a little bit of everything. He asked her about her schooling, she asked him about his work. She told him about some of the research she had been working on and some of the explorations she had been lucky enough to join. The one thing they both avoided talking about was their previous relationship or any current ones they might be in. Makayla didn't want to know for fear of bursting the fragile little world they had created for themselves in the café. She had noticed right away that he wasn't wearing a wedding ring, but in today's world, that didn't mean much.

"Have you heard from Tyrell lately?" Brian asked, sitting back with a sigh while a new waitress cleared their table.

Makayla shook her head. "I haven't talked to him in about six or seven months. For a guy who loves social media, he has been extremely quiet lately. The last time I saw him was at his grandmother's funeral. I know her death really hit him hard," she said.

"Oh, I didn't know she had passed away," Brian murmured with a sigh of regret. "A lot of things have changed in the past three years since I left the States."

"Yes," Makayla agreed. "I have to go. I promised Henry that I would be back in a couple of hours. I also don't want to get caught in the storm."

She started to reach for her purse, but Brian grunted that he had it covered. She murmured her thanks and slid out of her chair to gather the bags and her backpack. Brian quickly paid the waitress and helped her with her purchases. They exited the café and turned left to go back across the street. It didn't take long for them to return to the bike rack where Makayla had left her bike. Brian helped her load the baskets.

"It's a good thing there are three of them on this thing," he muttered. "I could put your bike in the back of my car and drop you off."

"No, that's okay. It isn't far to the marina and it is downhill, thank goodness, so it will be easier getting back," she said, suddenly feeling at a loss. "Brian...."

"Makayla," Brian said at the same time that she whispered his name. "Listen, I want to keep in touch with you. Here is my number. Call me."

Makayla took the paper he was holding out and nodded. She looked up at him, wondering... Her breath caught when he suddenly muttered a curse under his breath and wrapped his hands around her upper arms to pull her close.

"I can't believe I let you go," he muttered, pressing a hot kiss to her lips before he released her and stepped back. "Call me."

Makayla didn't say anything, she just nodded. At the moment, she was too overwhelmed with emotion, something that she hadn't experienced since the last time she had been with Brian. Turning, she quickly pushed the bike out onto the bike path and peddled away. Once she was back on the *Defiance,* she would deal with what had just happened. Until then, she would keep it safely locked away.

..*

Brian swallowed and watched Makayla ride away. He didn't realize his fingers were clenched until he felt his cell phone vibrate. Reaching into the front pocket of his jacket, he pulled it out and glanced at it.

No change, the message read.

Brian quickly tapped out a reply before pocketing the phone. Running a hand over his hair, he bit back a curse. Seeing Makayla again had shaken him more than he would have expected. His gaze automatically searched for her, but she was gone. Turning on his heel, he strode through the thinning crowd back to his car. The last few days had been hectic. He knew he probably should have ignored the urge to call out when he saw Makayla, but he had called her name before he had even realized it, held immobilized by shock and disbelief. At first, he had thought he was just imagining it was her. It wasn't until she had turned around and said his name that he felt like he had been sucker punched.

He reached into his pocket and pulled out his keys. Hitting the remote, he unlocked the car, pulled the door open, and slid into the driver's seat. Within minutes, he was navigating his way through traffic back toward the Consulate.

"Shit," he cursed, his mind unable to focus on anything but his encounter with Makayla. "Why now? Why here?"

Chapter 6

Makayla pedaled past the guard house after stopping to show him her identification. The wind was picking up and she could feel the first light sprinkle of rain. She knew her cheeks were a rosy color from the cold, stinging breeze coming in off the water and from her bike ride.

She coasted down the slight slope, turning at the end before pedaling the last few feet to the beginning of the dock where the *Defiance* was moored. It looked like she would just make it before the rains. She could see the line of showers over the mountains in the distance, and the bay, which had been smooth and calm earlier, was now covered in whitecaps.

Makayla threw her leg over the back of the bike and balanced on the left pedal while she coasted the last few feet before hopping off. She steadied the bike when it started to tilt, off-balance from the heavy load of groceries. Walking to the start of the dock, she frowned when she saw a man in black appear further down. It looked like he was on the *Defiance*.

Pushing the bike onto the dock, she slowed when she saw two other black men dressed in similar black clothing appear. It looked as if they were dragging someone between them. It only took a moment for her to realize that it was Henry. She stared at the men in stunned disbelief, unable to comprehend what was going on at first.

"Hey!" She yelled, leaning the bike up against one of the concrete dock posts. "Hey! What in the hell do you think you are doing?"

Makayla started forward in fury before she jerked to a stop when the tall, slender man turned to glare at her. Her eyes widened when he lifted his hand and she saw the gun he was holding. Her body was already in motion even before her brain screamed for her to run. She had turned and started back the way she had come when she felt a savage blow to her back. The force of it knocked her sideways and she felt herself stumble and lose her balance. A moment later, there was nothing but empty space before she hit the frigid water and sank beneath the surface.

* * *

"Get him to the boat," Ren Lu ordered in Cantonese to the two men with him.

He turned and strode down the dock, his gaze searching for the woman who had yelled at him. He silently cursed. It had taken longer than he had expected to extract the old man. The rest of the dock was empty thanks to the coming storm and time of year.

His gaze swept over the bicycle. It was obvious that the woman had just come from the market. He wondered which boat she was on and if there was anyone else that he would have to kill. He stopped and stared down at the dark water. Normally, it would be clear enough to see almost to the bottom, but the rough water and the dark cloud cover made it impossible to see more than a few feet below the surface.

The temperature of water was still warm enough to survive, but he had shot the woman in the center of the back, between her shoulder blades. More than likely, the bullet had severed her spine or punctured her heart. Either way, she would be dead. He waited several precious minutes, searching and listening for any unusual sounds in the wind before he finally turned, satisfied that she was dead.

He ignored the rain that began to fall. Within a matter of minutes, he was on the speedboat that had been docked a few berths down from the sailboat. He glanced back once over his shoulder, a frown creasing his brow as he stared at the receding line of the marina. He would have felt better if he had actually seen the woman's body. He hated loose ends. Turning back toward the bow of the speeding boat, he decided he would send a man to locate the woman's body and dispose of it. For now, he had a package to deliver to his employer.

***

Makayla clamped her lips tightly together to prevent the air in her lungs from escaping. She allowed the weight of the backpack to pull her down below the surface of the water. Once she felt sure that she was down far enough not to be seen, she struggled to push the straps weighing her down off her shoulders and let it drop to the bottom. Kicking her legs, she swam underwater until she could make out one of the pillars holding up the dock. Only then did she slowly release the air she was holding and silently rise to the surface.

It took every bit of her scuba diving training not to gasp out for air once she reached the surface. Instead, she treaded water, keeping her head above the waves, and peered through the slats in the dock. Just as she feared, a moment later she saw the dark shadow of a man in black. He stood on the dock above her, staring down at the water. She could see the black gun clenched firmly in his hand.

Makayla swallowed, fear threatening to drown her more than the choppy salt water. It seemed like forever before the man turned and walked away. She swam under the dock, trying to get a glimpse of the man whenever he crossed one of the drainage grates. There wouldn't be anything she could do, but she hoped for some sign that her grandfather was still alive.

She gripped a mooring line that was hanging down to hold herself in place when she saw the man jump down onto a speedboat. She couldn't see much of it, but she memorized every inch of what she could see, as well as the man who had taken Henry and shot at her. A few minutes later, the boat was speeding across the bay.

Makayla swam further down and grabbed another line. She didn't bother trying to climb out yet. She didn't want to take a chance on being seen and the men coming back. Only when she could no longer see the boat did she swim back to the nearest boat with a dive platform on it. It took several tries before she was able to kick herself far enough out of the water to roll onto it. Her wet clothes were heavy and tried to suck her down. Her back throbbed from where the bullet had struck her. She was just thankful that it had become lodged in one of the items that filled her backpack, probably one of the numerous canned goods or the slab of pork that she had purchased.

With difficulty, Makayla rolled onto her hands and knees before using the engine to help pull herself to a standing position. She was freezing, especially now that she was out of the water and the wind and the rain were in full force. Her teeth chattered and her body felt clumsy when she reached for the ladder. Forcing her body to move, she climbed up onto the dock. For a few precious seconds, her mind debated if she should run or if she should go to the *Defiance*. Finally, it was the freezing cold wind and rain that turned her toward the sailboat. She needed to get dry and warm. Already, she could see the tips of her fingers turning blue.

"Old man, what happened?" Makayla whispered, half climbing, half falling onto the *Defiance*. "What did those men want?"

* * *

Makayla didn't stay in the shower too long. She was afraid that the men might come back. She wanted to wash the salt water off her and she needed to get warm. The hot shower was the fastest and easiest way to accomplish both tasks. She quickly rinsed the soap from her hair and body before turning off the shower. Grabbing the towel, she dried her body before leaning over and wrapping the towel around her hair. It didn't take her long to dress in a fresh pair of panties, jeans, thick socks, bra, T-shirt, and heavy dark blue sweater.

Slowly opening the door, she listened before peeking out of the head. Only when she was satisfied that she was alone, did she step out. She bent and grabbed a pair of black hiking boots out from the storage cabinet under the bed. She sat down on the bench seat by the table and quickly slid her feet into them, weaving the laces through the hooks and tying them.

Her hands trembled when she saw the bloodstain on the floor near her wet clothes. Standing up, she walked over to the dark red stain and knelt. Her fingers hovered over the spot, but she didn't touch it. She glanced around the cabin. The men had been wearing gloves, so she doubted there would be any finger prints.

She needed to notify the police. Her fingers reached for the small purse that she always wore. It was soaked from her dunking in the water. She grabbed it off the floor. Turning, she pulled the towel off her head and spread it over the table. Her fingers trembled as she twisted the catch on her purse. Lifting it, she dumped the contents out onto the towel. Most of the things would be alright once they dried.

Makayla patted the end of the towel over her cell phone, wallet, and other miscellaneous items. Luckily, her cell phone was one of the new waterproof ones. Picking it up, she realized that she didn't have a clue how to contact the police in Hong Kong. Shoving the items back into her purse, she pulled the strap over her head and draped it across herself. She reached for one of the rain slickers that Henry kept near the steps leading up to the wheelhouse, pulled it on, and fastened it before pulling the hood up over her tangled hair.

Seconds later, she was tossing the soaked bags of wet groceries through the entrance of the companionway and onto the bench seat. Once the bike was empty of the heavy weight, she pushed it down the dock and jumped on. Several minutes later and a frantic plea with the security guard, Makayla was in a taxi heading to the nearest police department.

Chapter 7

Makayla rubbed her arms as a blast of chilly air swept through the door when it opened. She turned her head to watch two police officers guiding a very angry man and a pregnant woman into the room and up to the front desk. Despair filled her at the thought of how much time had passed already since the incident down at the marina.

"Mrs. Summerlin," a voice called out.

Makayla started when she heard her name and quickly rose to her feet. She tucked her hair back behind her ear and walked forward to the man standing near a swinging door. She stopped and waited when another officer called out to him. The man quickly answered the other officer before turning to look at her again with an apologetic smile.

"Mrs. Summerlin?" The police officer asked.

"Miss… I'm not married," Makayla replied.

"Miss Summerlin, please follow me," the officer said in a polite voice. "Detective Woo will take your statement."

"Thank you," Makayla whispered softly.

"Detective Woo is one of our finest," the officer assured her, stopping in front of a small office and waving for her to enter. "She will be with you in just a moment."

Makayla nodded and entered the room. She slid down into the hard, dark wood chair, suddenly exhausted. Her hand trembled and she clenched it. She would not fall apart. It wouldn't help. Henry was in trouble and she needed to keep herself under control. Drawing in a deep breath, Makayla focused on regaining her composure. After several deep breaths, she glanced down at her hand – it had stopped shaking. She would handle this just like she had handled the other difficult situations in her life – by staying calm and doing what needed to be done. Falling apart left you vulnerable and weak. She had learned that at a very, very young age.

She glanced over her shoulder when the door behind her opened again and a seemingly delicate woman who was probably only a few years older than Makayla stepped into the room. The woman didn't say anything. She walked past Makayla before pulling out the chair behind the desk and sitting down. She opened the file with the paperwork that Makayla had filled out.

Makayla silently studied the woman while she read over the report. The woman made several notes, glanced up at her a few times, before making several more notations. Since she wasn't familiar with police protocols in Hong Kong, Makayla decided it was better to remain quiet until the woman spoke.

"My name is Detective Helen Woo," the woman finally said, laying the pen in her hand down on the folder and staring at Makayla with a curious, intelligent gaze. "You are Makayla Summerlin?"

"Y… Yes," Makayla started to say. She cleared her throat when her voice broke. "Yes, that's right. I've come because my grandfather has been kidnapped."

"You saw the men who took your grandfather?" Detective Woo asked.

Makayla nodded. "Yes," she said, raising a hand to her throat. "I'm sorry. I was knocked into the water when the man shot me."

"You were shot?" Detective Woo asked, looking at Makayla with an intense gaze. "Where?"

"In the back," Makayla replied. "I had just come from the market. I was wearing my backpack. It was filled with canned goods. It is the only thing that saved my life."

Detective Woo rose from her seat and walked around the desk. "May I see your back?" She asked politely.

Makayla nodded and rose. She shrugged off the rain slicker and laid it across the arm of the chair. Next, she gripped the end of her sweater and T-shirt and pulled it upward, keeping her arms crossed in front of her. She watched Detective Woo walk behind her. Once the woman stopped, Makayla glanced over her shoulder.

"It felt like it hit me between the shoulder blades," Makayla said.

A shiver went through her when she felt the gentle touch of fingers between her shoulders. She winced when the fingers slid over a tender area. The woman's fingers froze and a second later she was returning to her seat.

Makayla frowned and pulled her T-shirt and sweater down before she sank once again into the hard chair. She pulled the slicker off the arm of the chair and carefully folded it in her lap. Biting her lip, she watched Detective Woo pick up the phone on her desk. She spoke rapidly to the person on the other end. Unfortunately for Makayla, the words were in Cantonese and she didn't understand a single thing that was being said.

Less than a minute later, there was a brisk knock on the door before it opened. The man who had escorted Makayla earlier stepped into the room carrying a tray with two cups and a steaming pot. He walked over and placed it on the desk before he murmured something to the woman. She nodded and replied before redirecting her attention to Makayla.

She carefully poured some of the hot tea into the two cups and held one out for Makayla. Makayla smiled her appreciation and reached for the cup. She shook her head when the woman offered milk and sugar. Sitting back in the chair, she studied the woman.

"Did you see a doctor? There is a very large bruise forming on your back and the area is red and swollen," Detective Woo asked.

Makayla shook her head. "No. I knew it wasn't bad enough to see a doctor. I just wanted to get here so I could get help for my grandfather," she said, sipping the tea to keep from saying anything rude – like quit asking questions and just do something!

Detective Woo glanced at the report and looked back at Makayla. "The report you gave is very detailed, but I would like for you to tell me exactly what happened. Sometimes, I'm able to pick up things you may have forgotten or didn't write down," Woo explained.

Makayla drew in a deep, calming breath and lowered the cup to her lap. She wrapped both hands around it, appreciating the warmth from the porcelain. Staring directly into the detective's eyes, she recounted everything that had happened, relaying every detail that she had memorized.

"I'm a scientist," she began. "… A marine biologist. It is important to pay attention to details. I left at thirteen hundred hours this afternoon to go to the market for supplies…."

..*

Detective Helen Woo listened intently to Makayla Summerlin. Every once in a while, she would pick up the pen and write a note on the summary. She was good at what she did because she listened to the people who came in. She also could tell a lot from their body language, a skill not many of her colleagues had developed.

At twenty-eight, she was one of the youngest members of the Hong Kong police force to make the rank of Detective. The only daughter of a district police administrator and British school teacher, she had excelled in all her classes. Her mother had been supportive of her decision to follow in her father's footsteps, though she had felt her mother's concern for her safety. Her father had been slightly less forgiving, drilling her over the dangers and finally taking her under his wing so he could train her himself. Only after she made detective, did he finally admit that he was very proud of her – but still worried for her well-being.

When the report had been first entered into the system, Officer Wang had immediately notified her of the report and that he was rerouting it directly to her inbox. He had said a young American woman had just reported an incident down at the Royal Hong Kong Yacht Club that involved a kidnapping and shooting. Such acts of violence in an exclusive area could have devastating effects to tourism and the economy.

If the area became known for being unsafe, it could quickly create a vacuum for gangs and increased crime. Her responsibility was to take a proactive stance on such crimes and mitigate the situation before it escalated. Over the last decade, crime had continued to decrease with the help of the revitalization of many parts of the city.

Helen was very impressed with the woman sitting across from her. She could tell that Makayla was upset, but she had an almost unnatural control of her emotions – especially considering the fact that she should be dead. The bruise on her back proved that she had been very fortunate. If Makayla had not been wearing the backpack filled with canned goods, Helen had no doubt that she would be dealing with a homicide as well as a kidnapping. The shot had been very precise – sever the spine, pierce the heart. It had been a kill shot. The description of the incident left no doubt in Helen's mind that killing her had been the attacker's intent.

"Are you aware of anyone your grandfather might have angered? Is he involved in anything illegal?" Helen asked, gazing into Makayla's eyes to see if she was telling her the truth.

Makayla held her gaze when she answered. "Henry is a little rough around the edges, but he has a good heart and people recognize that in him. As far as illegal, he is also one of the most honest men you'll ever meet," she replied, her gaze softening. "Our family isn't rich. The *Defiance* looks pitifully out of place in comparison to most of the boats at the marina, so it isn't like he was screaming 'I'm wealthy, come take me'. Detective Woo, I don't know much about crime, but the man who shot at me, there was something different about him – and, I can tell you that the speedboat they were in cost far more than the sailboat my grandfather owned. Something isn't right, I can feel it. I don't know what it is. I just want to find my grandfather."

Helen nodded and stood up. "I would like to see the sailboat," she instructed, picking up the file.

"Finally," Makayla muttered with a sigh of relief and rose to her feet.

Helen chuckled. It was the first uncontrolled response that Makayla had made. Walking to the door, she pulled the long raincoat off the hook and picked up her umbrella. Opening the door, Helen called to Officer Wang.

"Please update the information into the system. I've added detailed information about the suspects. I would like for you to run a search and cross match the description of the speedboat and the man. I would also like to see what you can find out about Henry Summerlin and Miss Summerlin," Helen instructed in Cantonese, handing him the file.

"Yes, Detective Woo," Officer Wang replied, taking the file.

"Mr. Wang," Helen said, touching his arm. "I'll need an expanded search completed – with discretion, of course."

"I will personally conduct it myself," Officer Wang assured her with a bow.

Helen turned back to where Makayla was silently waiting, staring intently at them. She smiled reassuringly and nodded to her. With a wave of her hand, she indicated which way they would go.

"We will take my car," Helen said. "Please follow me."

Makayla nodded and fell into step beside her. Helen slipped her raincoat on and pulled her keys out of the pocket. They walked down several different corridors and past offices filled with people. She was used to the hustle and bustle of the precinct. Several people nodded to her when they passed them in the hall, but like her, they were more focused on dealing with their own issues.

"What information do you want to know about Henry and me?" Makayla suddenly asked, surprising Helen.

Helen paused at the exit to the stairwell leading down to the secured parking garage reserved for employees. She turned to stare at Makayla with a raised eyebrow. Tilting her head, she gave her a curious expression.

"You understand Cantonese?" Helen asked.

Makayla shook her head. "No. I heard you say Henry's and my name to Officer Wang. It wasn't difficult to deduce that you were asking him to find out more about us. It is what I would do," she admitted. "I just thought I could speed up the process a little."

Helen chuckled and pushed open the door. "I hope you don't mind the stairs. I detest elevators," Helen replied, starting downward. "You are correct in your assumption. I like to have as much information as possible on any case. It is better to be informed so that I can make the right decisions. It would also speed up finding out what happened to your grandfather."

"There isn't much to tell," Makayla said, following her. "Henry had his own business for years working on boats. A little over a year ago, he decided to sail around the world. Everyone thought he was crazy, but it was something he's always wanted to do. I've been at college. I've met up with him a few times over the last year to sail with him on portions of his journey. I have a slightly longer break right now before I head out on my next internship with Harbor Branch Oceanographic and decided to make the trip from Hong Kong to Hawaii with him. We were supposed to leave this coming weekend, weather permitting."

Helen stopped and turned on the last step, her gaze lifting to lock on Makayla's face. Her eyes widened with sudden recognition and her lips parted. That was why the names sounded so familiar.

"You are Makayla Summerlin. You are the girl who stole her grandfather's sail boat," she whispered with a combination of awe and disbelief.

Makayla shifted from one foot to the other and glanced down at where she was holding the railing. Helen could see the slight embarrassment on the younger woman's face. Makayla finally nodded.

"I don't think I'll ever live that down," she said with a rueful expression. "I was sixteen."

Helen laughed and turned to the door marked 'Exit'. Through the window, the dark interior of the parking garage could be seen. The sky had grown darker outside and the lights flickered.

"I was at university when your adventure went viral," Helen admitted with a relaxed, warm smile. "I was conflicted by which career choice I should follow. I knew my parents wished for me to do something different, but my heart was in solving crimes and making the world a better place. A group of students were talking about what the boy and you were doing. I watched the videos that were posted."

"Tyrell called it our *'Voyage of the Defiance',*" Makayla muttered, walking over to the passenger side of the car. She paused and looked over at Helen. "I knew I should have drowned Tyrell. I didn't know he was plastering everything that was going on all over the Internet until we reached Tampa."

"I was captivated by your strength, courage, and passion," Helen admitted, staring over the roof of the car at Makayla.

Makayla shook her head. "I just wanted to go home," she whispered, lost in the memory.

"Your journey gave others the strength to believe in themselves, Makayla. I knew then that no voyage comes without danger. Mine was to follow in my father's footsteps. I just needed the courage to believe in myself," Helen replied in a soft voice.

"I still think I should have drowned Tyrell," Makayla stubbornly muttered, pulling open the door and sliding into the car.

Chapter 8

Henry shivered and rolled to his side. He didn't know what hurt worse, his head or his wrist. He decided that each part of his body hurt just as much as the next; so, he just checked off on the mental list he was making of his injuries that he was just in pain. He pushed himself up off the floor in a sitting position and scooted backwards until his back was pressed against the hull of the boat.

"More like a great big bloody ship, not a boat," he muttered, wincing when he tried to move his fingers. "Hell's bell's, you've got yourself into a doozy of a mess this time, Henry Summerlin."

He glanced around the area, trying to see if he could figure out what in the hell was going on and where he was. The room was lit by a single light bulb that swayed back and forth, and the floor rumbled under him. There was a slight dampness in the air. If he had to guess, he was either a long way from the dock or the bay was rougher than it had been.

The metal hull behind him was cool to the touch. He suspected he was below the water level. The room was bare for the most part. There were a few pieces of broken wood, probably left over from some wooden crate or pallet.

A loud hiss escaped him when he stood. The room rocked dangerously back and forth for a moment. Henry placed his good hand on the side of the hull to steady himself until the waves in his head settled down. The first thing he needed to do was stabilize his wrist.

Crossing over to where he could see the pieces of discarded wood, he found a couple that looked like they might work. He picked them up and staggered back to where he had first regained consciousness. Sliding down the metal wall, he pulled out the rag he had tucked into his back pocket earlier and folded it into a long two inch wide band.

Next, he braced his broken wrist on his knees and carefully felt it with his fingers. He could feel where the ulna was broken. It wasn't bad, but it would need to be pushed back into place if he wanted to stabilize it enough to wrap it. Sweat broke out on his brow and he gritted his teeth together. Aligning his thumb over the slight lump where the bone was broken, he wrapped his other fingers around his damaged wrist. He drew in a deep breath through his nose and pushed.

Tears clouded his vision and a low, guttural moan escaped him when the resulting wave of pain hit him, pushed the breath he had just drawn out of his lungs. A shudder went through his body. Tilting his head back, he closed his eyes, willing the pain to pass. In his mind, he tried to focus on all the horrible things he would love to inflict on the slender man with the Arctic expression and his mysterious employer.

"God, Mary Rose, that hurt," he muttered, opening his eyes and blinking away the tears. "Almost as much as the time I put a nail through my foot and you had to pull it out. Do you remember that? Of course, you do. You never forgot anything."

Feeling more composed, he shakily picked up the rag he had folded and placed it on his lap. Next, he placed one of the four-inch by one inch scraps of wood he had found on the rag. Laying his broken wrist on the wood, he braced it with another piece before he bent forward and used his teeth and his good hand to wrap the rag securely around his makeshift splint.

Only when he was finished did he relax back against the hull for a moment. A wry smile curved his lips and he felt along his pocket. His fingers closed over a small, round container. He clumsily reached in and pulled it out. Using his teeth, he gripped the top and twisted it free.

"This might not be morphine, but at least it's better than nothing," he grunted in triumph.

Henry tapped out two painkillers onto his lap. He picked up the small, red pills and popped them into his mouth. Recapping the plastic container, he slid it back into his pocket.

"So, what do you have to work with, Henry?" He quietly asked himself. "Pain killers, a dirty rag, a couple of pieces of broken wood, a pocketknife, and some change that you found when you were crawling on the floor. Not much, old boy," he answered himself with a shake of his head before he laid it back and closed his eyes. "Makayla, I hope you are safe, girl. I hope you are safe."

Henry could feel his body starting to relax. The pain medication was taking the edge off of his throbbing wrist and head, while the brace was providing some support and relief. He shifted on the hard, cold floor. At the moment, he felt every one of his almost seventy years on the planet. He shook his head. He couldn't stop the darkness that was clouding the edges of his vision. He finally gave up and gave into it.

* * *

Ren Lu stared through the binoculars at the marina. He had sent two men back to the sailboat. Their mission was to make sure that the body of the woman remained hidden and to search the sailboat for the canvas bags the old man had been carrying.

His gaze swept along the dock. He scanned over the bicycle the woman had been riding before moving on to the parking lot. A frown creased his brow and he quickly returned his attention back to the bike. He increased the zoom, staring at it. His lips tightened. He reached for the radio at his waist and pulled it free.

"Check the bike," he ordered. "The woman had bags filled with groceries."

His gaze followed the two men in the inflatable dinghy. They were tying off the boat and climbing up onto the dock. They separated, one heading down the dock toward the bike while the other one moved to the sailboat.

"The baskets are empty," the man checking the bike responded.

"There are bags of groceries scattered on the sailboat," the other man said. "Wet clothes are piled on the floor. It looks like they belong to a woman."

Ren Lu's hand tightened on the binoculars. A muscle in his jaw twitched. His gut feeling had been correct. The woman was alive – but, it was worse than that; she was connected with the old man. There had been nothing in the original manifests about two passengers. The report had just mentioned the old man.

"Check the bags for the package," he ordered in a terse tone.

"Affirmative," the man on the sailboat replied.

Ren Lu continued to scan the area. The first man had joined the other. He ignored the bite of the wind and the spray of the water that was kicked up. His focus was on the sailboat.

"Nothing," the man finally replied.

Ren Lu gritted his teeth in annoyance. A movement further up near the main building of the marina caught his attention. He turned his gaze to the dark blue car. It approached the parking area and slowed. He couldn't see the two occupants at first, just that there was a driver and one passenger. His gut twisted. Pressing the button on the side of the radio, he waited until the car pulled to a stop.

"You have company," he said.

"Affirmative," the man replied.

Ren Lu kept his attention on the car. The men were highly trained and would get out without being seen. A low hiss escaped him when the car doors opened and two women stepped out of it. He immediately recognized Detective Helen Woo. He made it his business to know who could and could not be bought. He turned the binoculars toward the other woman.

He immediately recognized her as well. She should be dead. He never missed his target. His gaze swept over her when she walked toward the dock. She was gesturing toward the bike and pointing to where she had fallen in the water. A minute later, both women disappeared from view when they climbed onto the sailboat.

Lowering the binoculars, he stared across the bay. He didn't move when he heard the sound of footsteps approaching over the wind. He finally turned when the man who had approached cleared his throat.

"What is it?" Ren Lu asked in a deadly quiet tone.

"The information you requested has arrived," the man stated.

Ren Lu turned away from the side. "There was a woman with the old man. Find out who she is," he ordered coldly. "And Mr. Arys, this time make sure I have all the information that I request."

"Yes, sir," Arys replied with a bow.

Ren Lu watched the man walk away. He had begun to personally vet all the members of the security team who had worked for his predecessor. Unfortunately, he had only been in this position for a few days and had not yet completed his review. The information that he had been relying on had come from reports generated before his promotion. Regardless, he knew his employer would not see it that way.

His hand automatically went to his pocket when his cell phone vibrated. He pulled it out, knowing that the very man he was thinking of would be on the other end. Tapping the access code, he held the phone to his ear and listened.

"No, the information has not yet been retrieved," Ren Lu replied in a voice devoid of emotion. "I am working on the situation. It will be resolved shortly. Yes, Mr. Sun, I am fully aware of the consequences if I should fail."

Ren Lu pressed the power button on the side of the phone when the line went dead. His gaze returned once more to the marina. Sometimes, it was just better to take care of things yourself, he thought.

Chapter 9

Makayla froze on the step leading down into the galley. Her gaze was locked on the scattered items that she had purchased from the market. Her hand trembled on the teak handle that she was holding. Her eyes zeroed in on her wet clothes. They had been moved.

"Someone's been here since I left," she whispered, turning to look at the woman with her. "Things have been moved."

Helen nodded and pulled the gun at her waist. Her gaze moved over the items. She jerked her head toward the bow of the sailboat.

"It's the sleeping area," Makayla murmured, glancing around. "I had thrown the bags on the bench seats, but all of the items were still in the bags. My clothes – I had dropped in a pile outside of the head."

"Stay here," Helen ordered, stepping over the items scattered all over the floor.

Makayla watched the detective search the front section of the sailboat. She returned and shook her head. Makayla glanced around the area.

"I found blood there," she said, pointing to the area near her clothes.

Helen glanced around to where she was pointing. She bent and studied the spot. Makayla started to look away when a scrap of paper sticking out from the pocket of her wet jeans caught her attention. She bent and gently pulled it free. It was the piece of paper Brian had given her earlier that afternoon. Her gaze moved to the darkness that had already descended outside. It seemed a lifetime ago.

She turned the paper over. The number was blurred from the water, but she could still read it. She carefully tucked it into the back pocket of her jeans with her cell phone before turning her gaze to Detective Woo.

"I've called for a crime scene team. Please do not touch anything else. They will need to go through the sailboat," Helen said.

Makayla glanced around her and shook her head. "The men were all wearing gloves. I don't imagine they changed that when they came back. It looks like they were searching for something," she said in a husky voice. "Can I at least put up the groceries?"

Makayla could see the hesitation on the other woman's face before she shook her head in apology. She understood why, it was just that she felt so helpless. The mess was making the situation seem even worse.

"The team will be here for several hours. Once they have completed their investigation, you can clean up the area," Helen explained in a tone filled with compassion.

Makayla nodded, looking out at the light rain that was falling. It almost seemed like a waste of time. Anything outside would have been washed away and the inside – well, she didn't have much confidence in the police finding anything there, either.

A shiver ran through her, followed by another one and then another one. Makayla knew that shock was beginning to set in. She suddenly needed to get away. She couldn't breathe. Turning, she climbed up the steps and out into the light rain. She pulled the hood up on the slicker she was wearing and stood indecisively looking around.

"Makayla…," Helen began, stopping when Makayla turned to look at her.

"You said that it would take the crew a couple of hours to do their thing, right?" Makayla asked in a strained voice.

"Yes," Helen replied.

"You have my number," Makayla said. "Call me when you are done and I'll come back."

"Where are you going?" Helen asked in concern. "It is not safe to be out on the streets alone at night."

"There's a café about a mile from here. I'll go there. I can get a cab to take me and bring me back," Makayla whispered, suddenly needing to be alone. "I'll stay in the café."

"I will have one of my men take you," Helen instructed, nodding to the assortment of vehicles pulling up in the parking lot. "I would take you, but I must oversee the investigation."

"I understand. Thank you," Makayla whispered, turning when several men and women came up to the stern of the *Defiance*.

Helen issued a swift order in Cantonese to one of the men. He nodded and looked at Makayla. Once again, Makayla felt the isolation of being in a foreign country.

"Officer Lee will take you to the café. I ask that you remain there until I call," Helen Woo emphasized. "Until we know what has happened to your grandfather, Makayla, you could also be in danger."

"I won't leave until you call," Makayla promised.

"Thank you, Makayla. I promise, we will do everything we can to find your grandfather," Helen said.

Makayla nodded and turned to follow Officer Lee. She kept her head down to shield her face from the rain. A brief smile of thanks curved her lips when Officer Lee opened the passenger door for her before hurrying around to the driver's side. The journey to the market was remarkably fast compared to riding the bike. Makayla murmured her thanks and slid out of the car. Minutes later, she was seated in the almost deserted café, her hands wrapped around another steaming hot cup of tea.

***

Ren Lu sat in his car that was parked across from the café. He had followed the long line of police vehicles into the marina and parked a short distance away. He wasn't afraid that the police would find the item that had been stolen by Harrington. Unless they knew what they were looking for, they would overlook it. It had not been in the bags, so either the old man had hidden it or the girl had it. His gut was telling him the latter.

He watched the girl through the window. She looked tired, sitting with her head bowed and her hands wrapped around her drink. He glanced down at his watch. It was twenty-one hundred hours. The café was open twenty-four hours and the few people that had ventured out were beginning to leave. He would wait until there were fewer witnesses to deal with, and then he would go inside.

Ren Lu glanced down and pulled up the file that he had requested. A frown creased his brow when he saw an image of the girl when she was younger, standing on the same sailboat from the marina. His gaze was focused on the expression on her face. It was a haunting image. She was at the helm with her hair blowing and the ocean behind her. Whoever had taken the photograph had captured the moment perfectly. Ren Lu was surprised at the jerk of emotion it drew from him. He began reading the attached article.

Makayla Summerlin stole her grandfather's sailboat in a single act of defiance that would change her life and touch the lives of millions….

Ren Lu glanced back at the image, feeling once again a spark of emotion. The frown on his brow deepened. He read the article. It gave him a better understanding of the woman on the dock who had defied death. When he was finished, he returned his gaze to the café. His eyes narrowed when he saw her paying the waitress and gathering her coat.

He opened the door to his car and slid out. Glancing back and forth, he waited until the traffic cleared to cross it. His hand slid into the pocket of his coat and he wrapped his fingers around the grip of the gun.

* * *

Makayla watched the police car pull away from the curb before she stepped up to the door of the café. Pulling the door open, she stepped inside and looked around. There were only a handful of people in it now. She walked over to one of the booths, slid her rain slicker off and tossed it on the seat before sitting down. Almost immediately, a waitress came to take her order.

"Hot tea, please," Makayla requested in a soft, tired voice.

"Would you like anything else?" the waitress asked when she placed the tea on the table.

"A time machine," Makayla responded before shaking her head in wry amusement. "No, nothing, thank you."

The waitress nodded and disappeared around the counter. Makayla tiredly pushed back her tangled hair with a grimace. She had forgotten that she still hadn't brushed it out. It was going to be a bear to get all the knots out now that it was dry.

She absently finger combed it with one hand while pulling out her cell phone out of her pocket with the other. A piece of paper dropped onto the table. It had been stuck to her cell phone when she pulled it out.

Unfolding the paper, she stared at the blurry numbers. Brian…. He worked at the US Consulate. He might know what to do and at the moment, he was the only one she knew in the country. A part of her was afraid to call him, but the rational side of her knew she had no other choice. This wasn't about her or the feelings she was trying to hide from – it was about Henry and bringing him home safe and sound.

She pulled her hand free from her hair and carefully pressed the numbers. Her hand trembled slightly when she lifted the phone and pressed it to her ear. He answered on the third ring.

"This is Brian," he said.

"Brian…," Makayla's voice faded when her throat tightened with emotion. "Brian… This is Makayla."

"Makayla, I'm glad you called," his voice brightened in surprise and pleasure, and she felt the familiar pull of his deep voice on her emotions.

"Brian, I need… I need your help…. Something… something's happened," she whispered in a thick voice, the tears and emotion she had been controlling threatening to break through the wall she had built around them. She cleared her throat. "I'm at the café we were in this afternoon."

"I'm on my way," Brian replied. "Don't leave. It will take me about forty-five minutes to get there."

"I won't – leave. I'll wait," Makayla promised.

"Are you in danger?" Brian asked in a clear, hard voice, sounding different than she remembered.

"I don't know. I might be," Makayla replied honestly.

"Stay where there are a lot of people," Brian ordered. "I'm on my way."

Makayla hung up the phone and bowed her head. Her hair fell forward, shielding her face in a curtain of dark, brown, tangled strands. She closed her eyes and drew in deep, calming breaths. It was important that she stayed focused.

She sat back and opened her purse to pull out the small notepad she had in it. A grimace escaped her when she realized it was still damp from her swim earlier. She pushed it back in, pausing when it wouldn't slide in as easily as it had slid out. She caught sight of the problem. It was the small box that had been in the canvas bag. She pulled the box out and tucked it in the inside pocket of her rain slicker. Once it was out of the way, the notepad slid into the small purse with no issues.

She pulled out a pen and fastened the clasp on her purse once more. Reaching for one of the paper menus from behind the box of napkins, she turned it over. It was blank on the back. With meticulous care, she began recording everything she could remember on it, including a small sketch of the face of the man who had shot at her.

She jumped when her cell phone vibrated. Glancing at it, she was surprised to see that almost forty minutes had passed. She touched the screen and saw the text message from Brian. He would be there in less than ten minutes.

Makayla looked up when she saw the waitress heading toward her table again and decided it would be best to pay and wait just outside the café. It had a large overhang that covered the metal chairs and small tables right in front of the large, pane glass window.

She reached over and grabbed her rain slicker. Pulling it on, she reached into her purse and drew out several coins. She picked up the bill and walked over to the cashier. With a murmur to keep the change, she pulled the hood of the slicker up over her head and pushed the door open.

Makayla turned left and walked to the end of the set of tables before stepping behind one and leaning against the rough bricks of the building. She was just by the edge of the window and could see the waitress talking to another worker behind the counter. A chilly breeze of damp mist blew past her and she shivered.

She reached into her pocket and pulled out her cell phone to check the time. It was a little after ten o'clock. She slid her hand and the phone back into her pocket, grateful for the warmth of her jacket, and glanced down the street in the direction she thought Brian would come from.

Her body stiffened suddenly when she felt a hand wrap around the inside of her arm, and something hard pressed against her side. She slowly turned her head until her gaze locked with a pair of cold, dark brown eyes. She automatically tried to pull free, but his fingers tightened in warning.

"I wouldn't, Miss Summerlin," the man remarked in a cool voice.

Makayla frowned, anger building up and overriding her fear – anger at the man for hurting Henry – anger at his callous disregard for life – anger that he felt he had the right to harm another. It was misguided, but it was there and she grabbed the emotion with everything she had inside her because she knew if she let the fear take over, she would be dead.

"Where is my grandfather?" She hissed. "What do you want?"

The man studied her mutinous face. She lifted her chin, daring him to deny that he was responsible for Henry's disappearance. For a brief moment, his cold anger changed to something else, something that she didn't understand before his face hardened again.

"You," he replied in a clipped tone before pressing his lips together in a tight, straight line as if he was surprised by his reply.

"Great! A pervert on top of being a criminal," she muttered under her breath with a shake of her head and looked away from him.

Chapter 10

Her softly muttered statement both amused Ren Lu and tantalized him. His fingers tightened on her arm and his eyes narrowed in annoyance at the unexpected reaction he had to the woman glaring back at him. This could create a problem if he wasn't careful.

Distracted by his thoughts, he didn't notice the car that suddenly swerved up onto the curb. His head turned toward the glare of headlights at the same time that pain exploded through his groin. He released his hold on Makayla's arm when she jerked her elbow down and pushed against his chest.

Ren Lu stumbled back into the shadows just as a man threw open the door of the car and jumped out. He slid further back into the alley when he saw the gun in the man's hand. Twisting, he disappeared into the darkness.

* * *

Makayla reacted instinctively when she saw the car coming. She used the distraction to turn into the man holding her and drove her knee into his groin.

She had hoped the move would put him on the ground, but it hadn't. It did give her the chance to pull away from him. Placing both hands on his chest, she had pushed him away from her before turning toward Brian.

She almost stopped when she saw Brian emerge from the car with a gun in his hand. Shocked, she forced her body into motion when he yelled at her to get in the car. A grunt of annoyance escaped her when she started for the wrong side of the car, forgetting in her moment of panic that the driver and passenger sides were reversed to the States.

Jerking the passenger side door open, she scrambled in and slammed the door, locking it for good measure. Her eyes widened when she saw Brian disappear into the dark alley. Afraid that something might happen to him, she fumbled to unlock the door. She was just opening the door again when he reappeared.

She watched him look both ways and slide the gun he was holding behind his back. Her gaze followed him as he walked back to the car. He pulled the door open further and slid into the car before shutting the door.

"Brian…," she started to say.

He shot her a look and shook his head. "Not yet, Makayla, I want to get you out of here," he muttered in a terse tone. "Then, I want to know what in the hell is going on."

Makayla nodded, glancing back at the café as he pulled away. The waitress from earlier and several other people were standing near the front window excitedly talking and pointing. She turned back around and sank back against the seat in exhaustion. Raising a hand to her brow, she rubbed it.

"Are you okay? Did he hurt you?" Brian asked in a harsh, clipped tone.

"What? No, well, yes, earlier, but not now," she admitted in a distracted voice.

"Earlier?" He gritted out the question between clenched teeth.

When he slid around a corner on the wet pavement, Makayla decided it might be safer to wait. She glanced at his face, then down to the hand on the stick shift. His knuckles were white. She fumbled for her seat belt when she realized that she had forgotten to put it on and an alarm began to ping.

They traveled several blocks at a dizzying speed before Brian slowed the car down. She noticed that he kept looking in the rearview mirror. Instinctively, she glanced over her shoulder to see if anyone was following them.

"No one's following us," he said, almost as if he was reading her mind.

"Oh, good," she murmured, folding her hands in her lap. "Thank you… for coming."

Brian took several more turns before he pulled to the side of the road along a line of empty parking spaces. Makayla glanced up, surprised to see that they were in what looked like a business district. Tall skyscrapers lined each side of the road, and unlike most popular tourist areas with their bright neon lights, the area was more subdued.

He shifted the car into neutral and sat looking out at the darkened streets. It had begun to rain again, causing the streets lights to take on an eerie glow through the windshield. She bit her bottom lip when she saw the muscle throbbing in his jaw and his fingers flexing on the steering wheel. He finally drew in a deep breath and released it before he let go of the steering wheel and turned to look at her.

"What happened?" He asked in a quiet, controlled voice.

Makayla pushed back the hood of her slicker and turned as much as she could to face him with the seat belt on. Swallowing, she slowly began telling him about the events that had occurred after she had returned from the market. She reached into her pocket and pulled out the folded menu and held it out.

"I wrote down everything I could remember so I wouldn't forget," she whispered, suddenly drained. "I tried, Brian…." Her voice broke on his name and she drew in a shuddering breath and wiped an impatient hand across her damp cheek, only then realizing that she was crying. "I tried to stop them from taking him, but I couldn't."

Brian took the folded paper from her hand and set it on the console between them. Reaching up, he slid his hand along her cheek. Makayla turned her face into his warmth, needing the contact.

"I know you did, Makayla," he replied in a rough tone. "You did the right thing. I'm just glad you're safe."

Makayla's gaze rose to meet Brian's eyes in the dim lighting. Her lips parted and she drew in a swift breath when he leaned forward and pressed a warm, gentle kiss to her lips. It had been a long time since she'd felt this way – three years to be exact.

..*

Two hours later, Brian quietly closed the door to the bedroom where Makayla was finally sleeping. He walked across the small efficiency apartment, grabbing the computer bag he had placed on the bar stool when they entered. Crossing over to the couch, he turned on the small lamp sitting on the end table next to the couch before he sank down onto the rich leather, and pulled the laptop out. He booted it up and entered his passcode.

He reached into his pocket and pulled out the folded menu that Makayla had given him in the car. He quickly scanned the information she had written down. A swift shaft of admiration shot through him at the details she had placed into categories, as if she were documenting information on a new species of marine life she had discovered.

His gaze froze on the sketch of the man she had drawn. Picking up the paper, he studied the face. She had gone into great detail on the man's eyes. He reached for his phone and snapped a picture of the image. Airdropping it to his account, he quickly accessed the databases he needed. Clicking and dragging the image, he dropped it into the search, he pressed the enter key. He minimized the screen while the facial recognition program ran and brought up another image, one that he had been working on late this afternoon.

His lips tightened when his phone buzzed. Picking it up, he slid his fingers across the screen. He held the phone to his ear and waited.

"No change," the voice stated.

"Increase security. No one who hasn't been cleared goes in or out of his room," Brian instructed, rising from the couch and walking over to the window.

"Already done. Have you found out anything?" The voice on the other end asked.

"Another incident came up that may be connected," Brian said, glancing at his computer screen. "I'm following a new lead."

"Report your findings as soon as you can confirm," the voice replied. "You are the only field agent assigned to this case now."

"Affirmative," Brian said in a toneless voice and disconnected the call.

Returning to the couch, he sat down and stared at the grainy image of Gabriel Harrington and an older man – a man who he knew all too well. His gaze moved down to Harrington's left hand that was partially hidden inside one of the canvas bags that

Henry Summerlin was holding while his right hand kept Henry still.

Brian lowered the screen when he heard the soft ping from the search he had been running. Pulling up the screen, he stared into the face of a young man – a young Chinese officer named Cheng Li Zhang. Brian clicked on the image. There was little information except for his possible date of birth; he had been in an orphanage until the age of nine, and the brief listing of his service record. What drew Brian's attention was Zhang's listed date of death. He clicked on it. Zhang was listed as having been killed when the helicopter carrying ten other men and him had crashed during a training mission. There were no survivors.

Brian closed the lid of the laptop when he heard a faint whimper. Rising up off the couch, he strode back across the living room. He paused outside of the bedroom door, his hand on the doorknob while his other hand pressed against the doorframe. Once again, a soft whimper sounded on the other side.

Twisting the door handle, he quietly pushed open the door and glanced toward the bed. Makayla was sitting up with her hands over her face and her hair falling forward to frame her face. She was breathing heavily and the bed sheets were twisted around her.

Brian walked across the room and sat down on the edge of the bed, grabbing Makayla's right hand when it shot out. A reluctant smile tugged at his lips at her wide-eyed expression. He reached up with his other hand and ran it tenderly across her cheek.

"You're safe," he promised, gently rubbing her cheek with his thumb.

"I was in the water again, only this time I couldn't swim to the top," she whispered, blinking several times to clear her vision. "I dreamed the bullet hit me."

"Shush," Brian murmured, shifting so he could pull her closer to him. "You're safe."

"What if they've killed him, Brian?" Makayla asked in a broken voice. "He's just an ornery old man. Henry wouldn't hurt anyone. What do they want with him?"

"I don't know," Brian said. "But, I'll do everything I can to find out. I promise, Makayla."

Makayla leaned her head against his shoulder and released a shuddering breath before she slowly lay back against the pillows, suddenly exhausted again. She knew part of it was because she was still suffering from jet lag, but the other part was just the emotional drain. Still, she didn't want to be alone.

"Brian, will you hold me?" She whispered, staring up at him.

Brian's throat tightened with emotion. He knew it took a lot for Makayla to admit that she didn't want to be alone, that she needed to be held – that she was feeling vulnerable. This was something he knew would be difficult for Makayla. The glimpse of her vulnerability and her hesitant plea only made his need to comfort her stronger.

He motioned for her to slide over and pulled back the covers. He kicked off his shoes and slid under the covers, pulling them up over the two of them and tucking the sides, making sure that Makayla was covered before he wrapped his arm around her when she turned her back to him. Bending forward, he pressed a kiss to the back of her head.

"What happened to you?" Makayla whispered, staring out the window. "When I saw you get out of the car…. What you did…. You've changed."

"I know," Brian replied in a soft voice, his arm tightening around her. "A lot… A lot has happened since I left three years ago."

"You don't just work for the Consulate, do you?" Makayla guessed, turning to look at him.

Brian was silent for several long minutes. He was torn between telling her the truth or denying it. He did work for the Consulate, just not in the way she thought.

"It's complicated," he admitted. "I do work for the Consulate, but there are some things I do that I'm not at liberty to talk about."

Makayla's lips curved in a rueful smile. "Guns, driving like a professional driver, confronting bad guys, works for the government… Secret Service type moves," she murmured, staring at him.

"Not Secret Service, those guys work for the White House," Brian chuckled.

The smile died on Makayla's lips and she looked at him with a solemn expression. He could feel his stomach clench and he groaned. He pressed a kiss to her forehead.

"More like spy stuff then," she whispered.

"Spies? No, not spies," he replied with a sigh.

"Intelligence," she asked with a smothered yawn.

"Did anyone ever say you are a very tenacious person?" Brian groaned.

"I've watched enough movies to understand when things aren't what they seem. I also know who you were before you left," she said, rolling back over to face the window. "You don't have to say, but I'll figure it out."

"I know you will. I just want to keep you safe," Brian whispered, staring out the window at the falling rain. "Get some rest. Tomorrow is probably going to be a long day."

"A Kingsman," she muttered sleepily.

Brian softly chuckled. "They were British," he said.

"It was still a good movie," she retorted in a barely audible voice.

It took almost ten minutes before he felt Makayla's body relax and she fell into a light sleep. He lay with his arm wrapped tightly around her. The feel of her in his arms and the sweet smell of her hair was a poignant reminder of all that he had pushed away three years ago.

His friendship with Makayla had gradually grown into something more – something richer and more precious – after her and Tyrell's fateful voyage. Like millions of other people, he had been caught up in the *Voyage of the Defiance* as it had become known. It was the voyage of two young people searching for who they were on a journey between life and almost certain death when they were caught in a late season hurricane in the Gulf of Mexico. Once again, Makayla had defied death – a fact that wasn't lost on Brian. His arm tightened around her waist and he pressed another kiss against her hair.

He had followed their journey on social media, mesmerized by the story that was unfolding. Tyrell Richards, a classmate of Makayla's, had almost proved the saying 'curiosity killed the cat' when he had decided to explore Henry Summerlin's sailboat and then fallen asleep on it. What Tyrell hadn't known was that Makayla was in the process of stealing the sailboat to sail from Fort Pierce, Florida to Tampa, via the Straits of Florida – not a smart move for a land-loving, non-swimmer.

Tyrell, being Tyrell, had decided to complete the classroom assignment the teacher had given them. It had been one of those group assignments that meant if they both didn't participate and turn it in, they both failed the assignment and more than likely the class. Tyrell had been desperate to make good enough grades to earn a scholarship.

He decided he would focus on Makayla and his own life since there weren't any other options. Of course, Makayla being Makayla, she hadn't given Tyrell much choice since she refused to turn back. She told Tyrell he could either sail with her or learn how to doggie paddle back to shore.

Tyrell's humorous but heartfelt stories, videos, and pictures had captured the hearts of millions when it went viral, much to Makayla's chagrin. During the journey, a rare and lasting friendship had formed between Makayla and Tyrell. Their friendship had later fired a jealousy inside Brian he didn't know he was capable of feeling, and had eventually driven a wedge between Makayla and himself.

A sigh of regret escaped him. The combination of his being three years older than Makayla and her being away at college hadn't helped. They had spent one amazing summer together after she had finished high school, but the pressures of his new job, her leaving for college, and a mysterious weekend with Tyrell that she refused to talk about, had eventually boiled over into a heated fight and he had walked away. He didn't find out until later – from Tyrell of all people – that Tyrell had been engaged to be married and his fiancée had taken off with his older brother. The incident had left Tyrell stunned, deeply hurt, and in need of a friend who could nurse him through a severe hangover and listen to him unload his anger without judging him.

His life had become more complicated in the last three years. He reluctantly pulled his arm from around her and carefully slid out of the bed. She had fallen into a deep, exhausted sleep. He tucked the covers around her again before he bent to pick up his shoes. Walking to the door, he pulled it open and stepped out once more. He needed to find the connection between Henry Summerlin, Gabriel Harrington, and a dead Chinese soldier. There was too much at stake to let emotions get in the way, but Brian knew it would be impossible now for that not to happen. He had known it the moment he had seen Makayla in the market. This assignment had just become personal.

Chapter 11

Makayla sleepily blinked and stared out the window with a frown. She rolled over onto her back and turned her head. It took a moment for her to remember where she was and why. Pushing herself up, she glanced down at her wrinkled T-shirt. She was still dressed in her jeans and T-shirt. She glanced around the bedroom and saw her sweater draped across a chair that was in the corner.

She lifted a hand and brushed her hair back from her face, grimacing when her fingers caught in a knot. Shoving the covers aside, she slid out of bed before quickly making it. She walked over to the chair and picked up her sweater before walking to the door and opening it. In the other room, she could hear Brian talking to someone in Cantonese.

A moment later he was turning to look at her. Her gaze shifted from his face to his hands where he was holding a bag with a well-known logo plastered across it. Her lips twitched and she raised an eyebrow at him.

"Old Navy?" She asked in a voice still husky from sleep.

Brian smiled at her and nodded. "I thought you might like to take a shower and change into some fresh clothes. I had a friend pick them up for me. I didn't want to leave you here alone," he explained. "I had her pick up some toiletries as well."

"What kind of friend?" Makayla asked before she could bite her tongue. "Never mind, I don't want to know."

"Makayla," Brian said, stepping forward and grabbing her hand when she started to turn away. "…My-seventy-two-year-old-neighbor-that-lives-across-the-hall-and-likes-to-mother-me-whenever-she-can-get-away-with-it kind of friend," he added in a soft voice. "Here, I'll fix us some breakfast while you get a shower."

Makayla stared at Brian for several long seconds before she reached out and took the bag he was holding out. A confused frown creased her brow as she looked back at him. Shaking her head, she looked away.

"You're different," she admitted, turning to gaze at him again.

"I've grown up a lot since I last saw you," he said, reaching up and touching her cheek.

"I have, too," she confessed.

Brian shook his head. "You were always what Mrs. Leu would call an old soul, Makayla. It is one of the things I always loved about you," he confessed before he dropped his hand and turned away. "Go get your shower."

"Yes, sir," Makayla retorted with a roll of her eyes before she could stop herself.

Brian's low chuckle told her that he hadn't missed the irritation in her response at being told what to do. Makayla's lips curved upward and she slowly walked to the bathroom. Shutting the door behind her, she turned the lock and began to undress.

She didn't take long in the shower. She washed her hair, thankful that Mrs. Leu had been thoughtful enough to purchase a bottle of conditioner as well as the shampoo. Rinsing, she turned off the shower and reached for the towel. She quickly dried off and slipped into the clothes that had been in the bag. She was impressed that everything fit, including the lingerie.

A smile tugged at her lips when she saw the brush and a new toothbrush and toothpaste at the bottom of the bag. She brushed her teeth, then brushed her hair out and braided it. Feeling more in control, she replaced the items in the bag. She would need to find out how much Brian had spent so she could reimburse him.

She opened the door and sniffed in appreciation when her stomach growled. Exiting the bathroom, she hurried across to the bedroom. She deposited the bag containing her dirty clothes and the toiletries by the door before grabbing her cell phone off the night stand. A soft groan escaped her when she saw that she had missed several calls from Helen Woo. She also needed to charge it.

She glanced around for her purse. Spying it on the chair along with her rain slicker, she grabbed it before heading out of the bedroom to the kitchen. Her footsteps slowed when Brian turned with the skillet in his hands and gave her a look that caused a light flush of pleasure to sweep through her before she glanced away.

"Thank you again for the clothes. They fit perfectly," she murmured, walking over to the bar and sliding onto one of the bar stools. "Do you have a place where I can plug this in?" She asked, holding up her cell phone.

"Sure, let me finish this and I'll get you an adaptor," he said, spooning some of the eggs onto a plate in front of her. "You liked them scrambled with cheese, right?"

"Yes," Makayla replied, watching him.

"Coffee or tea?" He asked, turning away to place the frying pan back on the stove after dumping the rest of the eggs on a plate for him.

"Tea," Makayla replied. "I'm still not much of a coffee drinker despite Henry's insistence that there is no other drink in the world – well, besides, rum and beer."

Brian chuckled. "I remember drinking all of that with him, and more," he replied, plugging in an adaptor into the wall and taking the cord she was holding out.

"I need to call Detective Woo," Makayla said, plugging her phone into the cord. "I forgot when everything that happened after…."

A shudder ran through her and she closed her eyes for a moment. Her eyelashes fluttered when she felt a warm hand on her chin. She opened her eyes and looked into Brian's warm, serious gaze.

"We'll find him," Brian promised, releasing her chin when she nodded. "Let's eat while the food is still hot, and then you can call Detective Woo. A few extra minutes won't make much difference."

"Okay," Makayla replied, turning her phone off and setting it aside. She picked up her fork, no longer hungry, but knowing she needed to eat. "I should probably call Uncle Jason and Mom and let them know what has happened. I just hate to worry them. There isn't anything they can do, but I think they should know what is going on."

Brian shook his head and his face hardened into the mask that she had seen last night when he had jumped out of the car. It was the face of a Brian that she didn't know. She raised the fork filled with the cheesy scrambled eggs to her mouth and took a bite, forcing her jaw to chew it before she swallowed.

"I think you should wait. No sense worrying them yet. We can find out what Detective Woo has discovered before we make a decision," he responded in a lighter tone. "Why don't you tell me what you've been up to since I last saw you?"

There were three things that Makayla recognized immediately. Primarily that Brian had changed from the carefree guy that she had known in the past, that he had used the word 'we' in reference to himself and her like they were a couple, and that he could change the subject with a skill that showed he was used to commanding a situation. The last observation took her back to the first one – Brian was different.

Makayla tried to pinpoint what was throwing her off balance about him. She glanced up at him and flushed when she saw that he was still waiting for her to tell him about her life. That was when what was different about him hit her – hard. There was an air of danger clinging to him now. Shocked, she lowered her eyes to her plate and stared down at the buttered toast.

"Not much, just school," she finally said, wondering what to do next. "You know I had opted for dual-enrollment, so I had my Associates Degree by the time I graduated from High School. I took as many classes as they would let me at the University of Florida and finished my Bachelor's degree in a year and a half after that. I started on my Master's degree and finished that six months ago. I've been taking classes toward my Ph.D. since then. It helped that some of the internships I've done have gone toward my degree requirements and I've received some very positive support from the scientists I've worked with," she said with a shrug. "I should be done in another year and a half. I would have been finished earlier, but I have taken various breaks to sail with Henry, this time from Hong Kong to Hawaii."

Brian sat back and smiled at her. She could see that he was impressed. For her, getting a good education and focusing on a career was a way of ensuring she was free. It gave her the power to control what happened in her life. She never wanted to have to worry about whether or not she could make it on her own or feel like she needed someone else for her to make it through the day. Deep down, she knew that was a result of her mom's struggle.

"Wow," he murmured.

"What about you?" She asked.

"Not much different," he responded in a light tone. "I'll clean up the kitchen and then you can call Detective Woo. I'd also like to go down to the marina and take a look around the *Defiance*."

"I'll help you," Makayla said, sliding off the bar stool and picking up her plate. "Oh, and Brian...." She paused to make sure he was looking at her before she spoke. "I do better if you ask me instead of telling me to do something."

The corner of his mouth tugged into a wry smile and he nodded. "Noted," he replied, turning to the sink.

They cleaned the kitchen in silence, both lost in their own thoughts. So much had happened in the past twenty four hours that she was still trying to process it. Just before she woke up, she'd had another dream. She couldn't remember what it was at first, but the faint images had returned when she was in the shower – the steely-eyed man from the dock who had shot at her. There was something about the way he had looked at her that reminded her of....

Makayla swallowed and glanced out of the corner of her eye at Brian. There had been the same sense of danger. Shaking her head, she decided she was either becoming paranoid or delusional.

"If you don't mind, can you put it on speaker so I can hear what she has to say?" Brian asked when she picked up her cell phone.

Makayla nodded and walked over to the couch. Sitting down, she touched the screen and accessed her recent calls. She touched the number. It had barely completed the first ring when it was picked up.

"Makayla, where are you?" Helen demanded.

Makayla looked at Brian and scowled. "She answers faster than you do. It took you three rings," she muttered. "I'm with a friend. He picked me up last night."

"You should have called me," Helen replied in a voice tinged with a slight reprimand.

"Detective Woo, this is Brian Jacobs. I work for the United States Consulate. Makayla was attacked outside of the café last night," Brian said in a hard tone edged with a warning – mess with Makayla, you mess with him. "It was the same man that took Henry and shot Makayla."

They could hear Helen Woo's swiftly inhaled breath over the phone. There was a moment of silence before she spoke again. This time, she was speaking in a quiet, urgent voice.

"Where are you?" Helen asked.

"I brought her back to my place," Brian said before Makayla could reply. "I would like to examine the *Defiance* and discuss any information that you have so far, if you don't mind. I have – resources that might help with the case."

"Who are you again?" Helen asked in a suspicious voice.

Brian looked at Makayla. "I've known Brian since I was sixteen. He lived down the street from my grandfather," she replied, staring into his eyes. "He… He can help us find Henry," Makayla replied in a soft voice before turning to look down at the phone in her hand. "I need you to share everything you know with him… please."

Once again, there was silence on the other end. Finally, Helen replied. Her voice was clipped, but professional.

"I will meet you down at the marina in twenty minutes," she said.

"Make it an hour. It will take us that long to get through the traffic," Brian replied.

"One hour," Helen agreed before politely ending the call.

Makayla looked up at Brian when he stood up. "What now?" She asked, rising to her feet.

"We go find out what she knows," he replied, reaching for her hand.

Makayla nodded. "Oh, I need to get my rain slicker. It looks like it is still drizzling," she said, releasing his hand and turning back toward the bedroom.

"Good idea," he murmured, staring out the window.

Chapter 12

Makayla gazed out the window of the car as Brian pulled into the parking lot of the marina an hour later. Detective Helen Woo was already there. She was standing on the dock looking out over the bay. Makayla opened the door of the car and slid out. Shutting the door, she waited until he walked around the car to where she was standing.

Reaching up, she tugged the hood of the slicker up to shield her face from the light rain that was falling. She began to move forward once he reached her side and they walked down the dock to where Helen was standing. In the back of her mind, Makayla couldn't help but think that everything appeared so much different today than it had yesterday.

Her footsteps slowed until she came to a stop. Her gaze was glued to the berth where the *Defiance* should have been. Instead, of the sailboat, there was nothing but an empty space and lapping salt water. Confusion swept through her and she glanced around, turning in a tight circle before coming to a stop when she was facing the detective again.

"Where… where is the *Defiance*?" Makayla asked, staring back at the detective with a puzzled expression.

"Gone," Helen replied in a terse tone.

"Gone? What the hell do you mean by gone?" Makayla demanded, taking a step closer to the woman. "How can a twenty-six foot sailboat just disappear?" She asked in an incredulous tone.

Helen's fingers tightened around the handle of the umbrella she was holding when a gust of wind swirled past them. She turned and glanced at Makayla with a frustrated expression clearly evident on her face. Pulling the collar of her raincoat higher, she shook her head.

"We found nothing last night," she replied. "I stayed the entire time. The investigation team didn't finish until after two this morning. They searched every centimeter of the sailboat and found nothing out of the ordinary."

"That doesn't explain how a sailboat can disappear," Makayla replied through gritted teeth. "You can't just put it into your pocket and walk away with it, for crying out loud!"

"I don't know where it is. It was here when I left earlier this morning," Helen admitted, releasing a deep sigh.

"What about the security cameras?" Brian asked, turning to look at the camera mounted on the pole.

"It doesn't cover this far," Helen said, turning to look out over the bay again. "It would catch anyone entering the dock, but it stops shortly after that. I checked it myself last night to see if I could find any leads that would help identify the men behind Henry Summerlin's abduction."

Makayla pushed pass Helen and stepped up to the edge of the dock. She knelt down and pulled one of the mooring lines up out of the water where it had fallen. Fingering the end, she glanced up at Brian.

"It was cut," she murmured, turning to look back at him.

She was just starting to stand up when Brian jerked and fell backwards several steps. His eyes widened and he immediately reached out for the gun at his side. Makayla grabbed Helen and pulled her to the side behind one of the large concrete pillars. Brian rolled when a piece of fiberglass from the boat behind him shattered.

"What's going on?" Makayla asked in a shocked whisper. "You're bleeding!"

Her gaze was locked on Brian's hand. A thin line of blood was running down from under his sleeve. She jerked her head up to look at his face. He was looking past her, scanning the bay.

"Did you see where the shots came from?" Helen asked. She gripped her gun in her hand. The umbrella she had been holding now lay in the boat behind them. "Three o'clock?" She asked, ducking when another bullet pierced the concrete pillar, cutting a thick section out of one of the corners.

"No," Brian replied, scanning each boat and calculating the trajectory. "There, five o'clock."

Makayla lifted her head just high enough to peer between the boat that had been moored next to the *Defiance* and the pillar. She saw the boat that Brian had pointed out. Drawing back, she looked at him.

"I'm pretty sure that is the same boat that was used to take Henry," she whispered.

"There is no way to hit it from here. Between the wind and the distance, we are no match for the firepower they are using," Brian responded, glancing around.

* * *

Three of the berths between them and the car were empty. Makayla didn't need to be a detective or whatever in the hell Brian was to figure out that they would be sitting ducks for whoever was shooting at them. Her gaze moved behind them before she turned back to the boat in front of them.

Grabbing the mooring line down by her foot, she quickly untied it. She motioned with her other hand for Brian to do the same. Turning, she glanced at the rope tied to the bow.

"I need to untie the bow rope," she said, wincing when Brian roughly jerked her back down just as another bullet hit the boat behind them.

"Keep your head down," he ordered, glancing at the rope she was talking about. "I'll take care of the bow rope. Can you get this thing started?"

"As long as they left the keys to it, I can," she retorted, sliding onto the back platform of the forty-five foot cabin Sports Cruiser.

"Check. If they did, start it," he said before glancing at Helen.

"What are you planning to do?" Helen asked.

"I want answers and they have them," Brian replied grimly.

..*

Brian ignored the stinging in his arm. He knew it was just a deep graze and not life threatening. His gaze swept over Makayla. Once again, he wondered how he could ever have been so stupid as to walk away from her. He watched her methodically searching the upper deck for the keys while still keeping low so that she wasn't a target.

The moment she turned with a triumphant expression on her face, he knew she had found the keys. Within seconds, she had the forty-five foot Sports Cruiser fired up. Brian turned to look at Helen again.

"Don't...," she hissed, reading the intention in his eyes even before he had a chance to express it. "If you are going to steal a boat, I can at least legitimize it by saying that it was necessary to confiscate it."

"Do you really think your commanding officers will agree?" He asked with a raised eyebrow.

"I'll find out," Helen bit out.

Helen slid her legs over the side of the dock and jumped down onto the platform. She grabbed the side when it rocked before quickly climbing the molded stairs to the upper wheelhouse.

Brian shook his head before he leaned to the side and aimed at the rope. It took three shots before he was able to cut through it enough to be confident it would snap when Makayla took off. Jumping onto the boat, he moved up the steps to stand next to Helen and Makayla.

"Go," he said, eyeing the boat in the distance.

"This thing is no match for that powerboat," Makayla warned. "We'll be lucky if the top speed hits thirty knots, especially in this weather. That speed boat can do at least fifty."

"I just need you to get me close enough to hit the engine compartment," Brian replied in a steely voice.

Makayla nodded. Pressing the throttle down a quarter of the way, she felt the cruiser's twin Volvo engines kick into gear. Her hands tightened on the wheel when she felt the tug of the front bow line. The line pulled the bow to the right before it snapped. Once she was clear of the pilings, she thrust the throttle all the way forward. The powerful engines responded and the Sports Cruiser went up onto a plane, cutting through the turbulent waters of the bay like a hot knife through butter.

Brian held onto the railing, his legs acting as shock absorbers when the Sports Cruiser rocked. His gaze flickered to Helen. She was doing the same. His research on Helen Woo last night said that she was a highly capable and hard-working member of the police force. She wasn't married, and she had a history of cracking some of the toughest unsolved crimes in Hong Kong.

He had completed a thorough background search on her. It had been necessary in his mind. He wasn't going to trust Makayla's life to anyone he didn't know. Helen Woo's background check had not only been spotless, but impressive. Top graduate in her class with honors, she had scored high on all of her evaluations and was one of the youngest police officers to ever make detective in a record number of years with the force.

Still, he had wanted to make sure that there hadn't been anyone that she owed. All of her bank records and living expenses were well within her pay grade. There were also no records of offshore accounts and no indication that she was on the payroll of any of the well documented local crime lords.

Turning his attention to Makayla, he saw her face was taut with determination. Her focus was on steering them toward the speedboat. All of them ducked down when the front windshield fractured under a hail of bullets. The tempered glass, instead of exploding, was littered with cracks and bullet holes from the high powered rifle.

Makayla swerved the Sports Cruiser as much as she could to make it more difficult to hit them. Brian gauged that they were about one hundred yards out. They were still too far for his handgun to do any damage.

"They are leaving," she said above the sound of the weather and the engines. "I can't go any faster."

Brian cursed under his breath. He grabbed at Makayla and pulled her down when he saw a man with a long range sniper rifle turn toward them. The choppiness of the water made it impossible for the man to get a clean shot. Still, the bullet that struck just three inches over their heads was enough to let him know they were dealing with a professional hitman.

He released his hold on Makayla and peered above the dash of the cabin cruiser through the windshield riddled with cracks and holes. Standing straight, he watched the speedboat disappear around the cove. Makayla must have realized it was impossible to pursue them and she pulled back on the throttle.

"What do we do now?" Makayla asked, staring into the distance.

"We find out who the speedboat belongs to," Helen replied, holding up a small camera with a wry smile. "According to my father, a good detective always carries a camera. Once again, he was right."

Brian nodded. "I want to know everything you know to date," he said.

"As do I, Mr. Jacobs, including what you really do for the United States Consulate and who authorized you to carry a military issue weapon," Helen replied.

***

Ren Lu stood on the deck of the large yacht anchored in the bay. His lips were pressed into a firm line, his face taut with anger. He had watched the scene unfold with a growing sense of fury. Lowering the binoculars he was looking through, Ren Lu turned sharply on his heel and strode across the covered deck to the salon below.

He pulled his cell phone out of his pocket and quickly dialed the number to Sun Yung-Wing. His mind ran through what he would say. He rejected most of his initial thoughts, as all they would do is get him killed.

"You've found it?" Yung demanded in greeting.

"No," Ren Lu snapped before drawing in a calming breath. "I have removed the sailboat to a secure port. Several of my most trusted men are currently searching it. If they find it, I will immediately inform you."

"Then, why did you call?" Yung snapped in annoyance.

"Who did you hire?" Ren Lu asked in a quiet voice.

There was a moment of silence on the other end. He could feel the tension radiating through the phone in his hand. He turned and clenched his fist before forcing himself to relax.

"The stakes are too high for failure. It was necessary to hire additional help," Yung replied in an icy tone.

"You have complicated the situation. I told you I would take care of retrieving the information," Ren Lu stated.

"Don't forget to whom you are speaking, Ren Lu," Yung snapped.

A nerve pulsed at Ren Lu's temple and he rubbed it. If he was to be successful in retrieving the information, then he needed to be careful. Sun Yung-Wing was a highly volatile man. He ran his corporation with fear and brutality, often making impulsive decisions that could prove lethal to anyone in his path. Money bought power, and Yung wielded that power like a fine edged sword.

"I have the situation under control. The American is unaware of what is going on," Ren Lu stated in a calm voice. "I have my men going over the sailboat. If Harrington gave the old man the information, it will be on there."

"How can you be sure? I told you I wanted the American brought to me," Yung reminded him in an angry voice.

"I interrogated him. I assure you, the old man knows nothing," Ren Lu asserted in a firm voice.

"What about the girl?" Yung demanded, revealing that he knew more about the situation than Ren Lu had thought.

"I will deal with her," Ren Lu replied in a quiet voice. "Call off your man. I will take care of this."

Again, there was silence before Yung replied. "I can't," Yung reluctantly admitted. "Eliminate the American and the girl, and find the information."

Ren Lu slowly lowered the cell phone when he heard the call disconnect. His fingers tightened around it. Sun's simple admission – *I can't* – signaled that he was nervous that word had already leaked out about the missing information. The situation was quickly becoming extremely dangerous for everyone involved.

* * *

Makayla carefully steered the Sports Cruiser back into its birth at the marina. Brian and Helen tied it off and she shut down the engines. A grimace crossed her face when she saw the damage to the expensive yacht. She really hoped the owners had insurance.

Pulling the keys out of the ignition, she climbed down the stairs to replace them in the cabin before joining Brian and Helen. Her footsteps faltered when she heard a familiar voice demanding to know what in the hell was going on.

"Tyrell?" Makayla gasped, staring up at the huge figure of her best friend.

"You've done gone off on another crazy adventure, haven't you, Makayla?" Tyrell's warm voice washed over her. "Come here so I can make sure you are okay."

"Oh, Tyrell," Makayla whispered, climbing up onto the dock and into his strong arms. "I was worried about you."

"Me?! I'm not the one getting shot at! When I pulled up and saw what was going on, I about had a heart attack, especially when I looked through my camera and saw it was you on that boat," Tyrell muttered, holding her tight. "Where in the hell is Henry and what is Brian doing here?"

Makayla leaned back and looked up into Tyrell's dark, worried face and shook her head. Her throat closed when she saw him glare over at Brian with a heated expression. She waited until he returned his attention to her before she spoke in a thick, tired voice.

"He's missing, Tyrell," Makayla said, turning to glance at the empty berth where the *Defiance* had been. "They took him and the *Defiance*."

Chapter 13

"Ouch," Brian hissed, wincing when Makayla pressed the cloth with iodine against the deep cut on his arm.

"Sorry," she muttered, frowning while she cleaned the wound.

Her gaze moved over his forearm. It was a lot more muscular than she remembered. In fact, his whole body was more solid than she recalled, an observation that was making her task more than a little distracting.

He had been lucky. The bullet had cut a slice through his upper arm about an inch from his shoulder. If the bullet had been a half-inch further to the right, it would have torn through flesh and muscle; possibly shattering the bone of his upper arm, or even worse, it could have pierced his chest.

She carefully cleaned the wound, making sure there were no fibers from his shirt in the abrasion before pulling it together and adding some topical antibiotic cream and several butterfly bandages to pull together the edges of skin along the wound.

A rueful smile curved her lips when she felt his knuckles brush against her skin. Lifting her chin, she stared back at him in silence. He leaned forward, his lips almost touching her when the door was pushed open behind them. Makayla drew back and lowered her gaze back to what she was doing.

"Brian, the speedboat is registered to Great Wall Industries. I've found very little information on them so far except that they deal in imports and exports, which does little to narrow the search considering half of Hong Kong companies do that," Helen mused before she looked up from the tablet she was carrying. She glanced up and paused when she saw Brian sitting on the commode. His back was to her and he had removed his shirt so Makayla could bandage his arm. "How bad is it?" She asked, staring over his shoulder at Makayla.

"Not as bad as it could have been," Makayla replied, picking up the piece of gauze from the First Aid kit that Helen had given her from her car.

"Yeah, he's still breathing," Tyrell muttered, glancing at Brian with a lopsided grin. "You'd think that a hitman would have a better aim, especially when they are shooting at such a …," Tyrell's voice faded when Makayla shot him an exasperated glance. "I was going to be nice," he muttered. "Sort of…."

Makayla's lips twitched at the blatant lie. "I'm sure you were," she retorted before glancing at Helen. "Thank you for the kit, it really came in handy," she added, winding the gauze around his arm.

"Standard protocol," Helen murmured, leaning against the door frame of the bathroom. "The boat was reported stolen, by the way. There appears to be a rash of that happening lately," she added with an ironic smile.

Makayla resisted the urge to roll her eyes – barely. She caught Brian's amused look and shook her head. Picking up the fabric tape, she wrapped a long piece around his arm to keep the gauze from slipping.

"All finished," she said, straightening up and stepping back so she could give her handiwork a critical look. "Not bad for a rookie."

Brian moved his arm and gave her an appreciative nod at her doctoring, his gaze serious. "Not bad at all," he agreed, reaching for the clean shirt he had brought into the bathroom and sliding it on before buttoning it.

Makayla glanced away and quickly collected the items she had taken out of the First Aid kit. She repacked everything, and stepped past Helen who was talking quietly with Brian about the information she had discovered. She had to push Tyrell, who was staring at her with a questioning expression, out of the way when he refused to move so she could escape to the living room. She could feel Helen and Brian's gaze on her back. She just needed to get out of the bathroom that suddenly felt far too cramped.

Placing the First Aid kit down on the bar, she walked over to stand at the window. She wrapped her arms around her waist and stared down at the street. Behind her, she could hear Tyrell quietly walk up to stand next to her. Brian and Helen entered the room a moment later, discussing what had happened. She overheard Brian murmur something about his position at the Consulate and that he had clearance to carry a concealed weapon in accordance with the law before she tuned them out. Returning her focus to the street, she raised a hand to wipe a strand of hair that had come free from her braid back behind her ear.

"Makayla," Tyrell murmured, shoving his hands into his pockets while he gazed out the window beside her.

Makayla wanted to shake her head and tell Tyrell to leave her alone for a moment so she could get a grip on her emotions, but she didn't. The overwhelming realization of how close she had come to losing Brian again, this time for good, had suddenly hit her when she was cleaning up the bloody washcloth and medical supplies.

Turning, she glanced at Tyrell for a brief second before she turned to gaze over at Brian with eyes filled with fear and determination. She wouldn't give up and she wouldn't give in. Whatever was going on, she was going to fight every inch of the way. She had faced difficult situations before and overcome them, and she would do it again.

"Is there any way to find out who owns this Hong Kong Industries?" Makayla asked, staring back and forth between Helen and Brian.

"I can," Brian murmured, glancing at Helen.

"I won't ask how, but that doesn't mean I won't figure it out," Helen replied, glancing at her phone and pursing her lips when she saw who was calling. "I need to take this in private."

"You can go in the bedroom," Brian said with a wave of his hand.

Makayla's gaze followed Helen until she disappeared into the bedroom before turning back to Brian. She was surprised that he was already sitting on the couch with his laptop open. Stepping around the coffee table, she sank down beside him. Tyrell glanced back and forth between where Helen had disappeared and Brian and her. She gave him an affectionate smile when she saw the confusion, exhaustion, and frustration sweeping across his face.

"When did you get here and why didn't you tell me you were coming?" Makayla asked in a quiet voice.

Tyrell walked over and sank down in the arm chair that was in the corner. He stretched out his long legs and folded his hands across his stomach. Well over six feet and built more like a football player than a photographer, Tyrell dwarfed the chair. He had gotten a new hair cut since she had last seen him. This time he was wearing it thicker on top with the sides shaved close. The thick, curly black hair made her want to run her fingers through it to see if it was as soft as a rabbit's tail.

"Knock it off," Tyrell mumbled with an exhausted grin when he saw her fingers twitch. "My hair is not a fluffy bunny."

"Knock… What about your hair?" Brian asked, glancing up at Tyrell in confusion before he scowled when he saw the expression on the other man's face and where he was staring. "What are you doing in Hong Kong?"

Tyrell glanced at Brian and raised an eyebrow. "I have a photo assignment for National Geographic. I was in Kenya for the last six months for a previous assignment and finally got back on social media. I saw a post from Henry that Makayla was joining him on a trip from here to Honolulu. He had tagged his location, so it wasn't all that hard to figure out where to find her. What's your story?"

Brian glanced down at the computer in front of him. "I work here," he muttered.

Makayla saw Tyrell's silent 'WTF does that mean?' and shook her head. Releasing a sigh, she swore she could almost see the tension between the two men like visible force fields colliding. She glanced at Tyrell with a look that she hoped he understood – truce.

Tyrell nodded and leaned his head back, gazing at them with an assessing look. A slow smile curved his lips when Brian reached over and absently rubbed Makayla's knee before returning his hand to the computer. Makayla glared back at Tyrell and mouthed for him to knock it off.

"Helen told me what happened while you were patching up lover boy," Tyrell finally said, his gaze turning sad. "I'm sorry, Makayla. I wish I had come a few days earlier."

"There wouldn't have been anything you could have done, except get yourself killed," Brian muttered, glancing over at Tyrell. "This wasn't a random act, Tyrell. Whoever is behind this wouldn't think twice about killing you or anyone else."

"Something tells me that you know quite a bit about the type of guys that did this," Tyrell observed, all traces of humor gone from his face.

"I do," Brian admitted, glancing over at Makayla before focusing back on what he was doing.

Makayla watched with a combination of fascination and confusion as he brought up screens that looked like something out of a movie. Her breath caught when she saw the grainy image on another screen before he could minimize it.

"Wait," she whispered, reaching out and touching his arm. "That's Henry."

"Yes," Brian acknowledged, sliding the cursor to the right corner.

"Stop," Makayla said a little more sharply, staring at the image. "Where did you get this? Why do you have a picture of Henry on your computer?"

A muscle in Brian's cheek throbbed when Tyrell rose and came to stand next to the arm of the couch near Makayla. The throbbing muscle was a telltale sign that Brian was agitated. She saw Brian glance over at Tyrell who was staring back at him with a dark, intense gaze of warning. Her fingers relaxed on Brian's arm and she slid her hand down to cover his, wrapping her fingers around it when he returned his attention to her.

"Brian, please. I need to know what is going on," Makayla said in a quiet voice.

Brian stared back into her eyes for several seconds before he pulled his hand away and stood up. He walked around the coffee table and over to the window. Staring at his stiff shoulders, she could tell he was trying to make up his mind. Once again, she wondered what had happened to the carefree young man she had once known.

He glanced toward the bedroom where Helen's muffled voice could be heard before flickering back to Tyrell. It sounded like Helen was dealing with her own issues. Drawing in a deep breath, he turned, shot Tyrell a heated glance, and focused on her face.

"This stays in this room. What I'm about to tell you both could endanger you more than you already have been." He waited for the meaning of his words to sink in. When they both nodded, he continued. "Five days ago one of our undercover agents here in Hong Kong was able to retrieve some highly sensitive information – information that could have a major impact on weapons being supplied to terrorists in strategic areas around the world. Sun Yung-Wing, a billionaire businessman and known crime lord here was a suspect. Our man has been working the last two years undercover," he replied in a quiet voice.

"The man...," her gaze turned to the image on the screen. There was the man facing Henry. It looked as if they had bumped into each other. Her gaze scrutinized the image, taking in every detail. A frown creased her brow and she leaned forward and enlarged it. It looked as if the man was putting something in one of the grocery bags Henry was carrying. "The bags…," she murmured, her eyes widening as the pieces fell into place. "Whoever took Henry saw this same picture didn't they? They think that this man, this agent, gave Henry whatever he stole."

"Yes," Brian said. "I need to find the information."

"What happened to your agent?" Tyrell asked in a quiet voice, searching Brian's face for the answer.

Brian bent his head and rubbed his hand over the back of his neck. He glanced at Makayla before looking away. His face was taut with tension and he looked older, harder than his almost twenty-six years.

"He was hit by a van while trying to escape. He's in a coma. We have security around him. His last words were that he would hide the information and give us directions for where to find it," he said.

Makayla's gaze returned to the computer screen and the blurry image of what looked like the man's hand reaching into one of the canvas bags. Her lips parted in a startled gasp. Instinctively, her hand reached for the small pocketbook at her side before she remembered that she had removed the item she had found in one of the shopping bags. She had placed it in the pocket of her slicker.

Trembling, she rose off the couch and stepped around Tyrell. She walked over to the bar stool where she had draped her coat. She bent, feeling in the pocket. Her fingers wrapped around the small box. She had thought it was a jewelry box with a trinket that Henry had picked up at the market. She pulled the box out and turned to look at Brian with a pale but composed expression.

"Is this...?" She swallowed past the thickness threatening to choke her and held out her hand. "I think this might be what you are looking for."

Both men's gazes moved to her outstretched hand. Brian's eyes widened when he saw the small, rectangular box sitting on her palm. He strode forward and stopped. His eyes were glued to the box before he slowly reached for it and turned his gaze to her.

"Where did you get this?" He asked in a slightly rough voice.

Makayla's hand dropped to her side. She shrugged and wrapped her arms around her waist. Her mind was trying to piece together how Henry must have been at the wrong place at the right time. She decided the Fates must be laughing at their little practical joke of messing with people's lives.

"It was in one of the shopping bags that I grabbed when I went to the market yesterday. I was folding them and I found it. Is it what you are looking for?" She asked, looking back at him again.

"I'm about to find out," he muttered, turning on his heel and walking back to the couch.

Makayla followed him, sinking down beside him and folding her hands together. Tyrell sat on the arm of the couch, looking over her shoulder at the computer. They watched in silence as Brian opened the box and removed a flash drive sealed in a small plastic bag. It was a good thing the flash drive had been wrapped in plastic, considering the box had been in her purse when she fell in the water.

Brian pulled it out of the plastic bag and inserted it into his computer's USB port. A message came up asking for a password. He growled in frustration. From the sound of his muttered curse, it wasn't going to be easy to access the information.

"I need to visit a friend," Brian finally muttered in frustration, running a hand through his hair and glancing up when Helen hurried into the room.

"We need to leave. Now!" She ordered, walking over to the window and angrily staring out.

"What's wrong?" Tyrell asked, standing up and watching Helen stride across to the window.

"What's going on?" Brian asked in a terse voice. He rose to his feet and walked over to stand next to Helen. He stared out of the window to the street below. A soft curse escaped him. "What happened?" He demanded.

Makayla stood up when Brian suddenly turned and strode over to a hall closet. She stood up and walked over to the window and glanced down. A moment later, Tyrell came to stand next to her to see what she was staring at. In the street below them, several vehicles had pulled up.

Brian's apartment was in the old, historic district of the city. The third floor window looked down across the busy street lined with a variety of small shops. The first floor of his apartment building contained a row of businesses with a narrow door and staircase leading up to the top five floors from the street level. There would be no way to avoid the men who were crossing the street.

"I know who is on the payroll of Sun Yung-Wing," Helen retorted, pulling her gun out and checking it. "My superior kept me on the phone for far longer than usual. I should have listened to my gut when it was telling me that something was wrong. He wanted to know where Makayla was and if you were with us," Helen explained, glancing over to where Brian was grabbing a backpack from the hall closet. "He should not have known about you. I never mentioned that you were with Makayla and me. Luckily, he didn't know about Tyrell."

"How many are there?" Brian asked.

Makayla glanced over her shoulder and watched while he shoved several things, including money, several passports, and additional ammo clips into the backpack before turning to grab the laptop off the coffee table. Snapping it shut, he removed the flash drive and slipped it into his pocket before he lifted the backpack to his shoulder.

"Three," Helen replied in a soft voice, glancing at him.

"Let's go," he said, pulling his gun out and jerking his head to Tyrell and both women.

"How are we going to get past them?" Makayla asked, crossing the room and grabbing the rain slicker off the stool before reaching for the First Aid kit, as well.

"There's an old service entrance that was closed off in Mrs. Leu's apartment. It goes down to the basement," he said, opening the door and glancing out before stepping out and motioning for them to follow him.

Makayla swallowed and stepped out into the hall. She saw Helen grab her coat while Tyrell slung the backpack he always carried over his shoulder. She glanced toward the stairs when she heard the sound of the door several floors below open and close. Brian passed her, leading the way. Helen stepped up behind her and Tyrell trailed behind them.

She moved as quietly as she could, wincing when the wood board under her foot creaked rather loudly. She bit her lip and glanced behind. Helen was walking sideways, keeping an eye on Makayla and Brian while also keeping her gun trained on the stairwell.

Brian paused outside of a door marked 303. He softly knocked on the door, paused, and knocked again. Almost immediately, the door opened. The older woman inside cracked the door before opening it and motioning for him and the others to come inside.

"How many?" Mrs. Leu asked before closing and locking the door.

"Three," Brian replied, brushing a kiss across Mrs. Leu's wrinkled cheek.

"You know where the exit is," she said with a curious smile at Helen and Tyrell. "Who are they?"

"Detective Helen Woo and Tyrell Richards," Brian replied, striding through the living room into the kitchen. He opened a narrow utility closet and began pulling several items out.

"A pleasure, my dears," Mrs. Leu said with a smile before it faded and she turned to Brian. "Do you need me to call for assistance?"

Brian shook his head and glanced at Helen before his gaze paused on Tyrell. "No, but if Tyrell can stay here until it is clear, I would appreciate it. They aren't aware that he is with us," he said.

"Like hell," Tyrell growled, shifting his shoulders. "I'm staying with Makayla. Where she goes, I go."

Makayla watched Brian return Tyrell's stubborn stare. A muscle jerked in the huge black man's jaw, and she knew that Brian had seen Tyrell's fingers tighten around the strap of his backpack. The look Tyrell gave Brian reminded her that Brian and she weren't the only ones who had changed over the last three years. There was a hardness in Tyrell's gaze that spoke of a man who had also seen and experienced some of life's darker side. Makayla breathed a sigh of relief when Brian turned back to Mrs. Leu.

"I'll make contact once we get to a safe house," Brian promised.

"Be safe, Brian," Mrs. Leu said.

"I will," he replied, pulling open the narrow door at the back of the closet and grabbing a small flashlight off the shelf.

Makayla paused, watching Brian squeeze through the tight opening and onto a narrow set of wooden stairs. She stepped through next, turning sideways to fit, followed by Helen. There was a muffled curse when Tyrell squeezed through the narrow opening. It wouldn't have been easy for him to get his big frame through the narrow space. The moment they were clear of the door, she heard Mrs. Leu close it behind them, replacing the broom, mop, and bucket that Brian had pulled out.

Except for the small flashlight, the staircase was devoid of any light. It was so tight that she could barely stand facing forward without both of her shoulders rubbing against the walls. Behind her, Tyrell wasn't so lucky.

None of them spoke while they descended the staircase. At the bottom was another door. The flashlight bobbed a little when Brian reached into his jacket pocket. He pulled out an old key and inserted it into the lock.

A moment later, he pulled open the door. There was an old wrought iron door in front of it. Brian selected another key on the key ring and inserted it into the master lock connecting the chain that was wrapped around the bars. He pulled the chain loose and pushed the iron door open. Scanning the area, he glanced at Makayla, Helen, and Tyrell.

"Let's go," he said in a quiet voice.

Makayla followed him through the basement. They skirted several machines and large pallets of boxes that the local businesses on the first floor stored there. Several minutes later, they emerged in a side alley. Once again, Makayla felt a disorienting sense of unreality. Where had Brian learned to do this kind of stuff? Who was Mrs. Leu? And what kind of job did

Brian have that included spies, crime lords, and international weapons? And what had she dragged Tyrell into?

She glanced over her shoulder. Tyrell's face was set into a hard mask. If seeing them being shot at had been a reality check for the dangers of the situation, then being targeted by hitmen sent by the Hong Kong police had sealed it. She refocused her gaze on Brian's back. Her eyes moved to his upper left shoulder where she had discovered another scar that hadn't been there three years ago – caused by a different bullet.

Chapter 14

Brian paused at the end of the alley. His car was blocked in by the vehicles the men had arrived in. He leaned back and gazed at the other three.

"My car is blocked," he muttered with a frown.

"Mine is back at the marina," Helen said before shaking her head. "We couldn't use it anyway. It has a GPS tracking system installed."

"I have mine," Tyrell suggested. "No one knows about me. If we took your car, they could trace it. Since no one knows about me, they won't know where we go."

A brief grin curved Brian's lips. He held out his hand when Tyrell pulled the keys out of his black leather coat pocket. Tyrell glared for a moment before he relented with a grudging nod.

"I know the city better," Brian explained. "Where did you park?"

Several minutes later, Brian pulled open the door to Tyrell's car and tossed the backpack into the back seat before sliding into the driver's seat. Makayla slid in behind him while Helen and Tyrell hurried around to the passenger side. Tyrell climbed in the back seat next to Makayla. Brian hadn't missed the inquisitive glance that she had shot him before she had climbed into the back seat. He knew that he would have a lot of explaining to do when they finally weren't running for their lives.

He gritted his teeth, wishing that they were alone for just a little while. He started the car and pulled away from the curb, slowing down when he passed two of the vehicles that the men had emerged from earlier. Helen must have understood his intent. She pulled the small camera out of her pocket and twisted, taking a photo of the front license tags for each vehicle.

"Tell me exactly what was said in your conversation with your commander," he ordered, taking the next left.

"I was about to ask you the same thing," Helen murmured before she released a sigh and leaned tiredly back against the seat and staring out of the window. "Commander Ying Ji Yeng is my superior. He is new and I don't know him very well. I should have taken the time," she murmured. "He was not happy about the incident at the marina. I was not surprised about that. He asked me routine questions about the case, which didn't concern me. Then, he started asking specific questions about my location, if Makayla was with me, and more pointedly, if you were there as well. That did raise a concern, as I had never mentioned you and there is nothing about you in any of my reports."

"How would he know about Brian?" Makayla asked, sitting forward between the seats.

Brian glanced over at Helen when she twisted in her seat slightly so she could face both Makayla and him. She glanced down at the gun in her lap for several seconds before she glanced at Brian. Her expression was stiff and held a trace of resignation.

"He bugged my phone," she said. "It was one issued by the department. Officer Wang delivered a new one to me shortly after Commander Yeng started. Wang warned me to be careful, that he had heard rumors of Yeng. I discarded his concern because Yeng had openly criticized Wang about his weight. Yeng wanted all detectives to use department issued cell phones. It was the only way he could have tracked me to your apartment. I never told him where I was," she said with a soft voice.

"Nice boss," Tyrell muttered, staring out of the window.

"Where is it now?" Brian asked, glancing at her before turning right.

"On the street outside of your apartment," she replied with a sardonic twist to her lips.

"Good," Brian muttered, glancing in the mirror at Makayla's pale face.

She returned his stare before glancing away. He felt his gut tighten at the look of wariness in her eyes. He returned his focus to the road. They needed answers – and soon – for Henry's sake, as well as their own.

***

Henry groaned and blinked through blurry eyes up at the man who had entered his prison cell. The man squatted down in front of him and stared into his face in silence. It took a few seconds before he could focus on the man's face.

"What the hell do you want?" He groused in a rough voice, raspy from thirst.

"Tell me about this man," the man demanded, holding up the blurry picture of two men.

Henry blinked and raised his good hand to rub it down his face. He needed his reading glasses. All he saw was two big masses in varying shades of gray. Shaking his head, he leaned back against the bulkhead.

"I can't see a damn thing without my reading glasses," he replied in a gruff voice. "It's hell getting old, but better than the alternative."

The man looked at Henry's unfocused eyes. He carefully returned the photo to the manila envelope he had pulled it from. Henry watched him, acting only slightly weaker than he really felt. Oh, he wasn't up to challenging the guy to another fight. No, he valued having at least one working arm. He just thought it might be better if he played the old man card in the hopes that they would get tired of his ass and dump it somewhere – preferably on dry land with him still breathing.

"Tell me about Makayla," the man requested in a deceptively quiet tone.

Henry felt his body jerk forward in surprise and alarm. He reached out and grabbed the front of the man's shirt with his good hand, his eyes clearing and his face stiffening in anger. The man didn't move or try to dislodge Henry's grip.

"You leave my granddaughter out of this," Henry growled in a harsh voice. "I don't know what you want, but you leave Makayla alone."

"What do you know about the man she is with?" The man asked, carefully pulling another image out of the folder.

This one was less grainy and blown up larger so that Henry could see it clearly enough to make out the image of Makayla standing next to a younger man. Confusion swept through Henry at the familiar features. He glanced at the photo before turning his gaze back to the man's face.

"Brian's here?" Henry asked, releasing the man's shirt and falling back against the cold wall again.

"Brian?" The man prompted, staring intently at Henry.

Henry licked his dry lips and nodded, suddenly feeling very old and very tired. He closed his eyes and drew in a deep breath. What the hell had he gotten Makayla and himself into and why was Brian here?

"Brian Jacobs," Henry muttered, opening his eyes. "He was a neighbor of ours back home. When he wasn't at college, he worked during the summer on the boats down at the boat yard. Nice kid until he broke Makayla's heart. After that, I just wanted to rip his heart out. If you want to kick some ass, I won't stop you from kicking his."

The man silently stared at Henry before rising to his feet. Henry didn't bother to look up at him. The cold and pain was hitting him hard. His hand and wrist were swollen and throbbing and the cold was playing hell with the rest of his body.

"Where would they go?" The man asked.

Henry shook his head to clear the fog from his mind. He had already forgotten what the man had been talking about. He glanced up in confusion.

"What?" He mumbled.

The man stared at his face. Henry didn't know if he was trying to decide if he was acting or not. The strength he had been hiding had drained from him when the man mentioned Makayla.

"Where would Brian have taken Makayla?" The man asked in a slightly impatient tone.

Henry shook his head, feeling it starting to droop again. "Don't know… The *Defiance,* maybe," he muttered, his eyes starting to feel weighted. "I didn't even know the boy was here."

With a low sigh, the man rose to his feet and turned away. Henry blinked, trying to focus on the man, but decided it was easier to give into the darkness. If Brian was here, he'd protect Makayla. As mad as he was at the boy for breaking her heart, Henry knew deep down that Brian would do everything in his power to keep Makayla safe.

"Please watch over her, Mary Rose," Henry whispered, sliding down to lay on the dirty floor.

* * *

Ren Lu strode down the narrow corridor of the freighter tied along the port. He snapped out an order to one of the men standing to the side. The man nodded and disappeared. Taking the steps two at a time, he ducked his head when he passed through the upper level hatch and stepped out onto the deck.

He had not been able to get as much information as he had hoped from the old man, but he had at least gotten a name to go with a face – Brian Jacobs. Pulling his cell phone out of his pocket, he pressed in an unlisted number and waited. Almost immediately, a voice answered on the other end.

"Brian Jacobs, American, connected to Makayla Summerlin," he said before disconnecting the call.

Ren Lu knew he would have information within the hour about the man who had been on the dock with Makayla. He thought about the way the man had moved. Even through the binoculars, he could see the man had been in control of the situation when Sun's hitman had fired on the women and him. He was about to slide the phone back into his pocket when it vibrated. Glancing down, his face stiffened.

"Yes," he answered, crossing the gangplank down to the dock and striding over to his car.

"Mr. Sun ordered a freelance hit," the man that he had assigned to Sun Yung-Wing said in a deep voice.

"Location," Ren Lu demanded, sliding behind the wheel.

He waited, listening to the information being relayed to him by a member of his security team.

Starting the car, he turned the wheel sharply to the right, spinning the tires and leaving a dark line when he accelerated. His lips tightened. He had been closer to his targets than he had realized. It was time to start cleaning up the mess that Sun had created before it got out of hand.

He spun the wheel, turning the black BMW sedan through the intersection. He barely missed a taxi. Pressing the accelerator, he made another left before turning down an alley and cutting between two main crossroads. He glanced to the left to make sure the coast was clear. Turning right, he glanced at the street sign. He had three blocks to go before he intercepted the men Sun had hired.

An unusual curse escaped him when he was forced to slam on his brakes when a group of adults and children crossed the road in front of him. Two women glared at him and motioned toward him in anger. The second they were clear, he shot around them. Less than ten minutes later, he pulled up in the narrow alley across from the address his man had told him was Jacobs' residence. He arrived just in time to see a group of men entering the building.

He turned off the car and thrust open the door. Locking it, he glanced both ways down the street, scanning it in case another man had stayed behind before crossing the road. His hand slid into the pocket of his long black coat and he pulled out a pair of black gloves. Pulling them on, he paused outside the door leading into the building and looked around once more before pulling the door open and stepping inside. Once he was in the narrow stairwell, he slipped the gun from the holster under his coat and pulled the silencer out of his pocket. He soundlessly climbed the stairs, attaching the silencer as he went.

Chapter 15

Makayla leaned back in the seat and stared out at the passing buildings. Her mind was sifting through Brian's behavior. He had been calm, confident, and obviously well prepared and well trained. Her brow creased when she remembered Mrs. Leu opening the door to his unusual knock, as if they had coordinated the move.

"Who is Mrs. Leu?" She asked quietly.

Brian briefly glanced at her in the rearview mirror before focusing back on the road. They were moving away from the city. The sign showed they were entering the Island Eastern Corridor that ran along Victoria Harbour.

"She is a sweet old lady who has had a very interesting life," Brian replied.

"I bet," Makayla muttered, sensing that he wouldn't tell her anything else. "Where are we going?"

"I need to see what is on the file. I have a friend who might be able to help break the encryption," Brian said, glancing at Helen. "What are you going to do? If your commander sent those men, you're in danger now, as well."

Helen gave him a taut smile that wasn't reflected in her eyes. "I have been temporarily relieved of my position," she replied, glancing back at Makayla. "It would appear stealing a yacht, even in the pursuit of justice, is against the law. He was also not impressed when I refused to bring Brian and you in for questioning."

"What did he say when you told him that you wouldn't?" Makayla asked, curious.

Helen gave her stiff smile. "That it could be hazardous to not only my career, but my life if I were to get in the way. That is when I saw the men pull up and put two and two together," she responded dryly.

"I'm sorry," Makayla whispered, glancing back and forth between the two of them.

"You know, I'm really not liking your boss too much at the moment," Tyrell said, glancing at Helen.

"I don't either," Helen admitted with a wry grin.

"Don't blame yourself, Makayla. If anything, the US and British governments are to blame for what has happened. Harrington never should have risked a civilian in this mission," Brian replied in a hard tone and he glanced at her again in the mirror, locking gazes for a brief, fierce moment before he concentrated on the road again.

Makayla swallowed. A brief flash of memory swept through her of Brian's eyes flashing with anger once before. That time, it had been directed at her. Her hand jerked in surprise until she realized that it was Tyrell reaching out to hold it in support. She glanced over at him before she turned away –

uncomfortable with the familiar look of compassion and understanding in his gaze.

She stared out the window, watching the whitecaps dance across the windblown bay. In the distance, she could see large freight ships moored, the skeletal frames of the cranes shifting the huge cargo containers and readying them for shipping. They looked alien against the landscape. A part of her mind processed the movement and she was amazed at how the dock workers could move such heavy containers with ease.

The other part was locked in a memory from three years ago. A shaft of pain pierced her and she briefly closed her eyes. Brian had been the only man she had ever allowed inside the wall she had built to protect herself – well, Tyrell and him. Her love for Tyrell was different. Their journey, and near death, had sealed their bond on a different, more spiritual level. They understood each other and accepted each other without fear of being rejected or ridiculed.

Makayla gazed out the window with sightless eyes, caught in the thread of memories. She had returned to Henry's house after graduating from high school and finishing her Associate of Arts degree at the local college. She had been taking online summer courses toward her Bachelor's degree, plus working with Henry down at the boatyard.

Brian had returned home for a short break before he was supposed to leave on an assignment. He'd had a new job working for some government agency she had never heard of before. He hadn't told her much about it, just that it would be a huge boost to his career and allow him to do some traveling aboard.

The budding, sometimes tense, attraction they had felt had grown, at least on her part. As much as she had tried to protect herself, Brian's sense of humor and gentle touch had awakened a feeling inside her that had left her excited and uncertain at first. As the summer had progressed, their love had grown and they had become lovers. It had been Makayla's first serious relationship and when they had broken up, it had left more than a few emotional scars behind.

Makayla blinked, pushing away the memories. She glanced at the sign when Brian turned onto Eastern Harbour Crossing. She frowned, trying to see where they were going. With everything that had happened, she hadn't seen very much of Hong Kong or the surrounding area.

"Where are we going?" Tyrell asked, leaning forward with a frown.

"Lei Yue Mun," Brian replied, glancing at him.

..*

Makayla paused before sliding her hand into Brian's when he opened the back door of the car and extended one hand to help her out. She grabbed his backpack at the same time, gripping the handle at the top. He reached over and took it from her, swinging the strap over his shoulder before reclaiming her hand.

She gazed around in awe. The narrow patch of land between a rugged forest-covered mountain and the bay was wall to wall buildings of all shapes, sizes, and building materials. The delicious smells of food mixed with the cool breeze blowing off the water. The weather front had cleared just as the weather channel had predicted and the late afternoon sky was a brilliant blue.

Along the shoreline, junks, sailboats, houseboats, and fishing boats littered the water as if a child had tossed an armful of toy boats into a bathtub, unsure of which one he or she wanted. She stumbled on the uneven ground, mesmerized by the sights, smells, and sounds of the village. It was a mixture of modern and old – creating an ageless scene.

There were a large number of tourists combined with the local residents strolling amid the numerous shops and restaurants. Several old men, their fingers stained from the cigarettes they were holding and their brown faces lined with wrinkles, sat at rickety wooden tables playing a game with pebbles, loudly talking and laughing while pigeons and seagulls fluttered around them, hoping to pick up a discarded tidbit from a passing diner.

"Are you okay?" Brian murmured, glancing down at her even as he pulled her closer.

"It's fascinating," she breathed, glancing up at the buildings. "I can't help but think that building code enforcement would have a field day here, not to mention the local Health and Fire Department. Yet, it is perfect," she added, waving a hand outward toward the scene in front of her.

Brian chuckled. "The food is some of the best, and freshest, in the world," he said.

"I'm sure," she acknowledged, wiggling her nose when she saw a young couple pick out a fresh fish, which was quickly wrapped in newspaper and handed to them, before walking into a restaurant behind the vendor. "Your friend lives here?" She asked, turning to look around him to the other side when they cut through a narrow slit between two buildings.

"Yes," he said, stepping onto an uneven dock that looked like it was about ready to collapse.

"I hope this is sturdier than it looks," Helen murmured, looking critically at the dock lined with old Junks, a traditional Chinese sailing boat designed and used primarily in the local waters that looked like they were one storm away from sinking.

"This is awesome," Tyrell muttered, raising the camera he had pulled out of his backpack and taking several shots. "The lighting, colors, and mixture of nature and humanity is awesome."

Brian glanced over his shoulder and smiled with reassurance at Helen before focusing on where he was going. Makayla decided that was a smart idea. She tightly gripped Brian's hand when the board under her foot moved.

"Uh, Tyrell, you might want to watch where you are going," Makayla called out when she glimpsed Helen grabbing Tyrell's jacket.

Brian paused when he reached the end of the dock. A large, beautifully restored junk with polished wood sat like a diamond among a pile of coal. It was obvious whoever owned this yacht had lovingly focused exacting attention to every detail when restoring it.

"Oh, man, I have got to do a photoshoot of this boat," Tyrell breathed, staring at the gleaming yacht.

Brian stepped onto the boat, keeping a firm grip on Makayla's hand before turning to help her cross the narrow span gap between the dock and the boat. He released her hand and assisted Helen next, cautioning them not to touch anything, including the railing. Tyrell followed at a slower pace, his mind still caught up in the images he wanted to capture. Makayla glanced at Brian and watched him shift the backpack on his shoulder and gaze warily down the companionway.

"What…?" Helen started to say when Brian shook his head and held out his arm to stop her from moving any further onto the boat.

"He has a very advanced security system," Brian muttered under his breath. "He'll let us know when we can go any further."

Makayla's eyes widened when a man in his early thirties suddenly appeared. His bright blue eyes glittered with wry amusement when he glanced at Brian before they turned to Helen and her. His expression quickly changed to appreciation and curiosity while he studied the two women. His eyes narrowed questioningly when he glanced over at Tyrell.

The man was wearing a pair of Bermuda shorts and a Jimmy Buffet T-shirt that looked like it had seen better days. His tan feet were bare despite the chilly weather and his sandy brown hair looked like he had just been in a wind tunnel. Her gaze flickered to his hands. He was holding what looked like a remote in one hand and a gun in the other.

"Brian, my man, what brings you here with two such beautiful women? I have to tell you, my hope for something extremely pleasurable quickly faded when I saw the heat you were packing," the man said with a wry smile and he jerked his head toward Tyrell. "Who's the camera buff?"

"I need your help, Kevin," Brian admitted, still not moving forward. "Can we come aboard?" He asked, glancing cautiously around.

"Oh, sure," Kevin replied with a wave of the hand holding the remote. "Come on in. I was expecting a delivery. I ordered plenty."

As if by magic, a young boy came running down the uneven dock toward them. They turned when the boy reached the end of the dock with two large bags in his hands. Makayla listened while the boy breathlessly rambled something in Cantonese. Kevin replied, sounding as if he was arguing with the boy. The two went back and forth for several long minutes before Kevin muttered a low curse under his breath and pulled some money out of his shorts' pocket.

Makayla blinked, wondering what he had done with the gun he was holding. His shorts didn't look tight enough around the waist to hold the weight of a gun. Helen's muffled chuckle told her that she had understood everything that Kevin had said.

"You are going to corrupt the boy," Helen remarked with a slightly amused hint of reproach.

Kevin flashed Helen a grin and shook his head. "That dock rat was born corrupt. He'd steal me blind while I was looking if I got too close to him and I wouldn't even know it," he retorted, holding up the two bags. "I hope you are hungry because I am!"

Brian motioned for Tyrell, Helen, and Makayla to follow Kevin across the deck and down the companionway. Makayla's breath caught. If she thought the ninety plus foot junk had been beautifully restored on the outside, it was nothing compared to what it looked like on the inside.

Rich wood, shining stainless steel and brass, leather, and fine silk adorned a luxurious but masculine interior. An electric fire burned in an ornate fireplace and soft jazz music came through hidden speakers. On the wall, a basketball game with the sound muted was playing.

Kevin pointed the remote to the television. The TV turned off and the screen disappeared behind the fireplace, revealing what looked suspiciously like a Marc Chagall painting. She swallowed and looked around the room with a more critical eye. Whoever Kevin was, the guy had some serious money.

"That just isn't right," Tyrell mumbled with a shake of his head, staring in awe at the interior. "This is sure a lot fancier than the *Defiance,* Makayla. If you'd had this, I wouldn't have ever nagged you about taking me back."

"Henry would have killed me if I stole something this nice," Makayla retorted.

"Anyone want a beer?" Kevin asked, placing the two bags on a bar set up to one side of the lounge area and grabbing two beers out from the refrigerator under it and holding them up. "I also have wine or the hard stuff."

"Hell, yeah, what kind do you have?" Tyrell replied with a grin, shrugging his backpack off and placing it on the floor near a large saltwater fish tank before rubbing his hands together in anticipation.

"Water," Makayla and Helen both said at the same time.

"I'll take a beer, too. Any kind is good with me," Brian grunted out, sliding the backpack off his arm and placing it next to a white leather sofa.

Makayla watched him casually reach under his jacket and slide his gun into the holster he had strapped to his belt. She started forward when Kevin placed several plates and some silverware on the bar. Silently picking them up, she carried them over to the table and set it while Helen carried the drinks over.

Several minutes later, they were all seated around the table. It was almost surreal in a way. They had been shot at and running for their lives the last two days and now they were sitting down having a delicious dinner on a million dollar junk with priceless paintings, jazz music, and a cozy fire. She couldn't help it when she slipped her hand down under the table to pinch her leg to make sure she wasn't having some kind of bizarre dream or hallucinating.

She glanced down at her plate, her fork suspended in midair when she felt the small stab of pain. No, she wasn't dreaming. Her gaze lifted when Brian casually poured a small amount of red wine into the wine glass that Kevin had placed in front of each of their plates.

"I'm Kevin Conner, by the way, resident bum of this floating palace," Kevin replied with a decidedly British accent and an easy grin, raising his glass of beer in salute.

"This is Makayla Summerlin and Detective Helen Woo. This giant is Tyrell Richards," Brian introduced before taking a bite of the fish on his plate. "This is good."

"Of course it is," Kevin replied, staring back and forth with a puzzled frown between the two women and Tyrell. "My curiosity is now completely engaged. Does Makayla work for…?" He started to ask when Brian interrupted him.

"No, she is a friend," Brian said in a rather abrupt tone.

"Okay, now I'm really fascinated," Kevin replied with a grin before turning his attention to Helen. His expression remained the same, but Makayla could see the wariness in his eyes. "So, what brings the Hong Kong police to my humble abode?"

"Hardly humble, Mr. Conner," Helen replied, looking around the room. Her gaze paused on several of the paintings, including the Chagall hanging over the fireplace. "What do you do for a living, Mr. Conner?" She asked, returning her gaze to Kevin.

"A little bit of this and that, all legal," he hastily added. "I have a phobia of dark, dirty cells."

Helen's eyebrow rose and she studied him for several long seconds. Makayla's lips twitched with humor when she saw Kevin move uncomfortably in his chair. He picked up his glass of beer and drained it before rising with a muttered question if anyone wanted another one.

"Are we talking *the* Kevin Conner? The guy that invented the NoVac satellite security system?" Tyrell asked with a frown, staring across the table at Kevin.

"Yes," Kevin replied before he froze and looked at Tyrell with wide eyes. "Are you the Tyrell Richards from the National Geographic magazines?"

"The one and only," Tyrell replied with a grin.

"I sponsored your trip to Bora Bora last year," Kevin replied with a deep laugh. "The way you capture an image is unbelievable. I feel like I can reach into the magazine and touch it."

Makayla listened while Brian, Tyrell, and Kevin talked about the different places they had been, some of Tyrell's favorite photo shoots, and sports. Between the delicious food and wine, the soft, mellow music, and the warmth of the fire, she could feel the tension of the day seeping out of her body, leaving her drained. A glance at Helen told her that the detective was feeling the same way.

"Brian, Tyrell, and I will take care of the dishes. Why don't you ladies relax and put your feet up," Kevin suggested with a pointed look at Brian who nodded in agreement.

"I'm not about to turn that down," Makayla replied, covering her mouth when a yawn escaped her.

"Neither will I," Helen murmured, surprised when Kevin stepped behind her and pulled the chair out when she started to rise. "Thank you," she said with a slightly suspicious expression.

"My pleasure," Kevin replied, sliding the chair back under the table once she had stepped to the side. "My mother always raised her boys to be gentlemen."

"I'm impressed," Helen murmured politely, walking over to the couch.

"Your mother…?" Brian muttered dryly under his breath with a raised eyebrow. "I thought you were an only child."."

"Shut up," Kevin mumbled, grabbing the dirty plates off the table.

Makayla chuckled and walked over to where Helen was sitting. She sank down onto the chair across from her, bending to unlace her boots before setting them next to the chair. Helen had removed her short boots, as well, and had curled her legs up beside her on the couch, her head tiredly resting against the palm of her hand.

"Who do you think those men were?" Makayla finally asked, staring into the fire.

Helen released a sigh and leaned her head back against the cushioned headrest. "They were professionals. The way they moved in formation spoke of military training," she reflected in a thoughtful voice. "The weapons they were carrying were not standard issue. I need to see if I can access the database and run the plate numbers I photographed. Unfortunately, I didn't get a good enough look at any of the men."

"What about the man who shot me?" Makayla asked. "I gave the paper to Brian. If you had a database of suspects, mug shots, maybe I could pick him out."

"That would help. I know that Brian brought his laptop," Helen started to say before she covered her mouth when another yawn escaped her. "I'm sorry. I've had very little sleep in the last forty-eight hours and it is beginning to catch up with me."

"I know. I hope the guys finish the dishes before we both fall asleep. I swear Kevin couldn't make it any harder to stay awake. I really shouldn't have had the wine, either. That isn't helping," Makayla murmured, pulling her legs up and turning in the oversized chair so she could lay her head against the soft leather.

Both women were silent, more from exhaustion than being deep in thought. Within minutes, that exhaustion had claimed them. Neither one heard the soft footsteps of the men, nor felt it when they were picked up and carried further down into the luxurious boat to the bedrooms below deck.

Chapter 16

Brian slid the rolling chair closer to the bank of computers in the small staging room that Kevin had set up below deck. The room was almost the size of Brian's small apartment and contained a sophisticated network of servers with a wall of computer screens. Tyrell had volunteered to take a stroll along the shops. He was taking photos and keeping an eye out for anyone who might appear suspicious. While they didn't believe anyone knew about Tyrell, they decided it would be good to have him keep an eye out just in case.

Brian had quietly explained what had happened the previous two days while they cleaned up the dishes. When they were finished, they returned to the salon to find the women sound asleep. A soft, concerned smile curved Brian's lips when he saw the dark shadows under Makayla's eyes.

Brian and Kevin had quickly settled the women in two of the bedrooms below deck. Then Tyrell had quietly murmured he would be back later. Brian grabbed his backpack from the salon and joined Kevin in his office. One row of computers to the left continually monitored the numerous cameras and heat sensitive monitors that Kevin had installed both above and below the water. Most of the old junks moored along the dock belonged to Kevin, decoys to keep any unwanted visitors from trying to sneak aboard to either kidnap him or try to rob him. Brian had eventually learned each boat was rigged with explosives that Kevin could set off with a touch on his watch or the remote that he carried.

Kidnapping was a huge issue for anyone in Kevin's position. Kevin was filthy rich, listed as one of the richest men in the world for his development of security software among other business ventures. He made a nice target for anyone wanting to ransom him. He also made a nice target for anyone wanting to tap into the information stored in his brain.

Kevin made sure that there was little information about his wealth or himself out in the world. He preferred to maintain the persona of a nameless bum who was lucky enough to be living as the caretaker on a rich man's boat. Brian and he had met during one of Brian's first assignments three years ago. Kevin, flush with his newly acquired wealth, had been targeted by an unscrupulous organization upset by having been shut down by him.

British Intelligence, working with the US Government, had been afraid that if Kevin fell into the wrong hands, he could become a liability. The British had asked for assistance in protecting Kevin. When a report had come through that the young, wealthy software magnet had been targeted while on vacation in Thailand, the British had asked for assistance. Since Brian had previously been assigned in Thailand, Brian had shadowed him. The organization had followed through on the reported threat. Brian had thwarted the kidnapping attempt, and had ended up taking the bullet meant for Kevin.

Shortly afterward, Kevin had disappeared from the public eye, erasing or burying information about himself on the Internet until there was very little left available or discoverable about Kevin Conner or his achievements. Brian had been transferred three months after that incident to Hong Kong, but not before an unlikely and rare friendship formed between the two men. It was that friendship that had helped Brian to understand and accept the relationship that had developed between Makayla and Tyrell. Unfortunately, with that knowledge had come the understanding of just how badly he had screwed up with her, making the pain of losing her even more excruciating.

Now, he had been given a second chance. He was smart enough to know that and wasn't about to blow it again. His biggest fear was not being able to protect her. Watching Zhang almost kidnap her and seeing the large bruise still evident on her back from where she had been shot was enough to drive him crazy if he allowed himself to dwell on it.

"Tyrell's a cool guy," Kevin said, turning toward the bank of computers. "I'm glad I got to meet him in person."

"He is. He's also a very good friend to Makayla," Brian admitted with a deep sigh.

"That sounds like you might have a little competition," Kevin remarked, glancing at Brian.

"Not in the way you think," Brian replied. "I screwed up with Makayla. I'm just hoping I can fix it."

"I hope so, too, for your sake. She seems like a pretty amazing woman. Now, where's the image you have?" Kevin asked, sliding the cursor over the software program he had developed. "I'll get it processing while I take a look at the flash drive you have. I'll also run those plate numbers if you hand me the SD card from the camera."

"Doesn't the local power authority complain about your usage? I can't even imagine how much broadband you use," Brian muttered, handing Kevin all the items that he had requested.

"I've got my own power company set up and I use my own satellite system so no one can piggyback on me or shut me down. It can't interfere with my games, either," Kevin added with a grin. "You might like getting shot at in real life, but I prefer the ones where I can press a button and reset myself if I get hit. Real blood and I do not care for each other."

"Yeah, I'll admit getting shot hurts like hell. I need you to access the security camera databases around Graham Marketplace as well if you can and the port areas. I'm looking for this speedboat," Brian said, showing the picture of the boat that Helen had taken. "Also, what can you tell me about Commander Yeng? He put a hit out on Helen, Makayla, and me. I want to know who he sent, if possible."

"Anything's possible if they put the information on a computer," Kevin remarked, slipping the camera's SD card into a reader.

Brian watched Kevin's fingers which were flying across the keyboard and his gaze moved between the screens, the computer, and the scanner. Kevin clicked on the image, enlarging it and copying the license plate numbers into the Hong Kong Transportation database that he had hacked. He did the same with the partial registration number on the side of the speedboat, before typing in a more detailed description.

Brian reached into his pocket and pulled out the flash drive Makayla had found. He placed it on the desk in front of Kevin. He could feel the tension in his shoulders and rolled them. Glancing at Kevin, he sat forward in his seat.

"Thank you," Brian said in a quiet tone. "I know every time you do anything like this, it endangers you."

Kevin shrugged his shoulders. "I swore I'd use this weird brain of mine to help make this world a little better. I figure that was why it was given to me. I don't like getting shot at in real life, but that doesn't mean I can't help out those who aren't afraid of it. Besides, it gets boring just developing shit, playing games, and polishing wood all day. I need something that can keep my brain on edge," he grinned before it faded. "I just hope I don't have to blow up this boat. I'm almost finished restoring it."

"I'll try to make sure it doesn't come down to that," Brian remarked dryly, watching Kevin slide the flash drive off the desk in front of him and plug it into the port on the computer. "Harrington encrypted it. He suspected that Sun Yung-Wing might be onto him a few days ago. Our bosses were reluctant to pull him until they knew for sure that he had all the information. There was a lot riding on his ability to integrate into Sun Yung-Wing's inner circle. It took him almost dying once to get him there."

"What happened to him? Can't you just ask him for it?" Kevin asked, pulling up another screen and dragging it over the box asking for the passcode.

"He's in a coma," Brian replied in a terse tone.

Brian glanced down at the dark screen of his cell phone. He had received a text when they were escaping the apartment, but hadn't had a chance to respond until a short while ago. Harrington had been taken back into surgery to relieve the swelling of his brain. His contact at the hospital had told him that Harrington had begun bleeding again and that things were very grave.

"Should I know what is on this or be blissfully ignorant?" Kevin asked, frowning when he saw a message come up. "Your guy was good, he used multiple safeguards, but I'm better. This might take a little while, but I'll get the information for you."

Brian nodded and stretched before he tiredly ran a hand down over his face. "I'm beat," he said with a yawn. "I'm going to go crash for a couple of hours."

"Security is on, but I've set it just to alert me. I'll keep an eye out for Tyrell. Once he is back, I'll increase it. The damn system is so sensitive it alerts me if a fish so much as farts near this boat, so we'll be safe," Kevin absently mumbled.

"Thanks again, Kevin," Brian murmured with a shake of his head and a dry laugh. He rose and slapped his friend on the shoulder before he quietly left Kevin to his computers.

Brian turned right when he exited the room and headed down the long, plush corridor toward the bow where the bedrooms were. He paused outside of the room where he had placed Makayla. A part of him was torn between finding another spot to grab a few hours of sleep or slipping in and staying with her.

His hand hovered over the doorknob for a brief second before he gripped it firmly in his hand and quietly turned it. The least he could do was check on her. Pushing the door, he glanced at the massive king sized bed where Makayla was sleeping. A frown creased his brow when he heard a soft whimper escape her and she restlessly moved under the covers.

Cursing softly under his breath, Brian pushed the door open further and stepped in before closing it. He padded across to the bed on silent feet. Kicking off his shoes and removing his jacket. He placed it across a chair in the corner. He unstrapped the holster and removed his gun, checking the clip and making sure the safety was on before placing it on the nightstand next to the bed.

He absently ran a hand over the bandage on his arm and rotated his shoulders to relax the tight muscles before he carefully pulled back the covers and slid in next to Makayla fully clothed. Almost immediately, she turned into his warmth and he wrapped his arms around her when she settled her head against his chest.

"Is everything okay?" She mumbled, her voice thick with sleep.

"Everything's fine," he whispered, stroking her side when she rolled and slid her leg over his.

"I missed you," she admitted with a sigh before brushing her nose against the cloth of his shirt and relaxing.

Brian felt her body melt against his when she fell back asleep. His arm tightened around her and he pulled her even closer. He rested his cheek against her hair, enjoying the feel of her in his arms.

"I missed you, too, Makayla," Brian whispered into the darkness of the room. "Far more than I ever could have imagined."

He stared up at the ceiling for several minutes, his mind replaying their last day together over and over while mentally kicking his own ass for being such a stubborn jerk. Soon, the tension melted away and he felt himself slip into a light dream dotted with floating images of sailboats, storm tossed seas, and Makayla's beautiful face.

***

Makayla slowly came awake and stared up at the ceiling of the cabin. She immediately realized that she wasn't alone. The heavy weight of an arm around her waist and the soft sound of breathing near her ear told her that Brian was with her. She carefully turned her head to look at his relaxed face. His face was covered in the shadow of almost two days' growth. His short hair was wildly tousled, reminding her of their days sailing on the *Defiance*.

Her fingers ached to trace his jaw. She had thought she was finally over him, but she knew now that she had just been deluding herself. Seeing him again had shaken her, and all the old feelings had rushed back through her with a vengeance. The only difference now was that they had both changed. They were older, more experienced with life, and both were focused on their own career paths.

"Good morning," Brian murmured, slowly opening his eyes to stare back at her.

"Morning," she whispered, staring back at him before she started to roll away.

"Wait," he ordered in a voice still husky with sleep. "I want to hold you for a minute."

A reluctant smile tugged at Makayla's lips at the familiar words. "Before the world realizes that we are here," she finished, relaxing back and allowing him to pull her close.

"Before the world knows that we are here," he repeated, pressing his lips to her forehead and closing his eyes. "I don't want to lose you again, Makayla," he whispered in a rough voice. "I can't."

Makayla's heart jerked at the heartfelt emotion in his voice. His strong arms were wrapped tightly around her, and, at that moment, she felt like he never would let her go. She trembled, almost afraid to believe him. Memories of how badly their last parting had hurt her swept through her. He must have felt her trying to pull away from him because his arms tightened even more.

"I'm sorry," he said, pulling back just far enough that he could see her face. "I was an ass. I should have trusted you and been more understanding. There is no excuse for the horrible words I said, except that I was a stupid idiot."

A reluctant smile curved the corner of Makayla's lips. "Yes, you should have, and yes, you were," she agreed, her gaze softening when she saw the regret flash across his face along with a touch of resignation. "We were both young. I should have trusted you as well. Tyrell gave me hell for being so stubborn. He wouldn't have cared if I had told you what was going on. He just didn't want the world to know. He called me a stubborn smart-ass who needed to realize that there were people who loved me and that I didn't need to do everything on my own."

A glimmer of amusement came into Brian's eyes and he chuckled. "I like Tyrell even more now," he teased.

Makayla laughed. "You wanted to kick his ass the last time you saw him," she pointed out.

"That was when I thought I had lost you to him," he replied. "I've never wanted to tear someone apart so much in my life, yet I couldn't because I knew how much you loved him."

"I never loved him the way I loved you, Brian," Makayla murmured before rolling away from him and sitting up.

She glanced over her shoulder when she felt Brian move behind her. He was sitting up, but turned toward her. Their eyes locked and she felt the familiar wave of longing sweep through her again.

"Have you stopped – loving me?" He asked quietly.

Makayla stared at him for several long seconds before she finally answered him. It was a question she had been afraid to ask herself. Did she still have feelings for him? If so, how did he feel and could they make it work? There was so much about him that she didn't know anymore. It was obvious that whatever his involvement with the government was, it was much more dangerous than simply working at the Consulate General.

"I don't know," she finally said, glancing away.

***

Brian's gaze followed Makayla as she crossed the room to the attached bathroom. He raised a hand and ran it through his disheveled hair when she quietly closed the door behind her. His mind raced over the conversation. She hadn't said she didn't love him – just that she didn't know if she did. That meant he still had a chance.

He dropped his hand and rolled out of the bed. Glancing back at the door, he could hear the water running. Turning away, he glanced at the clock. It was ten minutes to six in the morning. He would go see what Kevin had discovered and fix some breakfast. He had a feeling they were all going to need it.

Chapter 17

Sun Yung-Wing stared out of the windows of the tall high rise, looking out over Hong Kong and Victoria Bay. In the distance, he could see the large cargo freighters that belonged to his empire – an empire that he had built with a few million dollars from his father and a cruel, iron fist. Anyone that got in his way was ruthlessly destroyed.

He lifted his hand and blotted the sweat on his brow with the fine linen handkerchief crumpled between his stiff fingers. He'd had little sleep in the last week and it was showing, not only physically, but mentally. Somehow, one of his clients had discovered that the information he had compiled on them had been stolen by a government agent. He had been given an ultimatum, retrieve the information within the next twenty-four hours and eliminate those involved or he would forfeit his own life and that of his family. His client had been very explicit that they would set an example for others to see.

Pulling his cell phone out of his pocket, he dialed Ren Lu's number with trembling fingers. He wiped his forehead again while he waited for his new security chief to answer. Annoyance burned that it was taking him longer than it should.

"Yes, Mr. Sun," Ren Lu greeted.

"Have you found it yet?" Yung demanded in a voice edged with desperation.

"I would have informed you if I had," Ren Lu stated.

"The situation… The situation is graver than I originally thought," Yung said, pacing back and forth in front of the window. "My clients have threatened my family and myself."

"Do not call in anyone else. I told you I would handle this. I will see that your family is moved to a secure location," Ren Lu replied.

"There is one man… My client was the one that hired him, not me," Yung admitted. "I won't call in any others, but I can't do anything about him."

"I will deal with him," Ren Lu said after a slight pause. "And, Mr. Sun…."

"Yes," Yung said, pausing to look out of the window again.

"Do not stand in front of the windows. It can be very dangerous to your health," Ren Lu bit out before ending the call.

Yung slowly lowered the phone and stepped away from the window. His whole body was shaking now and sweat ran down from his hairline. He moved back until he was in the shadows of the office, but even there, he wasn't confident he couldn't be seen. His hand searched for the doorknob to his office door and he jerked it open and stepped into the outer office. Two of his bodyguards straightened and looked at him in inquiry.

"Make sure no one enters the conference room," he ordered in a hoarse tone. "No one!"

"Yes, sir," they both replied.

He could feel their puzzled gazes on his back when he turned and hurried down the corridor. Pressing his hand to the scanner, he pushed open the door when he heard the lock disengage and disappeared inside. Only when the door was firmly locked again did he move to the chair at the head of the long table and sink down onto the plush, black leather, his trembling legs unable to support him any longer.

* * *

Ren Lu dropped the cell phone he was holding onto the seat beside him. He stared down at the camera feed on the powerful tablet he was holding. His gaze moved from the figure of Sun Yung-Wing, sitting at the conference room table with his head bowed. His priority had shifted from keeping Sun alive. His focus was now on finding the information that had been stolen and the girl. Something told him if he found one, he would find the other.

Reducing the camera screen, he returned his attention to the information he had been reading on Brian Jacobs. He skimmed through the report, memorizing any information he thought would help him understand the young American better.

The man was an enigma. The information was sketchy at best, and rather disappointing. The man had never been in the military, had a degree in Political Science, and had worked as a Political Advisory at the Hong Kong Consulate for the past three years. There was nothing extraordinary there, yet something didn't ring quite true. He had watched the man in action. Brian moved like he had military training, not like some clerk who always had his nose buried in some political report. There was also no information about Jacobs having a relationship with Makayla Summerlin, excepting their connections to her grandfather. Henry Summerlin had hinted that there had been one, several years ago, and that Jacobs had hurt Makayla deeply. Frustration burned through his gut and he minimized the report he had requested on Jacobs.

Next, he opened the file he had on Helen Woo. The information was basic, citing Woo's education, a brief section on her family, how she excelled in her training with the police department, and that she seldom broke procedure. Again, her connection to Jacobs and Makayla came through Henry. For the first time, Ren Lu regretted following Sun's orders to kidnap the old man. At the time, he could not afford to create a rift between his employer and himself without risking his new position, a promotion he had been diligently working on achieving for the past year. He had seen the old man as only collateral damage.

Drawing in a deep breath, he decided it was time to use the old man as bait. He had followed the men that Sun had hired up to Jacobs' apartment and eliminated them. Jacobs and the others had already been gone by then. He had searched the apartment thoroughly, but except for finding a single bag of neatly folded women's clothing and toiletries in the bedroom, there was nothing to indicate that Makayla and Jacobs were together. Jacobs had had very few personal items there in the apartment. That was unusual for a man who had lived there for the past three years. He had discovered a discarded blood soaked dress shirt and used medical supplies. He knew that was because the sniper had grazed Jacobs on the dock.

A search of the area had turned up a shattered cell phone on the street below, probably the one Commander Yeng had issued to Helen Woo. The information on Yeng had proved slightly more interesting. He would have to make sure when all of this was over that he paid a visit to the Commander.

With time running out, he needed to draw out Jacobs and get the stolen information. Ren Lu touched the tab and pulled the screen back up. A contact number to reach Brian Jacobs through the Consulate was posted. Reaching into the glove box of the car, Ren Lu pulled out a disposal cell phone. He tapped in the number and waited.

"United States Consulate General, how may I direct your call?" The American-accented feminine voice on the other end asked.

"Brian Jacobs," Ren Lu responded.

"One moment, please," the woman replied.

Ren Lu listened to the phone beep several times before another voice answered. This time it was a male. The man introduced himself by the name, Michael Harmon, and stated that Mr. Jacobs was currently unavailable. Ren Lu waited for the man to finish speaking before he responded.

"I would like to leave a message for Brian Jacobs," Ren Lu replied politely. "Please tell him that I have something that belongs to Makayla. I will meet him at the Statue of Queen Victoria in Victoria Park at sixteen hundred hours to discuss the best possible way to return the item that has gone missing."

There was a brief pause before the man spoke. "Yes, sir. I will notify Mr. Jacobs immediately," the man assured him. "Is there anything else?"

Ren Lu paused for a fraction of a second. "Yes, tell him that it would be best if Makayla came with him," he added, his gaze narrowing on the street in front of him. "And, Detective Woo, as well."

"Yes, sir, I'll make sure that he is informed," the man replied before disconnecting the call.

Ren Lu looked at the clock, it was barely seven o'clock. The park would still be fairly crowded at that time of the day. It would provide good coverage. In the meantime, he would locate the hitman Sun's client had hired and take care of him.

He placed the tablet on the seat next to him and started the car. Making a tight U-turn on the nearly deserted street outside of Brian's apartment building, he paused and rolled down his window. With a flick of his wrist, he tossed the disposable cell phone into the trash can. He glanced in the rearview mirror. Further down the street, he could see the garbage collectors emptying the cans and tossing them into the back of an old truck.

Pressing the button, the window silently closed and he merged into traffic heading toward the Street Market district. He had cast the first lure to reel in Jacobs, now it was time to cast his second line for the hitman. If he planned this carefully, he might be able to eliminate both men at the same time, with the unwitting help of Helen Woo.

Chapter 18

Brian looked up from where he was talking to Kevin and Tyrell when Makayla entered the salon where they had had dinner the previous night. She had showered and changed into some new clothes. Brian turned and raised an eyebrow at Kevin.

"With the Internet and enough money, you can get anything you want delivered twenty-four hours a day," Kevin muttered, glancing over at where Helen was talking to Makayla. "It wasn't hard to figure out their sizes by the information on their driver's licenses. You were actually the hardest one to order for, man. You need to get your license updated. I know you've packed on some muscle in the last six years. You looked like you were still in high school. Tyrell already had his stuff in the car. That saved me trying to find anything for him."

"Now, you're just freaking me out," Brian retorted, grabbing several glasses and placing them on the counter so he could pour orange juice into them. "What did you find out?"

"A ton of shit," Kevin admitted, glancing over at the women. "Your dead guy has been very active since he died."

Brian nodded, not surprised. He finished pouring the orange juice and replaced the carton in the small refrigerator under the bar. He had taken a quick shower and changed in the bedroom next to the one Makayla and he had shared. Kevin had dropped off the clothes with a muttering about hoping they fit before disappearing. Despite being a hermit, Kevin kept a very well stocked guest bedroom and bath for his non-existent visitors.

"That smells wonderful," Makayla said politely, watching Kevin slide the scrambled eggs out of the frying pan onto the five plates.

"Survival," Kevin admitted with a grin. "I like eating out, but it gets a bit old after a while. With time on my hands, I started watching the Food Channel. They make it look a lot easier than it is. I spent a fortune on exotic spices and have used only about three or four of them."

Both women laughed at the comical expression of WTF on his face when he said the last sentence. Picking up their full plates, they each walked over and sat down at the table. Tyrell had set it with fresh napkins, silverware, and a large carafe of freshly ground and brewed coffee while Brian placed the glasses of orange juice in front of each setting.

"Thank you for the clothes," Helen said, smoothing a hand over the fine, cream-colored silk blouse she was wearing and soft blue jeans. "How did you know what size I wore?" She asked, pouring a touch of heavy cream into her coffee.

"Your driver's license," Kevin said, following her movement as if mesmerized by the gracefulness of it. "I hacked into the DMV."

Helen's hand paused and her eyes widened. She pressed her lips firmly together. It was obvious to Makayla and Brian that she was trying not to laugh.

"You know that is illegal," Helen responded casually, tapping the spoon carefully on the side of the cup before placing it on the small saucer.

"Just a little bit," Tyrell muttered under his breath, taking a large bite of toast covered with eggs.

"Oh, that's okay. I do it all the time," Kevin said, stabbing his fork into his eggs and taking a bite. "I never get caught," he mumbled around the mouthful of food.

"You just did," Helen pointed out, laying her napkin on her lap while politely ignoring the others, who were trying to hide their amusement. "Did you forget that I am a Detective with the Hong Kong Police Department?" She reminded him with a raised eyebrow.

Kevin paused, his eyes wide before he shook his head. "Not at the moment. You're wanted for the murder of three men," he said, swallowing. "They've got your fingerprints all over Brian's apartment. They have you as a suspect as well, Brian."

"What?!" Helen whispered, paling and setting her coffee cup down.

Kevin shook his head again. "No worries, it's all circumstantial. Commander Yeng has issued warrants for Brian, Makayla, and you. He wants you brought in for questioning. I seriously doubt you'd make it that far before they killed you, though. Sun Yung-Wing and the Taiwan cartel have placed a bigger bounty on you," he added, waving his fork around between eating and talking.

"Kevin," Brian muttered, glaring at his friend.

"What…?" Kevin asked, pausing on the last bite on his plate.

Brian watched his friend's gaze move around to the women's untouched meals. Kevin slowly swallowed before turning to look at Makayla and Helen with a grimace. Setting his fork on his empty plate, Brian waited until Kevin looked back at him.

Brian shook his head. "We'll finish this discussion after breakfast," he finally said, glancing at the two women. "It gets worse."

"My parents are going to be devastated. I know my father will have already heard about it," Helen whispered, staring across at Kevin with wide, stunned eyes and a pale face. "If you will excuse me, I need some fresh air."

Kevin rose when Helen suddenly pushed her chair back from the table and slipped from her chair. He watched her hurry out of the room and up the companionway to the deck. His gaze swung to her untouched plate before moving to Brian and Tyrell with an expression of panic.

"You'd better stay with her," Brian instructed with an intense look. "I hope to hell you've turned off your security system."

"Shit!" Kevin muttered, grabbing the remote on the table next to his plate before he turned on his heel and took off after Helen. "Helen! Don't go near the railing."

Brian, Makayla, and Tyrell watched Kevin disappear up the stairs. Brian slowly shook his head back and forth. Kevin was brilliant, but lacked a filter on his mouth sometimes. He glanced up to see Makayla still staring after the other two.

Reaching over, he cupped her hand in his and squeezed it. She turned to look at him with a look of resignation. Unable to resist, he leaned over and brushed a kiss across her slightly parted lips. She blinked.

"What did you do that for?" She asked with a puzzled frown.

"Because I wanted to…," he admitted, sliding his hand up her arm. "…and to let you know that everything will be okay."

Her brow creased and her eyes flashed with brief exasperation. "We are wanted for murder and have at least two people that I've never heard of who have placed a price on our heads and you think everything will be okay?" She asked in an incredulous tone.

"Yes," Brian replied, sitting back in his seat.

Makayla studied his expression intently when he released her hand and started eating. Brian could feel her staring at him, trying to understand how he could be so confident that everything would work out. His gaze followed her hand to her stomach when it growled.

"How do you know?" Makayla asked, continuing to stare at him.

Brian glanced up and gave her what he hoped was a reassuring smile. "I have one of the smartest, richest geeks in the world hacking into every computer, a Hong Kong Detective known for her tenacious ability to solve crimes, a girl who can kick ass and sail through hurricanes, and a very nosy award-winning photographer grinning at us at the moment. How can we lose?"

Makayla continued to stare at him for several long seconds before she shook her head and picked up her fork. Stabbing at the pile of cheesy scrambled eggs on her plate, she took a defiant bite and shot a glare at Tyrell, who was silently watching them with a huge grin on his face. Brian watched her swallow the mouthful before she turned her attention back to him and spoke, waving her fork between Tyrell and him as she did.

"You are both certifiably nuts," she finally said.

Brian released a low chuckle and grinned. "I'm not the one who stole a sailboat when I was sixteen instead of taking the bus," he teasingly retorted.

Makayla groaned and briefly closed her eyes. "I'm never going to live that down," she muttered, bowing her head and focusing on her food when both men burst out laughing.

* * *

Makayla helped Brian clean up the dishes while Tyrell checked the photos he had taken the night before. Kevin and Helen were still up on the deck. Kevin had briefly come downstairs to retrieve a cell phone from a basket on one of the shelves before disappearing again. Makayla figured it was for Helen from the slightly panicked expression on his face.

They were just finishing up when Brian's cell phone rang. He froze and glanced at where he had laid it on the counter. A frown creased his brow and he quickly dried his hands on the dish towel before tossing it on the counter and picking up his phone.

"Yes," he said.

Makayla watched him glance at her as he listened to the caller speak before he turned his back so she couldn't see his face. Stepping over to stand next to him, she touched his elbow. He turned, his expression hard and distant.

"Thank you," he said, ending the call.

"What is it? Henry…," her throat tightened before she could voice her fear.

He placed the cell phone on the counter and cupped her cheeks. She gazed up at him and drew in a deep breath. She didn't see any grief in his eyes, she saw anger. This was not the emotion of someone who had just received bad news, but someone who was filled with an icy rage.

"I don't know, but it does have to do with Henry," Brian said, staring intently into her eyes.

Makayla's hands rose and slid up his chest. Her fingers curled into the soft material of his shirt. She lifted her chin in determination.

Brian's gaze softened and he leaned down and brushed another kiss across her parted lips, this one a little longer, a little firmer, and a lot more possessive. Uncertainty swamped Makayla, but she pushed it away. He pulled back, releasing her and turning to grab one of her hands.

"It's time for Kevin to share with us what he found out," Brian muttered, reluctantly turning toward the stairs leading up to the deck.

Makayla nodded, her lips tingling from his kiss and her hand wrapped possessively in his. She squeezed his hand, the last of her doubt and fears melting away. Three years ago, they had both been young and insecure. Now, they realized how fragile life was and how quickly things could change. It was at that moment Makayla realized she hadn't been any more ready than Brian had been to commit to a long-term, permanent relationship. She had been focused on getting her education and she still had trust issues that she needed to deal with.

A new sense of determination filled her. She wanted a future with Brian and she was willing to fight for it this time. Straightening her shoulders, she followed him up the stairs and onto the deck where Helen and Kevin were standing by the railing. They turned when they heard Brian and her approaching.

"We need to know everything now," Brian ordered in a hard, clear voice.

"What happened?" Helen asked, seeing the expression on his face.

"Ren Lu or Zhang, whichever name he is going by at the moment, just contacted the Consulate. He wants to meet to discuss an exchange," Brian replied with a grim expression.

"Uh… oh, that's not good," Kevin muttered. "Let's go down to my office."

Chapter 19

Ren Lu lowered the cell phone and peered through the binoculars at his target from the roof of a nearby building. The hitman belonged to an elite group of mercenaries for hire. He had dealt before with men like the man he was watching.

Raul Chavez. There was no information about the man prior to two years ago. Chavez had been a suspect in the assassination of a minor diplomat from Hungary. Six months later, he had been sighted again in Venezuela. Three American Environmental workers had been killed in a suspected kidnapping gone bad. It might have been unquestioned if one of the families hadn't paid to have an exhaustive investigation done. It had turned out the CEO of the oil company had paid to have the workers removed because they had discovered a previously thought extinct bird in the location of a new oil well. A month after that, Chavez was spotted in Brazil.

The list went on and on. Government agencies had grainy images of Chavez, but nothing concrete. They could place him at some of the assassinations, but there was not enough evidence to convict, only enough to suspect him of being involved. Chavez was always gone before anything could be proven. Ren Lu was certain the man was a skilled paid assassin. His informants had flagged Chavez as a possible problem the moment he had entered the country on one of Sun Yung-Wing's freighters. Ren Lu watched Chavez reach for his cell phone at the same time as he paid for a purchase at an open air restaurant. Ren Lu glanced at his own phone, noting the bug he had placed in Sun Yung-Wing's cell phone flash the number Sun was calling across the screen. He was positive it was Chavez's number.

He watched Chavez slide the phone back into the front pocket of his shirt before he pulled the chopsticks out, and began eating while he walked through the crowded marketplace. Minutes later, Chavez crossed the street and entered the building where he had rented an apartment. Ren Lu moved along the edge of the roof. He skirted an abandoned makeshift boxed garden and jumped over the wall, landing on the slightly lower roof of the building next door.

Ren Lu knelt down behind a rusted, metal fire escape. From this angle, he could see into the sixth floor flat where Chavez was staying. The door to the dingy room swung open and Chavez entered, tossing the remains of the meal he had ordered into a trash can by the door. Ren Lu watched Chavez disappear into another room. He shifted and scanned to see if he could pick him up through the other window.

Chavez reappeared several minutes later with a large case. A satisfied smile curved Ren Lu's lips when he saw Chavez pull out the pieces of a sniper rifle. The bait had worked. Sliding back far enough to keep from drawing attention to himself, Ren Lu stood up, turned on his heel, and headed for the door leading down through the building.

His call to Sun Yung-Wing had worked. He knew if he told his employer that he had discovered that Harrington's contact was meeting up with Detective Woo from the Hong Kong police to exchange information on the missing American, Sun would notify the mercenary. He glanced down at his watch. He had six hours to finish setting the trap. Before the end of the day, he would have the information he had been trying to get for the past year, and he would have Makayla Summerlin. One he would deliver, the other he would keep for himself.

..*

"It's a trap, man. It has mousetrap written all over it," Kevin said with a shake of his head when Brian finished telling all of them about the phone call he had received a few minutes ago. "You'd be crazy to follow through and there's no way in hell I'd let you take Makayla and Helen along with you."

"I agree," Tyrell said from where he was sitting toward the back of the group. "The meeting does has 'trap' written all over it. Haven't you seen any of those movies where the bad guy demands a meeting just to knock off the good guy?"

Brian started to say something, but snapped his mouth shut when both women turned to glare at Kevin and Tyrell with a look of warning. A wry grin curved his lips when he saw Kevin sit back and raise his hands in the air and Tyrell snapped his mouth shut and leaned back in the chair with his arms crossed. Behind Kevin, more than a dozen computer screens mounted to the wall showed different images or bits of information that his friend had uncovered last night.

"Go over the information," Brian ordered, nodding to the first screen. "In order, so we can follow along with your thought process."

Kevin released a snort and swiveled in his chair. "Good luck with that! Okay, screen number one," Kevin said, touching a button on the keyboard so that only the first screen appeared. "I'd like to introduce Captain Cheng Li Zhang, of the Chinese People's Liberation Army. The man has more lives than a cat. I found the same info you did about him dying in the helicopter crash, but I also located six other aliases for him and six other tragic accidents."

Brian watched the screens light up one at a time with images of the same man, along with different names, occupations, and causes of death. It was the last one that held his attention. He recognized the man from the brief glimpse he had caught of him outside the café. It was obvious from Makayla's swiftly inhaled breath, that she recognized him, as well.

"Resurrected, he is now called Ren Lu. A week ago, he became Sun Yung-Wing's head of security," Kevin added, touching another button on the keyboard and bringing up the image of Sun Yung-Wing. "I ran a background check on this guy, and let me tell you, he's a piece of work. If you ever have a chance to do business with the guy, run like hell. If you don't believe me, ask his former head of security. Oh, right, you can't."

"What happened to his former head of security?" Makayla asked, a shiver going through her at the cold, dark eyes staring outward.

"I found a reference to a location offshore in about six hundred feet of water," Kevin muttered. "I think you could safely say the guy is fish food by now."

"Gross! Remind me to never eat seafood again," Makayla replied with a repulsed expression.

"What else did you find out?" Brian asked, leaning forward.

"Sun Yung-Wing is involved in some serious shit. I haven't been able to access everything, but I suspect that he isn't shipping the stuffed bunnies that are listed on the invoices. The shipment weights, numbers, and destinations are all wrong. I'll work on a program to see if I can't run some analysis to figure out what type of cargo is, but I'm guessing either human cargo or something more valuable," Kevin replied, pressing another button. "Getting back to Ren Lu, someone doesn't want him found. The information I showed you is all there is. If they have anything else, it isn't in digital form." Kevin moved the latest image of Ren Lu to another screen and the next series of images came up. "Your man, Harrington, was smart. He knew that the information he had was worth a fortune and would likely get him the weighted ankle bracelets next to the head of security if he was caught. The flash drive he was carrying was encrypted. I have had a few minor issues accessing it, but ultimately no one's a match for this brain," Kevin continued, tapping his finger against his head.

"Such modesty," Helen murmured with a raised eyebrow.

Kevin shook his head. "I've got the degrees, or lack of them to prove it," he quipped with a wink. "No, seriously, my brain eats encrypted code for breakfast. I love the challenge. Anyway, once I cracked it, it didn't make much sense at first. Take a look."

Brian sat back and stared at what looked like a bunch of lines. There was a picture of a single sheet of paper. On the paper was a series of numbers and lines, some straight, some curved. It almost looked like a child had scribbled on it.

"What is that supposed to mean?" Brian asked in frustration, shaking his head.

Kevin chuckled. "I had that same WTF moment when I first saw it" he admitted. "What guy would be willing to die for a picture of a bunch of scribbles? I told you that I love challenges, right? Well, I did some research on Harrington and discovered the guy loved to create puzzles."

"How did you find that out?" Helen asked in amazement.

"Old college yearbooks," Kevin replied, pressing a button on the mouse and pulling up a screen. "He was voted the most creative mind in puzzle design by his classmates. There were several comments about his ability to take an image and break it down to its most simple form, tear it apart, mix it up, and put it back together. It is kind of like those slide puzzles where they take a picture and mix up the tiles and you have to keep sliding them around until you get all the pieces in the right place to tell what it is."

Brian glanced at Kevin, who was grinning. "You were able to get the tiles in the right place," he guessed.

"Yep, all it took was understanding Harrington's capabilities for doing what he does best – breaking the image down, tearing it apart, putting each line on a tile, then moving it around until the picture appears. I wrote a program that ran about a hundred thousand different versions of it, which was productive because there was not one, but three individual puzzles hidden within the single image. Each puzzle is a clue to where I suspect Harrington hid the information that you are looking for," Kevin explained, pointing to the puzzles on the screens that were moving through the different positions.

"So, where did Harrington hide the information?" Helen asked with a frown, blinking in surprise when the screens went blank one by one until only three images remained. "That looks like a building."

"It is. This is the Engineer's Office of the Former Pumping Station, also known as The Red Brick House, on Shanghai Street in Yau Ma Tei, to be exact," Kevin replied. He clicked the mouse under his hand to bring up a transparent line drawing of the old building. "It was built in 1895 and is the oldest pumping station in Hong Kong. This is the only section of the original building still standing. It has been used for many things, including a Post Office and a homeless shelter, but is currently empty while the city decides what to do with it."

"Why would Harrington go there?" Makayla asked in confusion.

"I wondered the same thing until I cross referenced the building, along with some of the other clues in Harrington's puzzle. Do you see these combinations of letters and numbers at the bottom of the tiles? Unless you solve the puzzle correctly, they don't mean a thing, but if you put them in order, they make more sense," Kevin explained with a grin. "The guy loves puzzles. What better way to create one than to do it through Geocaching."

"Geocaching," Tyrell repeated, glancing at the numbers. "Isn't that where people do a scavenger hunt using GPS locations and landmarks to hide things?"

"Yep, you have to go to them in order if you want to get the clues where to go next," Kevin said, his voice softening as he stared up at the three screens. "He created a puzzle within a puzzle. Each one will lead you to the next clue until you find where he hid the cache. The flash drive you gave me contained the information on where to start. If you find the first cache, it will lead you to the next."

"Will we have enough time to find each one before we are supposed to meet Ren Lu in Victoria Park?" Makayla asked, biting her lip in worry.

Brian shook his head. "No," he replied in a quiet, thoughtful tone before he glanced at Kevin. "How long do you think it would take someone else to do what you did with the flash drive?"

Kevin shrugged and rubbed the back of his neck. He swiveled around in his chair to look at the others with an intense expression. Brian could almost see the wheels turning in Kevin's brain while his friend processed what he had done.

"Honestly? If they are even half as good as I am, forty-eight hours, at least. If they aren't as talented – longer," Kevin replied.

"And if they were just as good as you or better?" Helen asked in a quiet tone.

Kevin's brow furrowed and he pressed his lips together. Brian could tell Kevin was biting back a sharp retort. He had to hand it to his friend; Kevin did a good job of controlling himself.

"If they are as good or better, which is highly unlikely, by the way, then I would say twenty-four hours or less," Kevin reluctantly muttered.

"What are we going to do?" Makayla asked, turning to look at Brian with pleading eyes. "If he'll tell us where Henry is, we have to do something."

"We go to the first location and find the clue to the second one," Brian said, staring up at the screens before looking at the others. "Then, we'll meet Ren Lu at the statue in Victoria Park. I'll give him the flash drive and we'll get the information about Henry. Helen and I will go after Henry while Tyrell and you locate the second clue. Once we have Henry, we'll leave him here with Kevin and meet up with the two of you."

"I'll fit each of you with a GPS tracking device. That way I'll have real time access to you. I can hop on several different satellites to keep the feed live. I can also help guide you from here to the next location and tell you what to expect," Kevin said with a grim expression.

"It is almost ten o'clock, we need to get moving," Brian said, rising out of his seat.

Chapter 20

Brian and Tyrell walked along the dock ahead of Makayla and Helen. Makayla fingered the watch that Kevin had given her. Helen wore a matching one while the two guys had slightly larger, more masculine ones. It would appear that was another one of Kevin's soft spots, buying fake designer watches from the kids who littered the sidewalks peddling their collections to unsuspecting tourists.

Kevin had opened the back and inserted a small tracking device into each one before sealing it and syncing the times. Makayla glanced out over the water. The morning was a beautiful one, much different from the last couple of days. The weather had warmed up a little, moving into the low seventies, so all she needed was a light jacket over the dark purple silk blouse that Kevin had ordered for her. She wore a short, black leather jacket and matching black jeans. She had opted for her own hiking boots, which worked out well since they matched her jeans and jacket.

Makayla had braided her hair to keep it out of her way. She glanced over at the others. Helen was wearing the cream-colored silk blouse with a pair of dark blue jeans and low-cut cream-colored boots. She had a dark red leather jacket that really complemented her pale complexion and jet black, shoulder length black hair.

Kevin hadn't been as creative with Brian, settling for a pair of faded denim jeans, a black T-shirt, and a matching black jacket. Tyrell was dressed in his usual jeans, button up white dress shirt, and gray pullover sweater. Both men carried a backpack on their shoulders. Makayla bit her lip when she remembered that she'd forgotten to ask Brian about his arm. She should have offered to change the bandage on it this morning.

"Thank goodness we are off that dock," Helen muttered under her breath. "I keep expecting to fall through it at any time."

Makayla released a strained chuckle and nodded. "I know, but you have to admit that it probably helps deter wayward tourists from venturing down it," she reflected, walking over to Tyrell's car. "Thank you," she whispered when she saw Brian standing with the door open for her.

"Makayla," Brian said, reaching out and touching her arm.

"Yes?" she replied, looking up at him.

His hand slid up her arm to tenderly touch her cheek. She turned her face into his palm, feeling the warmth and soaking it up. At that moment, she knew she still loved him – that she had never stopped.

"Whatever happens, you make sure you stay safe. I want you to run like hell if things go south. Run and don't look back," Brian ordered in a slightly desperate tone. "I need to know that you are safe."

Makayla knew her eyes gave away her thoughts. He must have seen the rebellion in them, the fact that she wouldn't flee, she would fight. He bent and captured her lips in a passionate, desperate kiss. His fingers tangled in her braid, holding her to him. It took several long seconds before he reluctantly released her and stepped back. His face was grim with determination.

"I won't be stupid, Brian," she promised. "If I need to run, I'll run. But, I won't leave you or any of the others behind."

Brian's lips twisted into a bitter smile. "Not like I did," he muttered in a self-condemnation.

"We both made mistakes. It wasn't just you," she whispered before she reached up and pressed her lips against his to silence his protest.

She pulled back and gazed at him for a second before sliding into the back seat. Brian closed the door and slid into the seat in front of her. Their eyes locked in the rearview mirror before she pulled away, distracted by Tyrell's humming.

"Shut up," she muttered when he grinned at her.

"K-I-S-S-I-N-G," Tyrell teased. "It's good to see you together again."

Makayla shot Tyrell a scowl before she leaned over and brushed a kiss against his cheek. As crazy as he drove her at times, he was also the one to remind her to embrace life and not always be so serious. Straightening, she caught Brian staring at her again.

His eyes warm with humor and – love. She swallowed when a wave of heat filled her.

"You've got it bad," Tyrell whispered, his eyes glittering with amusement.

"I should have drowned you when I had the chance," she growled, rolling the window down so that the sounds of traffic and wind could drown out his laughter.

***

Makayla was glad Brian was the one doing the driving. Not only was her head still trying to get around the fact that the cars drove on the opposite side of the street like the British, but the traffic and number of signs made her head spin. Helen was giving Brian directions whenever they came to a gridlock on where to turn. It also helped having two people know where they were going and the different streets that would get them there.

She had learned over the last couple of days that Hong Kong had wide streets that were very, very busy and narrow streets that were – well, very, very busy. The narrow streets were made even more claustrophobic by the tall high rises that loomed up over them and the congestion of pedestrians as well as the motorized traffic.

A wave of longing swept through her. Henry and she should have been out on the open sea by now, heading east, then south along the shipping lanes. She closed her eyes and lifted her chin to the infrequent patches of sun that slipped between the buildings. With the motion of the car and the wind in her face, she could almost imagine that she was on the *Defiance,* cutting through the waves with nothing to stop her.

It was a nice dream until the smell of exhaust and the piercing sound of a motorcycle going by forced her to roll up the window. She gave Helen a wan smile when the other woman glanced at her with a worried frown. Makayla sat back against the seat and stared out the window.

"Do we have any idea of exactly what we are looking for at this place?" Tyrell asked.

"Kevin printed out the images. In the lower corner is a GPS location. Normally, most devices are only accurate to within ten feet. Kevin gave me a military grade unit accurate to within two," Brian said. "It's in my backpack."

"He already programmed in the wave points," Helen murmured. "Once we find what we are looking for, it should give us the location of the second site. Kevin said the image shows a Buddha, but it could mean anything. The wave points will give us the actual location. Harrington reversed the last puzzle. We need whatever clues he left at the second location to find the third spot – and the information that he stole. In the first puzzle, he gave us an image of the building. There isn't anything else. Kevin said we should find what we need inside the building, but there isn't much information to guide us, just the image of the building and a few lines with an arrow on it. He believes we need to locate the arrow inside the building to find the location of the second puzzle."

"Don't forget we've got to figure this out before the bad guys do," Tyrell pointed out.

Makayla shook her head. "Even if they do, without the first piece it will be virtually impossible for them to know where to look. They would have a much more difficult time solving the puzzle."

"Yes," Helen agreed. "Yet, not completely impossible."

"Which is why we are going to find the first one and solve where the second one is before we meet with Ren Lu this afternoon," Brian said, glancing up in the mirror.

"We should rent another car," Helen suggested. "We will need two vehicles."

"I'll stop after we finish at the Red Brick House," Brian said.

"If one of us rents it, won't they be able to trace us? Unless Tyrell rents another one," Makayla asked with a frown.

Brian flashed a wry grin. "I've got that covered," he promised, turning onto Shanghai Street.

"What are we going to do about this afternoon?" Tyrell asked, leaning forward and resting his hand on the back of the seat.

"Helen, Makayla, and I will meet with Ren Lu," Brian stated with a thread of steel in his voice. "You are going to use that powerful lens on your camera to capture some photos of Ren Lu and make sure that we don't have any other visitors."

"I hope these little microphones really work. They look more like toys," Tyrell mumbled, reaching into his pocket to finger the tiny box containing a wireless microphone and earpiece.

"If Kevin gave them to us, they'll work," Brian assured him.

Several minutes later, Brian pulled into a loading space across the street. Makayla marveled at not only his luck, but his skill at finding a spot in the lane lined with blue and green delivery trucks. Anxious to find what they were looking for, they all opened the doors to the car at almost the exact same time. Makayla's lips curved upward when she heard Tyrell mutter a curse under his breath that small cars and tall men were not compatible with each other.

"It should be illegal to make cars this small. It's worse than the head on the *Defiance*," he muttered and gave her the lopsided grin she loved.

Makayla shook her head in sympathy before turning to look around her. Each side of the street was lined with huge high rise apartments. Glancing down the street, she could see a small, red brick building that looked out of place among the towering buildings. Workmen, dressed in yellow and orange vests, worked nearby while metal railings ran along the roadway that looked like it was being worked on. Pedestrians walked by, going about their daily business.

Along the street, a truck slowed and pulled into a loading area. Workers stood ready to help unload items from the truck into the local Food and Environmental Hygiene Department. She turned when she felt Brian's hand on her arm. It took a second for her to realize the others were waiting for her.

"Sorry," she mumbled, stepping around the car.

Helen and Tyrell were already crossing the street. Makayla nodded to Brian when he shot her a questioning glance before they both darted across to join the other two. The four of them quickly walked along the sidewalk down to the two-story, colonial style building.

Makayla's gaze moved over the Chinese double-clay tile roof and down over the arches that showcased the beautiful ironwork of the second floor verandah. There was only one window on the first floor facing the street while there were three windows on the side closest to them. It was impossible to see inside the building through the glass, ironwork, and black shutters that covered them. They continued past and slipped behind a small brick wall to the black painted door on the other side.

Tyrell stood in front of Brian, his massive six foot two, two hundred and sixty pound frame blocking Brian from view. He fiddled with the camera he had hanging from his neck. Helen stood next to him while Makayla faced both Tyrell and Helen. To a casual observer, it would look like they were having a conversation.

Makayla kept her gaze glued on Brian. Within less than a minute, he had picked the lock on the door and slipped through it. Helen went next. Makayla glanced up at Tyrell, who nodded for her to go.

"I'll be the lookout and distract anyone if they come. Go find the next clue," he said with a grim smile.

"Thanks, Tyrell," she whispered, slipping behind him and disappearing into the building before she closed the door behind her.

The interior was completely devoid of light except for the twin glows from Brian's and Helen's cell phones. Makayla fumbled in her purse and pulled her phone out as well. Pressing the button, she swiped upward on her phone and tapped the flashlight.

She walked slowly forward, gazing around. The building had been renovated into a type of theater for the performing arts from the looks of it. The windows were covered on the inside so the interior was dark. A stage had been built against the back wall while a staircase across from it led to the upper floor.

"I'll check the upstairs," Brian murmured.

"I'll check along the walls," Helen said.

"I guess I'll check out the other rooms – and hope there are no monsters, bogeymen, or hired hitmen waiting in the shadows since I'm the only one without a gun," Makayla muttered under her breath while staring after the other two when they disappeared in opposite directions.

Makayla decided right then and there that she didn't have what it took to be a police officer, spy, or whatever the hell Brian was now. Give her the ocean and a boat under her feet and she was fine, give her an enclosed, dark area while being hunted by killers and she concluded she was ready to climb under the bed with the imaginary monsters and hide.

Shaking her head at her musings, she started across the room, heading in the direction of several doors she had noticed along the far wall. She stepped around several wooden boxes sitting on the floor and walked toward the first door.

Opening the door, she saw some faint light from outside coming through the window. It looked like they may have been offices at one time. She was about to step inside when she heard Brian call for Helen and her. Turning, she closed the door behind her and hurried back toward the stairs.

She paused at the foot of the staircase and gazed upward. Brian was on the landing separating the two floors. He motioned for Helen and Makayla to follow him. They climbed the stairs, their footsteps echoing in the stillness of the building.

"What is it?" She asked in a hushed voice.

"I'm not sure. I found a faint arrow on the wall upstairs," he admitted. "It looks like there is a piece of paper attached to one of the beams above it."

They shone the light from their phones up at the ceiling. Sure enough, along one of the beams there was a small piece of paper attached to it. Makayla looked at Brian and Helen. Helen wouldn't be tall enough, but she might be if Brian could boost her up.

"Do you think you could lift me up?" Makayla asked.

Brian nodded and handed his phone to Helen. Makayla tucked her phone back in the pocket of her jacket and moved over to Brian when he squatted down. Sliding her leg over his shoulder, she steadied herself using the wall. Once she was sitting on his shoulders, he stood up, holding her lower legs to keep her balanced.

Makayla stretched, her fingers barely touching the corner of the white piece of paper illuminated by the light from Helen's cell phone. It took her four tries before she was able to grab enough of it to pull it down. She held it tightly while Brian lowered her back to the floor.

She carefully climbed off of his shoulders, holding on to them so she wouldn't fall. She gave Brian a brief, triumphant smile and held up the paper before unfolding it. Her brow creased when she saw a jumble of letters and a small key taped to the paper.

"What is this supposed to mean?" She asked, blowing out a breath in frustration.

Brian took the paper and the key from her, studying it. Makayla bit her lip before she reached into her pocket and pulled out her phone. She quickly did a search for Geocaching in Hong Kong. A moment later, she grinned in triumph again, this time glancing at the encrypted code key from the website and the letters on the paper.

She copied the key to her notes before turning to him. "Read me the letters," she requested.

Brian read out the letters and she typed them in. Once he was finished, she started deciphering the code. Helen stood closer, watching what she was doing.

"No, that should be a W," Helen whispered, understanding what Makayla was doing. "Outside Kowloon Tong MTR station, Exit F, CLP Box, top left corner. That's about five kilometers from here."

"Let's go," Brian muttered, folding the paper and sliding it into his pocket.

The three of them made their way back down the stairs. Brian switched off his light when they reached the door. On the other side, they could hear the muted voice of Tyrell laughing and chatting with someone. They waited, growing frustrated as the minutes passed. Almost ten minutes later, Tyrell called out a goodbye. Brian carefully opened the door.

"Clear," Tyrell muttered, standing in front of the opening to cover their exit. "Damn, I didn't think that cop was ever going to leave."

"What happened?" Helen asked in concern.

"He was an amateur photographer," Tyrell replied with a sigh. "He liked my camera and started asking questions. Did you guys find the next clue?"

"Yes," Brian replied, glancing back and forth before crossing the road back to the car. "We need to head to the Kowloon Tong MTR station."

Chapter 21

Half an hour later, Brian pulled up on Somerset Road in front of the Kowloon Tong Station, a gleaming white building with blue accents. There was a small line standing at the front ticket area while exiting passengers either waited or walked down the street, heading for the next destination.

Makayla saw Brian's lips tightening in the mirror when he saw there was no place to park, even temporarily. His gaze flashed over the front of the building. He turned his head when she touched his shoulder.

"We'll go. You circle around. Give me the paper," she instructed.

"Here you go," Brian said, pulling the paper with the key attached out of his pocket and handing it to her. "I'll circle around and see if I can find a spot to park along the edge of the road."

"Hopefully, it won't take us long to find it," she said, taking the paper.

She glanced around to make sure it was safe to get out before opening the door and sliding out. Helen and Tyrell also pushed open their doors. The three of them hurried across the almost deserted street.

Glancing around, she turned, trying to see if she could make sense of what the note said. A frown of frustration creased her brow and she turned to Tyrell and Helen with an almost desperate expression. Helen looked just as puzzled as she did.

"What is a CLP Box?" Makayla asked.

"I don't know. I was hoping it would be something obvious," Helen admitted, glancing around.

"Power box," Tyrell muttered. "Look for some type of power box."

"Power box?" Makayla repeated with a puzzled glance.

"There," Tyrell said, pointing upward. "Follow the conduits. They have to lead to a junction, or CLP box."

"This way," Helen said, her gaze following the line of gray metal pipes protecting the electrical wires inside.

They started forward, cutting around the ticket booth. A transit worker called out to them when they started to go around one of the gates. Helen pulled out her identification and flashed it before speaking in rapid Cantonese. Whatever she said, it must have worked because the man hurried forward and opened the gate for them.

Helen motioned for them to follow her and they walked quickly around the curved wall, following the conduits. She slowed when they reached the far wall. Her gaze narrowed on a group of large electrical boxes on the wall next to a door marked **Danger – Do Not Enter: Electrical**.

They hurried over to them. From a distance, Makayla could see there was a tall, narrow, clear plastic box sitting on top of the one closest to the corner. Even from several feet away, she could see it had two labels taped to the side with the message Do Not Remove on it. Makayla looked at Tyrell with a doubtful expression.

"Really?" She asked in a questioning tone. "Would Harrington really hide something as important as the key to the next puzzle in such an obvious and risky place?"

"How am I supposed to know how spies think? I'm not crazy enough to get into a career where people try to kill me all the time," he retorted, reaching up and pulling down the box.

Makayla and Helen gathered around him, watching him unhook the plastic latch. Inside the container was a small notepad and an odd assortment of items, mostly junk. There was a souvenir Buddha keychain, several toys from a child's meal, a pen, some business cards, a dollar bill from the U.S. with a website written on it, and a metal pin with the words I love Hong Kong.

Makayla thumbed through the notepad. Written inside were comments from people from around the world who were doing the Geocaching. She shook her head at the other two, there was nothing that needed a key or had additional numbers on it. She handed the notepad back to Tyrell.

"Nothing," she said, glancing around the terminal again before pulling the paper and the key out of her pocket. She unfolded it and read the message again. "CLP Box...."

She touched the key. It was too large to go in the small lock on the box. Her gaze followed the conduit down to the box again. The wires stopped there, but they had to go somewhere else. Her gaze turned to the door marked Electrical. She ran her thumb over the key and glanced down at the lock on the door.

"What are you thinking?" Tyrell asked, replacing the plastic box.

"What if...," Makayla's voice faded and she pulled the key off the paper and walked over to the door.

Her hand wrapped round the long metal handle. It was locked. She fitted the key to the deadbolt just above the handle. Sure enough, it slid in. She twisted it and felt the lock give. Pulling open the door, she glanced over her shoulder at Tyrell and Helen before disappearing inside the small room.

***

Brian gazed down the street, waiting. His fingers flexed on the steering wheel while his gaze followed each person who entered and left the building. Looking up, he watched a city bus approach from the other end of the street. It passed him and pulled into the drop off space in front of the Metro station.

His mind wandered back to the night before while he impatiently waited. Holding Makayla in his arms again had been a combination of pure pleasure and agonizing torture. The more time he spent with her, the more he wanted. He had always had a physical attraction to her, but there had also been something deeper. Three years ago, he had been too stupid and callow to understand what it was until he had lost it.

His fingers itched to pull the ragged photo out of his wallet. Over the last few years, he had tortured himself with the urge to call or text her, but he had been too much of a coward. His job allowed him to access a lot of information, but even he couldn't stoop that low. If he was truthful with himself, he would've admitted that it was more out of fear of finding out Makayla had moved on and found someone – someone like Tyrell – than out of any moral or ethical code. As long as he didn't know, he could still hope and dream that one day he would get up enough nerve to see her again.

He hadn't been completely ignorant of what she was doing. Deep down, he figured his mom probably knew that he was hungry for any tidbit of gossip about Makayla. She often shared what she had heard from Henry with him in her emails. He had hungrily read over each piece, proud of Makayla's accomplishments, curious as to whether or not she missed him as much as he missed her, and wondering if she would ever forgive him for being a jealous fool.

Two days after they had broken up, he had made reservations to return home after he had had enough time to cool down and think things through, only he never made it. The afternoon he was supposed to leave he had been called into Senator Womack's office. Instead of the Senator, though, it had been two other men he had never met before offering him the chance of a lifetime to move up in his career working with foreign governments. The next thing he knew he was in an intensive six month training program before he was deployed on his first mission.

Brian glanced down at his fingers. He forced himself to draw in deep, calming breaths the way his handlers had taught him. His life had become too dangerous for him to think of having a long-term relationship with anyone, especially someone like Makayla who deserved a man who would always be there to cherish her.

He jerked when he felt the vibration of his cell phone. Pulling it out of his jacket pocket, he glanced at the message. His gut tightened and he slowly responded.

Harrington didn't make it, the message read. *Any more info?*

Affirmative, he typed, pausing before adding, *Soon.*

Brian sat back in the seat and stared out the front window. A part of his mind continued to process everything going on outside the Metro, while another part absorbed the information he had just received. The fact that two years' worth of undercover work and the lives of thousands of innocent people were at stake if they couldn't find the information Harrington had hidden, wasn't lost on him. What else wasn't lost was the fact that Harrington had recently confided in him that he had a wife and son – a wife who was now a widow and a son who would never know his father.

This was another reason Brian had avoided trying to contact Makayla. The thought of loving her and having to lie to her day in and day out, to leave and possibly never come home, or to have a family and know that not only was he risking his life, but theirs if his enemies discovered them had been too much to risk.

He had asked Harrington about it just days before over a beer at one of the local bars. It had been the night that Brian had given Harrington the orders from their handlers to proceed with stealing the information Harrington had uncovered on Sun Yung-Wing's private computer. They had concluded they would have one chance to copy the files containing the detailed lists of buyers, suppliers, amounts, and locations of shipments of weapons being dispersed to terrorist groups around the world.

Brian felt his stomach clench when he remembered their conversation and the happy, but also haunted look in Harrington's eyes. Personally, Brian had thought the man had been crazy, but there was nothing he could have done to change the situation. Harrington was in too deep to be pulled out without jeopardizing the mission. The only good thing was that Harrington's wife and son were in the States visiting her sister and brother-in-law.

Now, he would have to inform Harrington's handler that the British agent had left behind a family. Harrington's wife would be well compensated financially, but that could never compensate for losing her husband, or the fact that she would never know the truth of his career. Harrington insisted it was worth it, that having a wife and son made what he did worthwhile. Brian had been doubtful.

A movement out of the corner of his eye drew his attention. Once again, he felt a shaft of desire and the magnetic pull of some invisible force drawing him toward the slender young woman who had just emerged from the building. He wondered if this was what Harrington had felt for his wife.

Brian released a soft curse at his thoughts, shifted the car into drive, and pulled out onto the street. Within seconds, the small group was piling back into the car. He glanced over his shoulder at Makayla's smiling face. She held up a piece of paper with a series of numbers on it.

"Tian Tan Buddha," she said with a glow of triumph.

"We won't have time to get there and back before we meet with Ren Lu," Helen commented with concern. "It will take over an hour to get there, plus the time to locate the item and we still need to rent another car."

"We'll stick with the plan," Brian said, turning on his signal and merging into traffic. "You, Makayla, and I will meet with Ren Lu, while Tyrell watches our backs. I'll give Ren Lu the flash drive when he gives us Henry's location. The moment we have it, Tyrell and Makayla will go to the Tian Tan Buddha while we go after Henry. Then, we meet up once again when we know where the last location is. We'll get the information, and get the hell out."

Makayla leaned forward and rested her chin on her arm on the back of Brian's seat. He glanced in the mirror and could practically see her mind racing with questions and concerns. Turning left, he headed back to Victoria Park. There was a car rental place not far from the marina.

"What if he lies about Henry?" Makayla asked in a quiet voice, unable to keep the worry out of it. "What if you give him the flash drive and Henry isn't where he says he is?"

"I'll know," Brian assured her with more confidence than he felt. "Kevin will be listening in and can give me a heads up if Ren Lu tries to lie."

"How can he do that?" Tyrell asked, leaning forward as well.

Brian glanced in his side mirror before changing lanes and accelerating. There was a lot that Kevin could do remotely. He could keep a visual on them, listen in, and cross check information to see if Ren Lu was telling the truth. Some of the methods his friend would use were highly classified, his connections to some of the satellites were part of the security system he had helped develop for the government, while another was just crafty nerdiness and too much time on his hands.

"Whatever information Ren Lu relays about Henry's location, he can cross check to make sure Ren Lu is telling us the truth," Brian explained, merging onto the Eastern Harbour Crossway. "There is no guarantee, but my gut tells me that Ren Lu will tell us the truth about where Henry is."

"But… Why would he?" Makayla asked in a husky tone. "Why wouldn't he just kill him if he doesn't need him anymore?"

Brian glanced at her in the mirror before forcing himself to focus on the traffic ahead of him. Men like Ren Lu and he didn't kill unless they had to or were ordered to. If Henry wasn't dead yet, he most likely had not been ordered terminated. Once Ren Lu reported back to Sun Yung-Wing that he had the information, that could change. Brian was betting that Ren Lu wouldn't terminate Henry until he knew he had the information his employer was seeking in his hand. Henry alive, whether Ren Lu had him or he was somewhere else, was still a valuable pawn. Men like them were not restricted by releasing that pawn back out into the world. They knew they could always locate them again if they needed to.

"He can kill him anytime, Makayla," Brian finally replied. "He'll want to make sure he retrieves the information first."

Brian felt Makayla's hand tremble and she drew in a swift breath. "What happens when he finds out that we've got to it first?"

"I have to make sure Henry and you have disappeared before that happens," Brian said, turning into the parking lot of the car rental. "Then, I go hunting."

Chapter 22

Victoria Park: Fifteen Hundred Hours

Makayla nervously gazed around her. Brian and Tyrell had parked in the parking lot located in front of one of the large pavilions. Tyrell had grabbed his backpack and taken off in the opposite direction, pretending he didn't know them, while Brian, Helen, and she had exited and walked along one of the main stone paved paths near the South Pavilion Plaza.

They passed a long line of courts filled with late afternoon visitors playing basketball. Up ahead, Makayla could see a huge fountain where couples sat enjoying the fading sunlight while the children ran around squealing and trying to splash in the spray. She bit her lip, wondering if Ren Lu was already there, watching them.

"I spent many days playing in this park," Helen reflected, staring around her. "It seems like a lifetime ago. My parents would bring me here to race boats in the Model Boat Pool or to listen to the concerts at the bandstand. They still come here," she mused, watching an older couple walk by holding hands.

"Do you still come here?" Makayla asked, watching a couple of young boys turn to gawk at several giggling girls. It didn't matter where you lived, people were the same everywhere, she thought. "It looks like a huge park."

"It is. I haven't been here in years," Helen murmured. "There is a lot to do and some of the festivals they have here are magnificent."

"Did you get a chance to talk to your father?" Makayla asked, glancing at the other woman's calm expression.

"Yes, Kevin was kind enough to supply me with a cell phone," Helen replied in a soft voice. "My father is a very powerful, much respected member of the police force. Commander Yeng should have taken that into consideration when he made the accusations that he did. An investigation has been started and Commander Yeng has been relieved of duty. There is still concern over those on the force that may be on the same payroll as Yeng. Now that I know there is more to this case than Henry's disappearance, I've asked Commander Wang to allow me to continue the investigation alone until we know who could be trusted. Both he and my father agreed. I also thought it would be safer for Henry."

"Can you trust the person who has replaced him?" Brian asked, glancing around.

"Yes," Helen chuckled. "Captain Wang has been promoted. He is a good man with a kind heart. Yeng did not like Wang because he couldn't be bought. He used his weight as an excuse, but Wang has been with the force for over twenty years."

"There's the statue," Brian interjected with a nod of his head.

"And Ren Lu," Makayla murmured, slowing down when she saw the tall, menacing form of the man she just mentioned standing by the railing surrounding the statue of Queen Victoria.

Makayla felt a shiver run through her body when her gaze locked with his. Brian must have seen the possessive look that flashed across the other man's face before it disappeared because he reached over and grabbed her hand. She wanted to look up at Brian, but was afraid to take her eyes off the man who had not only kidnapped Henry, but had cold-bloodedly shot her.

They slowed to a standstill when they were within a few feet of Ren Lu. This was the first time that Makayla had a chance to really see the man up close and personal. The other two times, she had been fleeing for her life. She wrapped her arms around her waist when Brian released her hand.

"You are a very talented man for being a Political Advisory, Mr. Jacobs," Ren Lu stated in greeting, staring at Brian with an assessing gaze before turning to look at Makayla. "And you are a very resourceful young woman, Makayla Summerlin."

Makayla's chin jerked up and she raised her eyebrow at him, not missing the way he drew her name out or the narrowing of his eyes when he said it. She had all but forgotten what he had said to her the last time they had met when she asked him what he wanted. Her brow creased into a fierce frown when his silky words echoed through her mind and she pressed her lips together in defiance as she glared back at him.

"You would be too if someone was shooting at you or trying to kidnap you," she retorted in a scornful tone. "Where's my grandfather? I swear, if you've hurt one hair on that old man's cranky head, I'll do more than knee you in the groin."

Ren Lu lips twitched, even as his eyes hardened. "He's alive," he replied, turning his attention to Helen. "I see your father has taken care of Commander Yeng."

"How do you know…?" Helen started to demand before she pressed her lips together.

Ren Lu's intense, dark gaze sent a shaft of fear through Makayla. This guy wasn't someone you wanted to underestimate. Automatically her hand rose to push back the strand of hair from her face when the wind blew it. She could feel her face flush when his gaze followed the movement and quickly dropped it back to her side.

"Where is Henry Summerlin?" Brian demanded, stepping to the front and side so that he was slightly in front of Makayla.

Ren Lu's gaze flashed with irritation before he turned to stare back at Brian. Makayla swore she could feel the temperature drop from the frigid glare he shot Brian. Makayla hastily bit her lip before she made the mistake of making a nasty retort. Something along the lines of the two men reminding her of dogs peeing on trees.

"Harrington is dead," Ren Lu stated instead of answering Brian. "I want the information he gave to Summerlin. It was not on the old man or on the sailboat, so I would assume that Makayla has it. You give me the item I am looking for and I will give you the location of the old man."

"It won't do you much good," Brian said, pulling the flash drive out of his pocket. "Harrington encrypted it. As you said, Harrington is dead. Without the password, there is no way to retrieve the information."

"I will worry about that," Ren Lu replied, holding out his hand for the flash drive. "Give it to me and I will tell you where Summerlin is located."

Brian's hand paused, his fingers still wrapped tightly around the flash drive while his gaze was fixed on Ren Lu's face. Makayla could see the muscle twitching in his jaw. Her fingers curled until she could feel her nails biting into the flesh of her palm. All she wanted to do was rip the flash drive out of Brian's hand, give it to Ren Lu, then knock the crap out of the guy once he told her where Henry was being held.

She finally released the breath she was holding when Brian turned his hand over and dropped the flash drive into Ren Lu's opened palm. The other man didn't close his fingers around it or drop his hand. He continued to stare at Brian for several long seconds before a satisfied smile curved his lips at the corner.

"Container Terminal 8 West," Ren Lu stated in a quiet, even tone. "The Sea of Hong Kong; Deck Three."

Makayla, unable to stand not knowing, stepped past Brian when Ren Lu started to take a step back. Her hand reached out and she touched his arm. She knew her gaze was filled with worry, but she didn't care. They had what they needed – hopefully.

"Is he… Is my grandpa okay?" She asked in a hesitant voice, almost afraid of his answer.

Ren Lu paused and looked down at her. "His wrist is broken. Other than that, he is well," he promised.

"Broken… How…?" Makayla started to say when she heard Tyrell's sharp warning a moment before Brian jerked back against the railing. "Brian!"

Her cry was cut short when Ren Lu wrapped his hand around her arm and pulled her up against him. Another sound exploded around them, sending Helen diving to the ground. Makayla's eyes were glued to Brian. He had been struck in the chest. She could see the dark hole in the front of his shirt. The second impact knocked him backwards and over the short fencing surrounding the statue. Her lips parted to scream when she felt a slight sting followed by warmth.

"Makayla!" Tyrell's voice seemed to shout in her head even as it started to grow fuzzy.

It took a few precious seconds for Makayla to realize Ren Lu had drugged her. She fought against the effects, clenching her fist and swinging out at the same time as her legs started to give out from under her. Her body felt motionless for a second before an arm wrapped around her waist and she stumbled forward when Ren Lu turned and began hurrying them away from where Brian lay hidden behind a row of short hedges and Helen was behind a stone bench.

"Let me go!" She mumbled more than hissed, ineffectively trying to push away from him. "Brian…."

..*

Tyrell cursed and swung his camera over his shoulder. He reached down and grabbed his backpack off the ground before breaking into a fast sprint. Whoever in the hell was on the second floor had just taken out Brian and had Helen pinned down.

He had been taking photos of Ren Lu before scanning the area through the six hundred millimeter telephoto lens attached to his Canon EOS5. The flight of several doves and the open window drew his attention and he had zoomed in on it. He had called out a warning the moment he realized that he was staring down the end of a gun. His finger instinctively captured the man at the same time that he had fired.

Even with the warning, it had been too late. Tyrell had jerked his camera down in time to see Brian stagger backwards. The second shot had sent him over the railing. From this position, he could see Helen draw her own weapon and dive behind the bench. Tyrell knew that her pistol would be useless against the man with the high powered rifle.

A split second of indecision held him motionless when he saw Ren Lu grab Makayla. He finally made the decision to go after the gunman when he saw Brian crawl behind the statue and press his back against it. The gunman must have seen the slight movement as well because he fired another shot, cutting a piece of marble off the corner of the base.

Tyrell cut through several startled tourists and pushed open the door of the building. His gaze swept around the lower floor before he spied the staircase leading upstairs. He gripped his camera with one hand and slung the strap of his backpack over his shoulder before taking the stairs two at a time to the second floor.

He glanced back and forth when he reached the top, trying to gauge where the man would be. His gaze narrowed on the far end of the hallway facing the statue. Hurrying down the corridor, he glanced through the glass doors while he went. The second to the last one was an exercise room. Behind a pillar, Tyrell caught a glimpse of a shoe. He slid his backpack down off his shoulder and gripped it tightly by the handle before he pushed open the door and stepped in.

..*

Brian drew in a deep breath, wincing when his chest ached and a shaft of pain radiated through him at the movement. His fingers fumbled for the gun under his jacket before he wrapped them around the grip. Rolling onto his stomach, he glanced through the small bushes lining the inside of the fencing and peered at Helen. Their gazes locked, hers filled with worry, while he knew his eyes reflected his fury.

"Where's Makayla?" Brian asked in a furious voice.

"Ren Lu took her," Helen replied with relief and confusion. "How bad are you hit?"

"I'm good, just bruised," Brian said, glancing toward the statue. "Do we know where the gunman is?"

Helen shook her head. "No," she muttered, wincing when another bullet struck the bench above her and bits and pieces of concrete rained down on her.

Brian gritted his teeth. Pushing up, he rolled behind the statue and pressed his back to the smooth base. A fraction of a second later, another bullet struck inches from him.

"He could be anywhere," Helen shouted above the screams and shouts when the tourists close to them realized what was happening.

"I have to stop Ren Lu from taking Makayla," Brian yelled back, glancing around the other side of the statue.

"You can't save her if you are dead, Brian," Helen retorted.

Brian tried to glance around the side of the statue again. This time he was able to catch a glimpse of Ren

Lu and Makayla in the distance before they disappeared through the front entrance to the park. He leaned back and glanced around.

"Tyrell," Brian growled into the microphone.

"I'm on it," Tyrell replied in a breathless voice. "Second floor, last window to the west. I'm entering the building now."

Brian's mouth tightened and he glanced over at Helen. Her gaze was filled with concern as well. They were trained to handle people like the shooter, Tyrell wasn't. He saw Helen's expression change to determination. She drew her legs up under her so that she was now squatting. His gaze followed to where she was looking. There was a line of trees along the path that led to the building. He nodded to her when she shot him a look.

"Go!" Brian shouted, rising up and aiming for the window.

Helen took off when she heard Brian's gun discharge. She disappeared behind the large oak and out of direct line of sight of the gunman. Brian jerked back behind the statue when she was clear. Frustration gripped him. He was pinned down until Tyrell and Helen could stop the gunman. In the meantime, Ren Lu was getting further away with Makayla.

In the microphone in his ear, he heard Tyrell yell and the sounds of a scuffle. Rolling to his feet, he took off, jumping the short hedge and low fence. The sounds of sirens echoed in the background. He had to hope that Tyrell and Helen could take care of the man and get out. His focus was on finding Makayla.

"Kevin, I need you to track Makayla," Brian muttered, raising the watch on his arm to his mouth while he ran.

"I'm on it. Helen is in the building. I don't have a visual on them any longer," Kevin muttered. "I'm working on the security cameras inside, but they only have them on the first floor."

"Where did Ren Lu go?" Brian demanded.

"Cameras show them going across the foot bridge to the parking garage," Kevin replied.

"Don't lose them," Brian ordered.

"I'm tracking her, Brian," Kevin assured him. "Turn left and take the stairs down to the first level. I have them getting into a Black Audi."

Brian cut to the left and took the stairs down to the first level. He came out near the exit. Raising his gun, he listened to the sound of squealing tires approach. His eyes locked on Ren Lu. His finger squeezed the trigger. The car swerved, turning sharply before straightening. Brian barely had time to roll to the side before it roared past him and out onto the street.

Brian stood up and stared after the car. His heart thumped with fear and anguish while his mind raced. He needed to get to his car. As long as Makayla was wearing the watch Kevin had given her, he could track her.

"Brian, did you get Makayla?" Helen's voice echoed in his ear.

Brian touched his watch and raised it to his mouth. "Negative," he answered in a hard tone. "The gunman?"

"Dead," Helen replied. "We'll meet you at the car."

"Affirmative," he responded, sliding his gun into his pocket when several visitors to the park passed him talking excitedly about what was happening.

* * *

Tyrell pressed a tissue to the cut at the corner of his right eye. His other hand gripped the strap of his camera. He dropped his shoulder and reached for the black bag he was carrying so he could store the remains of his camera in it. He grimaced when he saw the bent angle of his two thousand dollar lens. It was shot.

He unzipped the bag and removed the lens with a press of a button and a twist. Staring down at it, he released a sigh before he dropped the bloodstained lens into a nearby trash can. It would be a little difficult to explain to the insurance adjuster that he had broken the lens upside someone's head. Sliding the camera into the bag, he quickly zipped it and applied pressure back to the cut near his eye which was beginning to swell.

"Thank you," he muttered to Helen.

Helen glanced at him and gave him a tight smile. "It is my job," she replied before releasing a sigh. "You're welcome."

Tyrell grunted an acknowledgment. He was lucky he had just walked away with some bruises and a cut above the eye. If Helen hadn't shown up when she had, he would be the one being removed in a body bag, not the gunman. Helen had entered the room in time to shoot the bad guy who was doing a pretty good job of kicking Tyrell's ass.

Tyrell had surprised the man and struck him with his camera. He was pretty sure getting hit upside the head by a hundred and sixty millimeter heavy-duty telephoto lens would have knocked most men out. Unfortunately, the man Tyrell had confronted had already looked like he'd been hit upside the head by a Mack truck and was still going.

The man had kicked him from one end of the room to the other. He was just turning the rifle on Tyrell when Helen stepped into the room and shot the man in the shoulder. The force of the impact had caught the assassin off-guard and he had tripped over the gun case on the floor and fallen out of the second floor window to the sidewalk below. In the meantime, Tyrell was still trying to capture all the damn bats in his belfry that the man had stirred up in Tyrell's brain from the last blow to his temple.

He turned and followed Helen when she stepped across to a less used path. His gaze swept over the policemen running by them. Brian, Makayla, and Helen were still fugitives, as far as they knew. He listened to Helen when she reached out to Brian.

"What happens now?" Tyrell asked when they neared the cars.

"We split up," Helen said, turning to watch Brian stride toward them at a brisk pace. "Brian goes after Makayla, I go after Henry, and you go find the second piece of the puzzle."

Tyrell stopped and looked down at Helen. He glanced around. On the corner, there was a small shop set up with motorbikes out front for rent. They were going to need another vehicle.

"I want both of you to go after Henry," Brian instructed, pulling his gun out, changing the clip, pulling a silencer out of his jacket pocket, and attaching it before holding it out to Tyrell. "I'll go after Makayla."

"What about the second piece to the puzzle?" Tyrell asked in surprise.

"To hell with the information. I'm not leaving Makayla or Henry to die for some…." Brian bit off the rest of his statement. "Go after Henry. After I get Makayla, she and I will go find the next piece."

"What if something happens?" Helen asked in a quiet voice.

Brian looked at her. "Then, you and Tyrell know what to do," he said, walking over to the car.

"Does Kevin have a fix on Makayla, yet?" Tyrell asked, watching Brian pull a bag out of the trunk of the car and open it.

"Yes," Brian replied with a hard edge to his voice.

Tyrell watched Brian pull out several guns and check them before concealing one in his jacket pocket and two more at his waist. He also pulled out a knife and clipped it to his belt. Tyrell swallowed. This was a man who knew what he was doing and did it with a calm that left no doubt that he was ready to do whatever was necessary to get Makayla back – even if it meant killing.

"Good luck and let us know once you get her," Tyrell muttered, turning when Helen pulled open the door to the other rental car.

Brian didn't answer. He was already in the car and pulling out by the time Helen started the one they had climbed into. Tyrell stared down at the gun in his hands. If getting his ass kicked wasn't enough to tell him he was in way over his head, holding a gun with a silencer attached was.

Chapter 23

Makayla shook her head and silently stared out of the window. The wind blew into the car from the shattered back window behind Ren Lu. Her head was beginning to clear with the cool breeze. Thank goodness whatever the man sitting next to her had given her hadn't lasted very long.

"You know, anyone can do bad things," she said in a quiet voice, not really expecting him to listen to her.

He shot her a puzzled glance before turning down another busy road. Silence followed her statement and she turned her head to stare out the window. Behind her, she gently rubbed her wrist to make sure the watch she was wearing was still attached. A relieved sigh escaped her when she felt it. She didn't think she was fortunate enough to have retained the earpiece, though. There was no way to check it with her hands tied behind her back.

"What do you mean?" Ren Lu finally asked, glancing at her again.

Makayla blinked in surprise at the curiosity in his voice. She turned to look at him again. He was older than she had originally thought, perhaps in his early thirties.

"It was just a random thought," she replied with a shrug. "Anyone can do something bad. It takes someone stronger to do something good. It's something Henry once said."

Ren Lu frowned and slowed down a little to Makayla's relief. She wasn't buckled in and didn't relish going through the windshield if he were to have an accident. She could feel the muscles in her legs relax a little.

"The old man, you call him by his given name instead of grandfather. Why?" Ren Lu asked.

Makayla stared out over the water. They were traveling along the bay again. She felt a sense of déjà vu strike her. She had definitely seen more of Hong Kong in the last forty-eight hours than she had the first two days.

Makayla's lips curved into a rueful smile that didn't reach her eyes. If anything, she could feel the sadness deep inside threatening to drown her. She lowered her head, her eyes locked on the gun sitting on the seat between his legs.

"You wouldn't be interested," she muttered.

"Tell me. I read about you. You stole your grandfather's sailboat when you were sixteen. Why? The place you wanted to go was two hours by car and much safer. Why would you do something so reckless?" He demanded, turning on his signal and pulling down a narrow road lined with warehouses.

Makayla groaned and leaned her head back against the seat. "I swear I'm never going to live that down. Robert Ballard once said he wished he could find a UFO at the bottom of the ocean so people would quit asking him about the Titanic. I can totally appreciate why now," she muttered, staring at the buildings. "Are you going to kill me? If you are, I think I'd like to know first."

Ren Lu's lips twitched. He drew the car to a stop in front of a building. It looked like they were at one of the commercial ports. She could see a glimpse of water ahead of them.

"No, I do not plan on killing you," he replied, turning the car off and shifting toward her to study her mutinous expression. "I find you attractive."

Makayla slowly lifted her head and turned to look at him with a disbelieving stare. She knew her mouth had to be hanging open and she forced it closed. Shaking her head, she tried to see if she was in some delusional state brought on by whatever drug he had injected into her. She didn't feel weird, but this was definitely one of the strangest moments of her life.

"I beg your pardon?" She muttered, blinking and frowning at him.

Ren Lu reached out to touch her. Makayla drew back, her gaze moving from his hand to his face. She braced herself for his touch, unsure of what to expect. She was shocked when he barely skimmed his fingertips along her cheek.

"I find you attractive," Ren Lu replied, slowly pulling his hand back. "I want to know why."

Makayla raised an eyebrow and stared at him in silence. She didn't want to touch that statement with a ten foot pole. In fact, she could think of any number of other things she would rather do – and places she would rather be – than dealing with a confused psychopathic killer who thought she was attractive.

"You don't get out much, do you?" Makayla asked.

Ren Lu's startled chuckle caused her to jump and scoot closer to the door. His eyes glittered with amusement. Makayla warily followed his hand when he reached down for the gun before he opened the driver's door. It wasn't until he closed the door that she released the breath she hadn't been aware that she'd been holding. Like Henry, she had a tendency to open her mouth and insert her foot before her brain could stop her.

She watched Ren Lu walk around to the passenger side and open the door. She wanted to resist getting out, but knew it would be futile. Instead, she swung her long legs out and stood up. As long as she kept her head clear, her mouth shut, and waited for –

The image of Brian falling backwards, a dark hole in his chest, suddenly washed through her mind. She stiffened, jerking back when the world momentarily tilted sideways. Her legs suddenly felt too weak to hold her and she could feel her body sliding down the side of the car that she had just exited while she struggled to pull oxygen into her lungs.

"Makayla," Ren Lu said, grabbing her by her forearms and steadying her. He knelt in front of her and lifted her chin so he could see her face. "What is it?"

Makayla slowly opened her eyes. Unexpected pain clenched her chest and her eyes filled with tears. The tears were caused by grief and rage. A guttural cry escaped her and she struck out with the only weapon she had – her body. She threw her body forward, knocking a surprised Ren Lu off balance. Kicking out, she tried to knee him while her teeth bit deeply into his wrist.

A soft grunt escaped him and he rolled, pinning her body under his muscular frame while she struggled to do whatever damage she could with her head, legs, and teeth. A sob escaped her before she drew in a deep, shuddering breath when he held her immobilized. She hiccupped inelegantly and tried to wipe away with her shoulder the tear that had escaped.

"What happened?" He demanded, staring down at her.

"Brian…," her voice broke and she sniffed again, her gaze burning with grief and anger. "You had someone shoot him."

Ren Lu's face stiffened and he cautiously rolled off of her. She stared up at him before she sat up and rolled onto her knees. He didn't help her when she struggled to stand. She couldn't really blame him for that. She was a little proud of how much she had roughed him up with her hands tied behind her back. His pristine black pants and shirt were coated in dust and debris from the road. He was absently rubbing the arm she had bitten.

"I did not hire the gunman to target Jacobs – my employer did," Ren Lu stated, staring at her.

"Oh," Makayla mumbled, glancing down at the ground before she glared back at him. "You still deserved it for working for such a jerk, not to mention drugging me, kidnapping me, and tying me up."

Ren Lu stepped forward and gripped her arm in a bruising grip. "I may not have hired the man, but I led him to Jacobs and Detective Woo. Men like us are not easy to kill, Makayla. Jacobs must not have been injured too badly since he was able to try to kill me in the parking garage. As for your other reasons, I will give you this one act of rebellion. But, if you try to attack me again, I won't be so forgiving."

Makayla stared back at him for several seconds before she finally looked away. The warning was clear: she needed to behave if she valued her life. Once again, her fingers caressed the watch on her wrist.

Chapter 24

Brian slowly braked the car to a stop, turned off the engine, and slid out of the car. He looked down the long row of warehouses. In front of the last one, a black Audi sat...empty.

Several minutes later, he was standing next to the car. He pulled his cell phone out of his jacket and pressed the number he had programmed into it. Almost immediately, Kevin picked up.

"Where is she?" Brian demanded, gazing out across the water.

The city lights were beginning to light up the sky in the growing dusk. The wind coming off the water was cool, but Brian didn't feel it. It was a little over an hour since the shooting at the park. It had taken longer than Kevin or he had expected to reach the location where Kevin had tracked Makayla and Ren Lu. The area around the park had been practically shut down, creating a gridlock with people traveling home for the night.

"I have her showing up in the middle of the water on the maps. Not like in it, but you get what I mean. I'm not talking fish food like Sun's last Head of Security," Kevin hastily muttered in his ear. "I won't have an exact location until the other satellite I'm waiting for comes within range so I can activate it. I didn't want to report until I knew for sure where she was at. I was hoping she was there."

"How long will that take?" Brian asked in frustration, walking toward the edge.

"Twenty-two minutes, forty-six seconds, if you want to know the exact time," Kevin said. "Whatever I find, you're going to need a boat."

Brian glanced around. The only thing here was an old tugboat. He raised his hand and ran it through his hair in frustration, staring across the bay.

"Brian, in case you have forgotten, I've got plenty of them here," Kevin gently reminded him. "By the time you get back here, I'll have everything you need."

"I'll need one fully loaded," Brian replied, dropping his hand to his side.

"I wouldn't give you anything less," Kevin promised.

Brian turned and strode back to his car. "Have you heard from Helen and Tyrell yet?" He asked in a tone fraught with tension.

"I'm listening and watching, but keeping silent," Kevin admitted. "They are going in now."

"Keep me posted," Brian instructed.

"I will," Kevin replied. "See you in forty-five."

Brian hung up the phone and slipped it into his pocket. He unlocked the door to his car and slid in behind the wheel. Within seconds, he was making a wide U-turn and cutting through the back streets, back to Lei Yue Mun and Kevin's place.

His fingers tightened on the steering wheel and he quickly shifted. He couldn't erase the image of Ren Lu pulling Makayla away from him. His mind kept replaying the last few days. It hadn't mattered that he had stayed away from her. It hadn't mattered that he had gone halfway around the world. His way of life had still tangled with Makayla's, unwittingly endangering her.

A soft curse slipped from his lips when he remembered something that Harrington had said to him. It hadn't made much sense to him at the time, but that might have been because he didn't have anything comparable to what Harrington was talking about then. Now, he did and Harrington's sentiments made perfect sense.

"You only get one shot at this life, Brian. When you find something as perfect as the woman you love, you realize that some things are worth the risk. Besides, you never really know when your time will be up. I could do this for thirty years and never get hurt. If there is one thing I've learned about living here in Hong Kong, it is that life is to be lived and appreciated every day as if it were my last."

Harrington hadn't let his job keep him from having a life. He didn't know if the man had ever told his wife what he did for a living, but deep down, Brian hoped that the other man had. If Harrington's wife was anything like Makayla, he imagined that she would have supported him.

Once again, it dawned on Brian that he had underestimated Makayla. She had not questioned what he was doing, complained, or had a meltdown. In all honesty, it hadn't been his fear of her doing any of that, but his own fears that had held him back.

One thing he didn't want was to end up like Harrington. Once he had Makayla and Henry safe, and the information in the proper hands, he was requesting a reassignment. He wanted that life with Makayla. He wanted the happily ever after, and, he didn't want to go to work wondering if he might never come home again. There were other things in life that were more important, and Makayla was at the top of his bucket list when it came to everything else. He'd screwed up once, he wouldn't do it again.

A flash of memory swept through him of Makayla's face the afternoon Tyrell and she had sailed into Tampa Bay. The sun had been shining down on her and she had handled the *Defiance* as if she were one with the sailboat. He'd never forget her face when she had seen all the people lining the pier cheering for Tyrell and her. Her eyes had flashed with confusion and a touch of fear until she had seen Henry, her mom – and him standing on the dock waiting for her.

He had kissed her like he would never let her go, but he had. When he had a chance to kiss her again, he was going to make sure she knew it was forever. It wasn't often that someone was given a second chance and he was smart enough now to know to hold onto it with both hands. He just needed to get her back first.

***

Tyrell wiped his sweaty palm across the denim of his jeans before shifting the gun in his other hand to the one he had just wiped so he could do his other one. He glanced at Helen. She looked like she was ready to go shopping instead of climbing aboard a huge ass cargo freighter with armed guards.

"Okay, how are we supposed to get on that thing without being seen?" Tyrell asked for the fifth time, glancing around the cargo container that they had slipped up behind. "I see two gangplanks going up to the deck and they both have guys with bigger guns than we do."

Helen glanced over her shoulder at him and shook her head in amusement. What she could find so amusing at the moment was beyond him. Personally, all he could think about was he hoped he didn't piss his pants. He'd been in some scary situations before, but nothing like this. The other times, he hadn't been one of the ones toting a gun.

He knew it was a throwback to his life before his journey on the *Defiance*. Before he had fallen asleep on the sailboat and woken to find himself at sea, he had only dreamed of becoming a professional photographer. In reality, his life had been one step away from being dragged down into the gangs that his older brother had gotten caught up in. A life that had come close to getting not only his older brother killed, but Tyrell and their grandmother.

When one of their high school teachers had assigned Makayla and him a class project to show how social media can be used to share extraordinary events in a person's life, he had never expected that event to be the *Voyage of the Defiance*. He had inadvertently stowed away on the boat when Makayla had stolen it and their subsequent journey had gone viral when he'd shared it. The fact that they had made it through not only a storm at sea, but a hurricane had captured the attention of millions of viewers following their journey – a journey that Makayla and he hadn't thought they would survive.

Swallowing, Tyrell gazed down at the long black barrel of the gun. It was vastly different from the camera lens. He had decided years ago that he didn't want the violent life that had killed his father, lured his mother and brother away, and had come close to taking everything he held dear. Now, he would have to use some of those skills to rescue Henry Summerlin.

"Do you see that?" Helen whispered, nodding to where a crane was loading cargo.

"You want to ride on a cargo container?" Tyrell asked in disbelief, his gaze following the swaying metal container that was hundreds of feet in the air.

"No, I want to go through the opening where they load the smaller crates under it," she retorted in quiet exasperation. "Look down."

Tyrell's gaze dropped to where a section of the cargo ship was open on the side and wooden crates were being lifted by a forklift which disappeared through the opening in the side of the ship. It looked like there was only one person working at the moment. His gaze followed the forklift. It looked like what the big cruise lines did when one of them was getting ready to leave port.

"So, what's the plan?" He asked, glancing down at Helen.

Helen smiled at him. "Do you know how to drive a forklift?" She asked with a raised eyebrow.

Fifteen minutes later, the former driver of the forklift was tied up behind one of the crates, and Tyrell was wearing the man's vest and hard hat. He was grateful for the growing darkness, because the vest was at least one size too small. It didn't take him long to remember how to drive the small piece of machinery. He had spent a couple of summers helping down at the boatyard, thanks to Henry's reference and helpful guidance.

He loaded several crates before he picked up the one with Helen in it. Turning the forklift, he guided it over the metal platform bridging the dock and the freighter. He guided the forklift over to where he had stacked the other crates and gently lowered the wooden container to the floor. Leaning forward, he turned off the machine and climbed out.

"Clear," he murmured after double checking to make sure they were alone.

Helen peered around the side of the crate. In the bright lights of the cargo hold, the gun she was holding looked huge and menacing. Tyrell swallowed and reached for the one Brian had given him that he had tucked into the back of his pants. He also reached for his cell phone. Kevin had sent each of them a blueprint of the cargo ship so they could find their way around the massive ship. He glanced at the map before turning to get his bearings. A silent curse escaped him when he saw Helen was already heading for a set of stairs leading up.

"That's right, just leave the rookie behind," he muttered with a shake of his head. He shoved his cell phone back in his pocket and hurried to follow her.

Together, they climbed the metal stairs. At first, he thought they should be stealthy. It wasn't until Helen gave him an inquisitive glance over her shoulder that he realized that acting like they were supposed to be there would draw less attention than two people slinking around. She kept her weapon by her side so it wasn't as visible, but he could tell she was ready for any unexpected encounters.

"What do we do if we meet someone?" Tyrell whispered.

Helen glanced up at him. "We try to avoid that. I would prefer not to have to kill anyone if I can. If they shoot at us, we shoot back. Otherwise, we try to do what we did with the other worker," she replied in a barely audible voice. "I have found from previous experience that most vessels like this have a minimum crew while at port."

"Yeah, but do most of them have a person that they've kidnapped on board?" Tyrell asked with a skeptical expression.

Helen's lips twisted in a slightly bitter smile. "You would be surprised, Tyrell. Human trafficking is a huge business," she said in a somber tone.

Tyrell stared after Helen. He knew a little about human trafficking. In some of the other countries he had visited, he'd heard about it, but he had never thought about it being an issue in a city as modern as Hong Kong. He didn't know why. After all, it was a hub for activity between China, the Philippines, and other surrounding Asian countries where he knew human trafficking was a major issue.

Once again, he realized that if he didn't pay attention, he could find himself left behind. They had to stop twice and hide when they heard the sound of approaching footsteps. The first time, Helen and he had remained frozen under the stairwell when two men came down. Fortunately, the men were too busy arguing and laughing over a recent sporting event to pay attention to anything but their conversation and where they were going. Tyrell was able to pick out enough of the words they were speaking to understand what they were talking about thanks to the months he had spent in China a couple of years ago.

The second time, they were able to slip into a room. Tyrell nodded when Helen indicated the coast was clear again. They walked down the narrow passage and he breathed a sigh of relief when he saw the huge **3** painted along the dull, gray walls. Helen moved more slowly now with her gun up and ready. Tyrell copied her, glancing back over his shoulder.

"The door on the left is closed," Helen murmured. "The others are open."

"I hear footsteps," Tyrell warned.

Helen nodded and motioned for Tyrell to follow her. They slipped through the open door across from the one that was locked and pressed up against the wall just inside the door. Less than a minute later, they heard the sound of a man's voice humming a song growing closer.

Tyrell glanced in the distorted mirror mounted over a small sink across from them. He could see the door across the hall. Seconds later, a young Asian man stopped in front of the door. The man was carrying a tray that looked like it had some food on it. White earbuds hung from the man's ears and the muted sound of pop music could be heard. The man bent and set the tray down on the floor before reaching into his pocket and pulling out a set of keys. They could hear him fumble with his key and the lock on the door before he removed the key. Replacing the keys in his pocket, he retrieved the tray.

Helen quickly moved once the man stepped into the room and muttered to the occupant. She stepped over the lip of the doorway, her gun raised. Then she crossed the corridor and went through the now unlocked door. The man carrying the tray froze when he felt the hard tip of her gun pressed against the back of his head.

Tyrell stepped through behind her and glanced around. The room was barren except for a small sink, toilet, and metal framed bunk attached to the far wall. A grin lit Tyrell's face when he saw the weathered face of Henry Summerlin scowling back at him.

"Hey, Mr. S.," Tyrell greeted with a wave of his hand before he realized he had the gun in it. "Are you ready to get out of here?"

Henry slowly sat up, the blanket he had draped over him falling to the side when he slid his feet over the edge of the bed. Tyrell's gaze darkened with worry when he saw the old man was in a lot of pain. He stepped closer, noticing the old man's good hand tremble when it dropped to the bed so he could push up. Tyrell wrapped an arm around Henry's waist and helped him to stand.

"Thanks, Tyrell," Henry replied in a rough, slightly uneven voice. "What the hell are you doing here?"

"Rescuing you," Tyrell replied in a quiet voice.

"How did you know where to find me?" Henry asked in a slightly stronger voice before he looked at Helen. "Who is she?"

"Detective Helen Woo, Hong Kong Police," Helen replied in a clipped tone. "I suggest we get out of here. We'll leave the same way we came. If we are lucky, no one will even know Mr. Summerlin is missing until we are long gone."

Tyrell heard Helen order the young man quietly standing with his hands up to give her the keys and his phone. The man reached into his pocket and withdrew the keys and his cell phone, pulling the earbuds out of his ears at the same time. Helen had the man turn the music off before she took the phone and told the man to sit on the bed. With a nod of her head, they backed out of the room, making sure the passageway was clear first.

Tyrell started slowly making his way back down the long metal corridor. Behind him, Helen closed and locked the door to the room where Henry had been held before falling in behind them. Tyrell worriedly glanced over his shoulder to make sure Henry was doing alright. The corridors were too narrow for them to walk side by side, so he couldn't assist Henry. He could see the old man's face was pale and etched with lines of pain, but he didn't make a sound while they threaded their way back to the cargo hold and freedom.

Chapter 25

Brian strode down the long dock back to Kevin's yacht. He slowed and stopped when he saw movement in one of the boats moored several slips before the yacht. In the muted glow from the restaurant lights, he could see Kevin's familiar shape moving around.

Kevin glanced up at him and nodded. "I found her," he said with satisfaction. "Let me finish with this. I've got you some heavy duty fireworks here."

"Thanks. Where is she?" Brian asked, reaching down and giving Kevin a hand back onto the dock.

"I have to tell you, when your girlfriend gets kidnapped, she does it in style," Kevin muttered. "Come on."

Brian followed Kevin back to his boat. Within minutes, he was staring up at the bank of computer screens again. Kevin had dimmed the lights and switched the screens to nighttime mode to help reduce the time it would take for Brian's night vision to return. The soft glow of red lights gave an eerie feel to the control room.

"Ren Lu has to be more than Sun Yung-Wing's Chief of Security," Kevin commented with a shake of his head. "The yacht he is on is listed with a British company. I'm still working on peeling back all the layers, but the yacht the man is on makes this thing look like a life raft."

"Where is Makayla?" Brian demanded, gritting his teeth. "I don't care how luxurious a prison is, it is still a prison and Makayla is in danger."

Kevin nodded, glancing back up at the screens. Brian stared at the one in the center. A frown creased his brow. He recognized the Royal Hong Kong Marina where the Defiance had been moored. His gaze followed the cursor when Kevin slid it just to the east; anchored less than a kilometer from the marina was a large yacht. An angry expletive burst from his lips when he realized that Ren Lu had had a front row seat to everything that had been happening.

"Yeah, I said pretty much the same thing when I saw it, too," Kevin muttered, staring up at the image. "Oh, Helen and Tyrell are on their way back."

"Henry…?" Brian asked, turning to look at Kevin with a concerned frown.

"He's a little beat up. I've called a doctor friend to come check him over," Kevin said. "I figured it would be safer here. Helen seemed to think that the worst was a broken wrist, a cut to his head, and exhaustion. I told Karl to be prepared to sedate the old man. Helen said Henry was ready to kick some ass when he found out that Ren Lu had Makayla."

Brian's lips twitched. "I can imagine," he replied.

Kevin opened his mouth to say something. Brian saw his friend blink and lean forward. He glanced down and winced when he felt Kevin poke his finger through the hole in his shirt.

"Is this a bullet hole?" Kevin asked with a scowl.

"Yes," Brian replied, running his hand down over the hole before sliding it up to the other one. "Thanks for the vest, by the way. It saved my ass today."

Kevin shook his head. "I told you I don't like getting shot at," he said. "You must be hell on clothes."

"Not normally," Brian said. "Kevin, I need to get Makayla back."

Kevin nodded. "Here is the blueprint of the yacht. I can only guess where he has her based on the specs I was able to download. I've included a pair of infrared, night vision goggles for you. I calculated you have a better chance of success the darker it is. Luckily, it's a new moon so you'll only have to deal with the artificial lights. Since the yacht is self-contained, there is no way I can cut the power or anything. Once you get there, you will be pretty much on your own," he said.

Brian nodded. "I'm not sure I should even ask what you are doing with half the stuff you've got," he retorted.

Kevin turned and grinned. "I get bored easily. When you have as much money as I do, any new gadget looks cool on eBay," he quipped, rising out of his chair. "Come on, I'll show you what I've packed. I've got a Zodiac BayRunner 420 for you. It has both a kick-ass Yamaha F50 EFI 4-Stroke on the back, as well as a powerful electric trolling motor. The water is pretty smooth now that the winds have died down. Your biggest enemy will be the light if they have the yacht lit up like downtown. It's kind of hard to sneak up on someone in a bright room."

"I'll figure out a way to deal with it," Brian promised.

"I figured that. I also included my paddle board. I'd like it back if at all possible," Kevin added, walking back up the stairs.

"Paddle board?" Brian asked.

Kevin nodded. "I figured it would be easier to get closer. It can fit two people, but you aren't going to be going anywhere fast. I'm trying to think of every scenario."

Brian nodded. They looked up when they saw a flash of car lights. Brian saw Tyrell emerge from the passenger side of the car. He walked around to the back and opened it. Brian's jaw clenched in anger when he saw Henry Summerlin slowly emerge from the back seat of the car; it was obvious, even from this distance, that the old man was in pain.

"Looks like they made it back," Kevin murmured.

"Yeah," Brian replied.

Several minutes later, the three were making their way slowly down the dock. Every once in a while, Brian would hear Henry curse at Tyrell, who was following behind him, to keep his damn hands off him, that he was old, not dead, and could walk unassisted.

"Hi Henry," Brian greeted, scanning the old man's face.

"What the hell are you doing in Hong Kong?" Henry asked in a gruff tone.

"Working," Brian replied. "I'm sorry you were drawn into this mess. You shouldn't have been."

"Not your fault," Henry groused with a tired sigh. "I'd better find a place to park my ass, otherwise I might be needing Tyrell's help after all," he added.

"I've got a doctor on the way," Kevin said, motioning for everyone to follow him.

"I just hope he's got some painkillers with him," Henry muttered, wincing when Brian and Tyrell helped him aboard the junk. "This is a hell of a lot nicer than the last place I was at."

Brian saw Kevin's lips twitch in amusement. Henry's muttered observations and snappy retorts made Brian more confident that the old man would be alright. Now, he needed to bring Makayla home. Almost as if Henry was reading his mind, the old man turned to glare at him with a pain-filled expression.

"You're going to bring my granddaughter back safe, aren't you?" Henry asked in a slightly uneven voice.

"Yes, sir," Brian responded. "Tyrell, I'm going to need your help."

Tyrell looked up in surprise from where he had helped Henry down onto the couch. "Me? Sure," he replied, glancing over at Helen. "You know I'd do anything for Makayla, but I don't know much about using a gun."

"I don't need you to use a gun. I can do that. I need you to operate the boat," Brian said in a grim tone.

Tyrell nodded. "Now that I can do," he replied. "When are we leaving?"

"Now," Brian said.

* * *

Makayla sat on the edge of the plush couch. She rubbed her wrists and glanced at where Ren Lu had stepped over to the bar. Her fingers caressed the watch still strapped to her wrist. She had been terrified Ren Lu would remove it when he had tied her wrists together, but he had tied the bindings slightly above the watch.

Her gaze scanned the time. It was after twenty-one hundred hours, almost five hours since they had arrived at the park earlier this afternoon. Folding her hands together, she watched Ren Lu pour a glass of red wine. He picked up the glass and walked back to her.

She stared at him when he held it out before reluctantly reaching for it. Their fingers briefly touched before she pulled the glass toward her. She didn't take a sip of the wine, afraid he might have drugged it. Her mistrust must have been evident in her expression because his lips curved in wry amusement.

"You don't like wine?" He asked.

"Not really," she admitted with a grimace of distaste. "It's right up there with coffee. Henry tried to get me to drink the stuff when I was a teenager, but I never did like it."

Ren Lu stepped back and sat in the white leather chair across from her. She resisted the urge to roll her eyes at him when he continued to stare at her in silence. Instead, she placed the glass of wine on the table next to her and sat back on the couch and crossed her arms in front of her. She was perfectly happy to sit and wait in silence to be rescued. She never had been one for idle conversation if it wasn't necessary.

"Why did you steal the sailboat?" Ren Lu suddenly asked.

Makayla didn't bother smothering the groan that escaped her. She lifted a hand and brushed the loose strands of hair back from her face before she sat forward. Folding her hands together and resting her elbows on her knees, she thought about how she should answer the question that she had already been asked a million times.

"I don't know," she finally whispered, not looking at Ren Lu. "I was sixteen, angry, hurt, and wanted to escape the world. I think that pretty much is the same for most kids that age."

"Why were you angry?" Ren Lu persisted, not letting her off the hook.

Makayla glanced up at him and scowled. Why did a hired hitmen care why she had stolen a sailboat or been angry? That had been six years ago, after all.

Rising up off the couch, Makayla shot Ren Lu a dark look before turning to walk over to the glass doors that looked out over the deck and the water below. She wrapped her arms around her waist inside her jacket and dug her fingers into her side to keep them from trembling.

"I was living with my mom and her loser boyfriend at the time," Makayla murmured in a distant voice. "He was enabling her addiction to pain pills. And if that wasn't bad enough, he was an abusive prick as well." Her hand rose to touch her face when she remembered her mom's ex hitting her. She didn't realize that Ren Lu could see her clearly in the reflection of the glass or that his gaze followed the movement. She was too lost in her memories. Her hand slid back down to her waist and she shook her head. "Anyway, there is a saying that you have to hit rock bottom before you can pick yourself up. My mom hit it and I found myself with the option of going to live with a grandfather I didn't remember or foster care." A bitter laugh escaped Makayla and she turned to face Ren Lu. "That wasn't much of choice. You can imagine what living in a state-run system would be like. I spent the summer helping Henry refurbish the Defiance. He taught me to sail and I learned more about my mom."

"That still does not explain why you would steal the sailboat," Ren Lu stated, tilting his head and staring intently at her face.

Makayla shrugged. "I thought I would be going home at the end of the summer. I missed my mom and my friends. It was my last year of high school and I wanted to be with them. My mom wasn't ready for me to come home. I had some trouble adjusting to my new school and Henry and I got into an argument. One thing led to another and I acted on impulse," she replied in a curt tone.

She lifted her chin when Ren Lu stood up and walked toward her. She didn't like telling people her life story. What she had told him was plastered all over the Internet, so it wasn't anything he couldn't have read already. She forced her body to remain still when he reached up and tenderly touched her cheek.

"What about the boy who was on board with you? The one that stowed away," Ren Lu asked in a quiet voice.

Makayla's brow creased into a puzzled frown. "Tyrell?" She shook her head and her lips curved at the memory of Tyrell's face when he had realized they were out to sea. "He freaked out at first. He didn't know how to swim and had never been on a boat in his life."

"You care for this person?" Ren Lu asked with a raised eyebrow.

Makayla's gaze softened and she tilted her head to stare up at Ren Lu. "You tend to care about someone when your lives depend on it. I saved Tyrell's life, but he also saved mine.... We're friends, but it is more than that. I can't really explain it. There is a connection there that I don't think happens very often between two people," she finally admitted after a pause.

"What about Brian?" Ren Lu asked in a deceptively quiet tone. "What are your feelings for him?"

Makayla pressed her lips together. She didn't miss the slight change in his voice or the look in Ren Lu's eyes when he mentioned Brian's name. She stared back at him in silence.

"A shame," he murmured, his thumb caressing her cheek.

"Why do you say that?" Makayla finally asked, not moving when he slid his hand further down to her neck.

"As I said before, I find you very attractive," Ren Lu replied in a quiet voice, slowly leaning forward.

"I wouldn't," Makayla whispered, pressing her hands against his chest. "I don't do well when people invade my personal space. If you don't want me to knee you again, I suggest you stop."

Ren Lu paused, his gaze locked with Makayla's serious one. His lips curved upward in a humorous smile before he slid his hand back along her jaw. He straightened and stepped back, allowing his fingers to caress her before he dropped his hand.

"As I said before – a shame," he replied with a slight bow of his head. "I have work that I must attend to. If you will follow me, I will escort you to a stateroom where you can freshen up and rest."

Makayla watched the cold, distant expression return to Ren Lu's face, reminding her again that this was a cold blooded killer who hadn't thought twice about shooting her in the back. She swallowed, her gaze following him when he turned and began to walk away. She started when he turned to look at her in silence.

"Will you… Are you going to let me go?" Makayla asked, clenching her fists by her side.

Ren Lu returned her steady gaze before he answered. "I'm not sure. Now follow me," he ordered, turning away from her again.

Makayla glanced at the doors leading out to the upper deck. A part of her wanted to make a dash for it and see if she could make it over the railing and into the dark waters of the bay. The only thing stopping her was knowing that she would need to get to the lower level to make that possible and she seriously doubted she would be fast enough. Reluctantly turning, she strode across the salon and down the stairs on the far side.

Brian will come, she thought with renewed hope, her fingers caressing the watch.

Chapter 26

Brian motioned for Tyrell to slow down the fourteen foot Zodiac when they neared the cove where the Royal Hong Kong Yacht Club and Marina was located. They moved through the channel barely causing a wake. They were running dark, so they didn't have the bow or stern lights turned on.

"Are you sure about this?" Tyrell asked in a quiet voice steering the boat into the slip where the *Defiance* should have been.

"Yes," Brian replied, slipping the straps of the waterproof black backpack onto his back.

Together they looped the bow rope around one of the pillars to keep the boat steady. Brian reached down and grabbed the long paddle, and with Tyrell's help, they slid the paddle board into the water. Brian carefully stepped onto the board, balancing himself by holding onto Tyrell's arm.

"I'll let you know when I'm near the yacht. You come up and set up like you are fishing. While you distract them, I'll climb aboard and find Makayla. Be prepared to come in fast once I do," Brian instructed.

"How will I know when you find her?" Tyrell asked with a nervous expression.

Brian glanced at him. "Look for the fireworks," he said before pushing off.

"Good luck, man," Tyrell whispered, shaking his head and sitting down on the padded seat to wait for Brian's call.

Brian paddled the board across the gently lapping water. He would have enjoyed the peace and quiet if it wasn't for the fact that he was on the most important mission of his life. He stayed focused on the yacht gleaming like a pearl against the black water. All around him, the shoreline was lit with colorful lights, washing out the stars that shone above. If he had been just a mile off shore, he would have observed an astronomical display that would have put the lights of Hong Kong to shame.

It didn't take him long to cover the half mile distance to the yacht. He lowered his body down to the board and lifted the watch on his wrist to his mouth. With a soft murmur, he spoke.

"I'm twenty feet out," he told Tyrell. "There are three men on the top deck and one moving along the lower deck. There is a helicopter on the top. I don't see any sign of Makayla or Ren Lu."

"Affirmative," Tyrell replied. "I'm on my way."

"Roger, that," Brian acknowledged.

Brian shifted the paddle and used it to keep the board just far enough away to be out of reach of the spotlight that he had seen mounted to the top near the bridge. Almost ten minutes later, he heard the soft purr of a motor. He glanced over his shoulder and saw the telltale red and green lights of a small boat coming closer. It was moving slowly and he could make out Tyrell's huge form in the soft white light of the navigation light attached to the windshield. In his hands was a lightweight fishing rod.

He paused and turned off the four-stroke engine and moved to the front where he could operate the trolling motor with his foot while he sat in a chair near the bow. Brian watched Tyrell skillfully maneuver the boat closer and closer in a non-threatening manner while casting the fishing pole and listening to music he had turned on.

A grudging smile curved Brian's lips. He had to give it to Tyrell, he wouldn't suspect the other man of being anything but a fisherman enjoying a night out on the water. He knew Tyrell had crossed the invisible line drawn around the yacht when the spotlight came on and the men patrolling the top and the one on the bottom deck moved toward the stern.

Brian quietly cut through the shadows cast by the bow and moved to the anchor. He clipped the paddle to the board and used the small rope attached to the front of the paddle to tie it to the chain hanging down. Gripping the chain, he stood up on the board. Within seconds, he was climbing up the side.

***

"What is it?" Ren Lu asked, glancing up when one of his men tapped lightly on the door.

"A man fishing," the guard replied. "You asked that we notify you immediately if anyone approached the yacht."

Ren Lu frowned in irritation and rose from the computer. The software was running to try to decipher the code that Harrington had used on it. So far, Jacobs had been telling the truth. Ren Lu picked up the pistol next to the computer, stepped out of his office, and glanced down the hallway. There had been no sound from the room where he had escorted Makayla. She was locked inside, but Ren Lu knew from experience that locks were never a guarantee.

He knew instinctively that Jacobs would try to find Makayla. A sense of unease swept through him. There was no way for Makayla to contact Jacobs or for Jacobs to locate her, at least not this quickly unless she had a way to do so.

Turning, he passed the man waiting for him and climbed the stairs to the main deck. He slid open the door and stepped out into the cool air. Striding to the side, he looked out at the boat. The man sitting on the front was shielding his eyes and yelling for them to quit blinding him with the spotlight.

"Waa gwaan. Come on, man, you gonna scare all the fish away and blind me," the man said with a distinctive Jamaican accent.

"You need to move away," one of Ren Lu's men shouted.

"You rich men think you all own the water, but this Jamaican knows better," the large black man shouted back. "We've fished the waters and not one damn fish has your name on it."

"We will not warn you again," the guard replied in a clipped tone.

"One night away from my woman to get out and you go and ruin it. That's just not right, man. That's just not right," the fisherman grumbled, rising and reeling in his fishing pole before turning the trolling motor and steering the boat away from the yacht. "Vacation in Hong Kong. The people are friendly and the waters are clear. Yeah, right."

Ren Lu watched the boat moving further away. A short time later, the soft sound of a weight hitting the water and the man's off-key, accented voice singing along with a song could be heard drifting across the water. He turned and glanced at the man beside him.

"Keep an eye on him," Ren Lu ordered, turning away. "And search the yacht."

"Yes, sir," the man said with a nod.

***

Brian placed another remote charge under the railing when he passed by a section on the far side. A door leading into the salon on the main deck opened on well-greased hinges. He slipped inside and glanced around. An elegant set of stairs led down to the staterooms below.

He glanced down at the small, waterproof GPS in his hand. Makayla was down there. He strode across the salon, his fingers tightening around the grip of the gun in his hand. He paused, listening and scanning the area before proceeding. He calculated he had maybe seven minutes before Tyrell left. Brian had caught a glimpse of Ren Lu through the window out on the deck.

He glanced in each room when he passed by them. The familiar screen of Harrington's passcode caught his attention when he walked past one door. His fingers itched to place a small explosive under the desk, but that would be too easy. The key next to the computer was another matter, though.

Brian glanced over his shoulder before he stepped into the room and wrapped his fingers around the key. He glanced out the door before stepping back out moving down the hallway. Two doors down, the knob refused to turn. He slipped the key into the lock and turned it.

Pushing it open, his gaze swept over the bed where a figure lay. His breath released when Makayla leaned up on one arm to stare back at him, her expression changing from mutinous to relief and joy. He watched her slide off the bed and rush toward him.

Brian stepped inside the room and closed the door behind him. He opened his arms and wrapped them around her, pulling her tight against his body while he buried his face against her shoulder. A shudder ran through his body and he knew he was breathing heavily in an effort to control his emotions.

"You're okay," she breathed, drawing back so that she could search his face even while she ran her hands over his chest. "I saw the hole in your shirt."

"Kevin lent me his Kevlar vest," Brian said with a rueful smile. "It worked just as good as your grocery-filled bulletproof backpack."

"Thank goodness for a thick pork roast. I love you, Brian," she whispered, staring up at him before throwing her arms around his neck. "I never stopped."

Brian's throat constricted and his eyes burned. His arms tightened around her until he was afraid he would crush her, but he swore he could never hold her tight enough or long enough. He turned his head and pressed his lips against her temple.

"I love you more, Makayla," he whispered before reluctantly releasing her. "We need to get out of here."

Makayla nodded. "Henry?" She asked, staring back at him with a touch of fear.

Brian touched her cheek. "He wanted to come and kick some ass, but Kevin was having the doctor sedate his cantankerous butt," he murmured. "Wait here."

Makayla nodded. Brian brushed a hard kiss across her lips before carefully opening the door to the stateroom. He peered down the hall before motioning for her to follow him. Together, they went the opposite way he had originally come. Instead, he headed for the front salon and sunroom located near the bow.

They were almost to the front staircase when a sense of danger made Brian glance over his shoulder. Ren Lu was striding down the hall toward them. His head jerked up at the same time that Brian turned on the stairs. Brian's arm holding the gun immediately came up and he fired at the man. Ren Lu dove for the opened door of the office.

"Move!" Brian growled to Makayla, twisting and gripping her hand.

The two of them took the rest of the stairs two at a time. They raced across the front salon to the door leading out to the bow. Makayla bounced back into Brian when the door didn't open under her hand. She reached out and twisted the lock in exasperation before pushing it open. Once on the deck, she frantically glanced around.

Brian reached into his pocket and pressed the detonator to set off a delayed series of small explosives which he had planted in various areas of the yacht. They would activate with five second intervals between them, causing more confusion than damage. He needed to talk to Kevin about working with real explosives instead of the black powder kind he had been creating from the fireworks he had been buying.

A small cry of warning escaped Makayla when a guard came around the corner. Brian turned and fired at the man. Out of the corner of his eye, Brian saw an expression of determination sweep across Makayla's face. He turned in time to see Makayla's body hit the door they had just exited with enough force to knock

Ren Lu back a step. The man's eyes were glued to Makayla's mutinous face. Deciding he had had enough of this, Brian raised his gun and pulled Makayla back. Ren Lu stared back at Brian with a challenging glare before he raised his hands and stepped away from the door.

"Time to go," Brian muttered.

"Where?" Makayla asked breathlessly when he dragged her over to the railing.

"Over the side," Brian said, lowering his arm long enough to pick her up and hold her over the water before he released her.

A second later, he jumped over the railing after her. The dark water felt like it rose up to greet him. The chill in it forced out the air in his lungs. He kicked upward with strong, powerful strokes. His head broke the surface and he twisted in a tight circle, searching for Makayla. He turned his head when he felt a hand on his shoulder.

"Wh… What now?" She asked.

"Get on the board and hang on," Brian said, swimming for the anchor.

Their location shielded them from the spotlight. Brian helped Makayla up onto the board and untied it from the chain. Using the side of the yacht to help give him momentum, he pushed off with his legs and began swimming. The shouts coming from the men on the yacht warned them that they had been spotted. A round of bullets littered the water around them a second before they were drowned out by the hum of a motor.

"Grab her!" Brian yelled to Tyrell the second the Zodiac was close enough.

"I've got her," Tyrell said, leaning over and grabbing Makayla under the arms and lifting her out of the water like she was a child's doll.

Brian rolled into the boat and onto his back. He motioned for Tyrell to go. Within seconds, they were speeding across the dark water of the bay. Brian grimaced when he felt the rope to the paddle board slip out of his numb fingers. He was going to owe Kevin a new one.

"Brian," Makayla whispered, climbing along the bouncing boat on her hands and knees to where he was lying.

Brian rolled and shrugged off the backpack and opened his arms. He hugged Makayla's shivering form against him. Twisting, he sat down with his back against the side and her in his lap. He nodded his thanks to Tyrell when the other man reached into the compartment under the console and handed him a thin blanket.

"Are you okay?" She whispered, turning her face up to him.

Brian looked down into her worried face and raised a hand to run his fingers down along her damp, chilled cheek. She was safe. He cupped her face with his hand and kissed her like he would never let her go.

Chapter 27

Makayla sighed and snuggled closer to the hard, warm body pressed against her back. Her hand slid down the hairy arm encircling her until she could wrap her fingers around the hand splayed across her stomach. She dragged the large hand upward until it was free of the covers and pressed a kiss to the knuckles.

"Morning," Brian murmured, his voice husky from sleep.

"Good morning," she whispered, rolling onto her back so she could see his face. "You really are here."

Brian raised his eyelids, suddenly wide awake. He stared into Makayla's dark brown eyes for several long seconds, thinking the same thing. A smile tugged at the corner of his mouth when she raised her eyebrow at him.

"Yeah, I'm really here," he said, leaning forward and pressing a kiss to the tip of her nose. "What time is it?"

Makayla turned her head to check the clock on the nightstand and groaned. It was almost seven. They had only been asleep for a few hours. She winced when she felt some of the bruises and sore muscles that she had accumulated in the last few days.

Tilting her head, a soft giggle escaped her when she heard Henry's loud snores echoing through the wall. She looked up when Brian rolled over on top of her. He held his weight up on his elbows while he slid the lower half of his body between her legs.

"Thank you," she said, gazing up at him.

Brian shook his head. His throat worked up and down several times before he bowed his head and drew in a deep breath. She lifted her hands to cup his face. Her thumbs caressed the deep lines etched at the corner of his eyes.

"This job is going to make you an old man fast," she observed, partially teasing and partially being brutally honest.

"I feel it," he replied. "I love you, Makayla. I have to finish this assignment, but I promise things will change after it."

Makayla shook her head. "I don't want you to change unless it is what you want. And to clarify, we will finish this together," she said. "We make a good team, Brian."

Brian's gaze softened. "Yeah, we do," he replied in a soft voice, lowering his head to press a hard kiss against her lips.

They both turned their heads when a knock sounded on the door before it opened. Kevin peeked in and grinned. Makayla bit her lip when Brian scowled at his friend.

"Sorry, love birds, but daylight is a'wasting. You need to get a move on. Your dastardly friend either is as good as I am or has a friend who is because they have hacked the code and are on the move to The Red Brick House," Kevin said.

"How do you know they hacked it?" Brian asked, rolling off of Makayla and sitting up.

"I might have slipped a little added script in there to alert me," Kevin replied with a grin. "Tyrell and Helen are waiting for you two."

"Thanks," Brian said, throwing the covers back and rising out of the bed when Kevin closed the door behind him.

Makayla rolled out of the other side and drew up the covers. She grabbed her clothes while Brian disappeared into the bathroom to change out of the jogging pants he was wearing and into some jeans. Makayla quickly removed the oversized T-shirt and sweatpants she was wearing and pulled on a fresh pair of jeans, bra, panties, and blouse from the closet.

Brian came out of the bathroom buttoning a black dress shirt. Her eyes greedily ran over his lean frame. A rosy blush swept over her cheeks when he looked up and caught her staring at him.

"I'll be right out," she muttered, stepping toward the bathroom.

"Makayla," Brian murmured, touching her arm when she started by him.

"Yes?"

"I like the way you look at me," he said, lifting his hand to brush the back of his knuckles along her cheek. "I like looking at you, too."

The blush on her cheeks deepened and she ran her fingers along the rough whiskers lining his jaw in answer. She stepped away and hurried into the bathroom. Behind her, she heard the soft click of the bedroom door. She quickly used the bathroom and brushed her teeth and hair before pulling it up into a messy ponytail.

Makayla grabbed her purse, socks, and boots off the floor and hurried out the door. She gave the others an apologetic smile before sinking down into one of the chairs and slipping her socks on before pulling her boots on and tying them.

"Ready," she said, glancing around the room, skipping over Tyrell's grinning mug.

"Here's something for you to eat," Kevin said with a somewhat self-conscious look. "I may not be good at espionage stuff, but I make a damn good egg and cheese biscuit."

"I think you do a marvelous job with espionage," Helen murmured, reaching for the small bag he was holding.

Makayla grinned when Tyrell whistled under his breath. "I think there is some kind of love potion in the water around here," he muttered, grabbing one of the bags off the counter. "I'll meet you guys up at the car."

Makayla smiled her thanks at Kevin when he walked over and handed her a bag. "I'll keep an eye on Henry. Kyle is supposed to come by again later this morning to check on how he is doing. I'll also be following your progress and helping remotely if I can," Kevin muttered, glancing over at where Brian was checking weapons. "Good luck."

Makayla rose and brushed a kiss across Kevin's cheek. She could tell that the other man, for all his brash talk, was really just a shy nerd trying to cover it up. She squeezed his hand when he shot Helen a glance before looking away.

"Are you ready?" Brian asked.

"Yes," Makayla said, picking up her purse and sliding it over her shoulder.

Kevin walked with them as far as the end of the dock. "Don't you guys get kidnapped or shot or anything," he called out from behind them.

"Yes, dear," Tyrell called down from the car.

They all laughed when Kevin lifted both hands and shot Tyrell a double middle finger. Makayla knew she was still grinning when she reached the car. Tyrell gazed at her with a raised eyebrow.

"Shut up," she retorted before he could open his mouth. "Just… shut up."

Tyrell's laughter was infectious. Brian pulled out of the parking lot while Tyrell told Helen about what had happened the night before again, this time with a little more exaggeration. Makayla sat back against the seat and pulled out one of the egg and cheese sandwiches in the bag and took a bite. Hopefully, today would be the end of this adventure and life would return to normal.

***

Ren Lu stood in the empty red brick building. The muscle in his jaw tightened before he forced himself to relax. Pulling out his cell phone, he looked at the image of the puzzles once again.

He drew in a deep breath, turned, and retraced his steps. The incident last night had shown him that he had underestimated Jacobs. The fisherman in the boat had turned out to be none other than Tyrell Richards. He had to hand it to the small group, considering that Detective Woo and Jacobs were the only ones trained and experienced enough to carry out such an operation, they had accomplished a very surprisingly successful mission. Makayla's resourcefulness was also not lost on him.

He stepped out of the building and closed the door behind him. Crossing the street, he pulled his cell phone out when it vibrated. A look of distaste crossed his face when he saw Sun Yung-Wing's number. He slid his finger across the screen and raised the phone to his ear.

"Yes," he answered.

"They… They say time is up," Sun Yung-Wing muttered in a desperate, disorganized sentence. "I'm out of time. You have to have the information."

"Even with the information, your time is up, Mr. Sun," Ren Lu stated, opening the door to his car and sliding in.

"You promised…," Yung choked out.

"I promised I would protect your family and I have done that. My employment with you is now completed," Ren Lu replied. "I suspect you will be dead by the end of the day."

"You can't quit," Yung screamed into the phone.

Ren Lu ended the call. There was nothing he could do to save the other man even if he had wanted to. Sun Yung-Wing had made some deadly enemies, including some of the most powerful and ruthless governments in the world. He had kept his promise to protect the man's wife and daughter. Both had been sent to live in a province outside of Beijing. In a country with almost ten million people, it was easy to get lost.

Ren Lu merged into traffic. A few minutes later, he accessed the GPS in the rental car belonging to Tyrell Richards. A satisfied smile curved his lips. He would simply follow them and let them lead him to the information he had been assigned to retrieve.

Chapter 28

The sun was shining by the time they arrived at Tian Tan Buddha in Ngong Ping on Lantau Island. The massive, thirty-four meter, bronze statue rose up into the air and could be seen for miles. Makayla read through the information about the statue online.

"According to the Internet, this is one of five large Buddha statues in China, but the only one facing north," she said, reading the information out loud. "There are two hundred and sixty eight steps and three floors behind the statue."

"That's a whole lot of steps to climb. We have the GPS location that Harrington left, so that should help," Tyrell said, peering inside her breakfast bag and grinning when he saw another biscuit. "Are you going to eat this?"

"No, go ahead," Makayla replied with a wave of her hand. "The three floors are the halls of the Universe, the hall of Benevolent Merit, and the hall of Remembrance."

"What time does it open?" Brian asked with a frown, turning to follow the signs leading to the park.

"This says ten o'clock," Makayla replied, glancing at her watch. "We should be okay. It is five after ten."

"Should we split up?" Helen asked.

"No, I think it would be better to stick together. We have the location. We just need to find the next clue, solve it, and get to the final location where Harrington stashed the information," Brian muttered.

"What about Ren Lu? Do you think he will be able to figure anything out based on the information he has?" Makayla asked, leaning forward.

"I wouldn't put anything past him. We need to keep our eyes open," Brian replied, turning into the nearly deserted parking lot and parking the car.

Makayla opened the door and slid out of the car. She glanced around. There was hardly anyone at the temple yet. Adjusting her purse, she closed the door and walked around the other side with Brian.

Together, the small group made their way across the parking lot to the ticket and information center. Makayla reached into her purse and pulled out her sunglasses. Slipping them on, she gripped Brian's hand and started climbing the stairs. From a distance, they looked like a young couple on vacation.

***

The top of the temple was circular and offered a breathtaking view of the mountains surrounding the temple. Six smaller statues, three on each side of the staircase stood as silent sentinels. Makayla read that they were known as the Six Devas and symbolized the Six Perfections. Makayla walked over and studied each one. She wished they had more time and really were here as tourists.

"Makayla," Brian called to her.

She turned and gave him an apologetic smile. "It's beautiful," she said.

Brian held his hand out to her. She slid her hand into his and felt his strong fingers wrap around her hand. He drew her close to his side and let go of her hand to wrap his arm around her waist. A shiver ran through her when he caressed her hip. For once, she was grateful that Tyrell was distracted and in heaven taking pictures.

"Brian, Makayla, this way," Helen called out.

Makayla saw Helen holding the small GPS that Kevin had given them. They walked around the circle of the Buddha to the other side. Helen moved back and forth, until she stopped in front of one of the small statues. This one was holding incense.

"Morality," Helen murmured, looking up at the statue.

"Harrington said you never knew when your time was up and you had to make the right choice based on how you wanted to live your life. He refused to stop living because of his job. He had a wife and son," Brian remarked in a quiet voice.

"There has to be some type of message and location," Tyrell said.

They spread out to look around. Makayla studied the statue. Harrington must have left them some type of clue, something to guide them. She stopped to look at the bronze plaque. Squatting down, she read the bottom of it. She was about to stand up again when a tiny spec of plastic caught her eye. Glancing around, she shifted and knelt on one knee. It took several tries before she could get a good enough grasp on the tip of the plastic that was barely visible and gently pull it out. Her heart sped up when she saw a piece of paper in the tiny plastic bag.

"Brian," Makayla called out, standing back up. "Brian, I think I found something."

The other three hurried over to her. She carefully opened the zip lock top and withdrew the paper. Unfolding it, she saw a set of numbers and the words.

The White Rabbit

"What does that mean?" Makayla asked, looking up at Brian.

"The coordinates are to Tai Po. That is over ten hours from here," Helen said.

"I'll let Kevin know," Brian replied, sliding his cell phone out of his pocket. "He'll be able to pinpoint the location."

"Kevin, we have the last clue," Brian muttered. He relayed the coordinates and glanced at the other three while he waited for Kevin's response. "We're headed there now. I'll keep you posted as to what we find."

"What did he say?" Tyrell asked, shifting the camera bag on his shoulder.

"Fong Ma Po Tsuen. It is in the Lam Tsuen Valley," Brian said.

"What is there?" Makayla asked, puzzled.

"The Wishing Tree," Helen answered. "It is a very respected place. The tree is believed to be a medium, allowing us to communicate between the gods and spirits. When I was young, my father took me there to hang a wish from the tree."

"Did it come true?" Tyrell asked, tilting his head to stare down at Helen's bemused face.

Helen blinked and nodded. "Yes," she replied with a serene smile. "Yes, it did."

..*

Ren Lu sat in his car in the parking lot. He had located the car that Tyrell Richards had rented, and parked so that he could keep an eye on it. For the hundredth time, he looked down at the drawing of the Buddha. If he was to believe the information Harrington had left, there should be one last place – the place with either the final clue or the actual information.

His hand moved to the gun he had laid across his lap. He checked the clip. Laying it on the seat next to him, he covered the gun with the coat he had removed.

He didn't have long to wait before he saw Brian Jacobs and the others winding their way through the cars. His gaze followed Makayla. Jacobs was holding her hand and smiling down at her. A shaft of emotion, possibly jealousy, shot through him. His fingers itched to erase the smile from Jacobs' face.

Ren Lu frowned. He had never experienced such strong emotion before. He focused his gaze on Makayla when she brushed a strand of hair back from her cheek. The memory of her touching that cheek when she had spoken of the man who had hurt her mother ignited a slow, burning rage at the unknown man who would hurt Makayla. Her comment about having the choice of either going to live with her grandfather or the state-run facility had hit home. Up until his ninth year, that was exactly where he had grown up. It had shaped who he was to become, especially after he was recruited.

Ren Lu started the car. He would give them plenty of leeway. Since the rental car had GPS tracking in case the car was stolen, there was no need to keep a visual on them. He waited ten minutes before he left. His gaze moved to the device mounted on the dashboard of his car. He relaxed and breathed deeply. Instead of working out the details of his assignment, he let his mind roam. This was something he seldom allowed and focused on more pleasurable thoughts, like Makayla.

Chapter 29

The sound of traffic woke Makayla the next morning. She glanced over at Brian's relaxed face. He was exhausted from driving all day yesterday. There had been sections of the road under construction, and it had been after midnight before they had finally reached their destination.

Helen had booked three rooms for them. The innkeeper had been very sweet when she saw how weary they were, and ushered them inside. Makayla had barely had the energy to change before she collapsed on the full sized bed. Brian hadn't been far behind her.

She slipped out of the bed and walked over to the tiny bathroom. She using the facilities, then brushed her teeth and her hair. She had slept in her T-shirt which was now very wrinkled. Shrugging, she quietly pushed back the curtain covering the bathroom. She walked over to the bed where Brian was lying propped up with his arm behind his head.

"Hey," she whispered, sliding across the soft fabric until she was facing him.

"Hey, yourself," he replied.

Makayla briefly closed her eyes when he ran his fingers along her cheek. A smile tugged at her lips when she opened them to stare at him. Her gaze softened when she saw the searching look in his eyes.

"I could get used to this," she said, kneeling next to him.

"Good, because I was planning on making this permanent," Brian said, drawing her closer. "Will you marry me, Makayla Summerlin?"

Makayla drew in a startled breath. Her eyes widened and she stared at him in shock. She had expected that they would be a couple, but she had never expected him to ask her to marry him. Her lips parted and she felt a moment of panic. So much had happened in the last few days, and now Brian was asking her to marry him.

"I…," she started to say before her voice faded.

"Say yes… please," Brian murmured.

Makayla's head started moving on its own – or at least without her being consciously aware that it was answering him. Brian drew in a deep breath before he released it. Leaning forward, he brushed a kiss across her lips before he jerked her forward with a soft chuckle.

"I love you, Makayla Summerlin," Brian murmured, rolling with her until she was caged beneath him.

"Yes," Makayla finally forced out, her eyes glittered with love. "I love you, too, Brian, more than you can ever know."

"How about you show me?" He asked with a wicked grin.

"You sure are bossy," Makayla teased and ran her hands down over his shoulders before moving across his chest.

"I could definitely get used to this," he murmured, sliding his hands around her waist and pulling her down so he could brush a series of kisses along her jaw.

..*

It was over an hour later before Makayla and Brian came downstairs. Tyrell and Helen were seated at a table near the corner. From Tyrell's empty plate and Helen's almost empty one, Makayla knew they had given up waiting for them.

"Morning," Makayla said, not looking at Tyrell's pointed gaze.

"Brian, I hope you plan on making an honest woman out of Makayla," Tyrell growled playfully, turning on Brian when Makayla refused to be baited.

Makayla leaned over, picked up the knife off of Helen's plate, and pointed it at Tyrell. She gave him a look that warned him to be careful what words he said next. Helen's amused chuckle told her that the innkeeper was watching with a wide, unsure expression.

"Glad you're having some fun, my friend," Tyrell said with a chuckle before slapping Brian on the shoulder. "I'll assume from Makayla's threat that things are going well."

"I asked her to marry me and she said yes," Brian retorted, reaching for the coffee.

"Whoa! I didn't see that one coming," Tyrell replied. His face lit up in a huge smile and he rose from his chair to pull a reluctant Makayla into a bear hug. "I'm happy for you, Makayla. Congratulations."

"Congratulations, Makayla," Helen added with a smile.

"You know, Brian is part of this too," Makayla mumbled against Tyrell's chest.

"You are one lucky man, Brian. I just want you to know if you break her heart, Henry and I will be there to.... Ow!" Tyrell broke off when Makayla pinched him hard.

"Congratulations do not come with threats," Makayla growled, returning to her seat.

"Congratulations, man," Tyrell muttered to Brian holding his hand out and shaking Brian's with a firm grip.

"Thanks, Tyrell," Brian replied with a hard squeeze to Tyrell's hand before letting it go.

"Damn, you're stronger than you look," Tyrell grumbled, rubbing his hand in mock agony.

"Just remember that," Brian retorted with a grin.

"After you eat, we should head to the Wishing Tree. I'll drive," Helen said.

"What happens when you get the information we've been searching for?" Makayla asked, smiling in appreciation and murmuring her thanks to the innkeeper when she brought a fresh pot of tea and two more cups.

"I turn it in," Brian replied, pouring a cup of coffee into his cup and grabbing several slices of pineapple bread, some thin slices of marinated fish, and fresh fruit.

"I talked to my father and Commander Wang this morning," Helen said, glancing at Brian. "We have been cleared, thanks to a very well respected witness who came forward."

"Mrs. Leu?" Makayla asked in surprise.

"Yes," Helen said.

"Do we have any idea of where Ren Lu is?" Tyrell asked, leaning forward and bracing his elbows on the table. "And what of the guy that ordered Henry's kidnapping?"

"Sun Yung-Wing committed suicide yesterday afternoon," Helen said, folding her napkin and placing it next to her plate.

"Suicide?!" Makayla exclaimed, her eyes wide with disbelief.

Helen nodded. "It would appear he fell out of his office window, a very difficult task with impact resistant windows," she added with a wry curve to her lips. "His bodyguards insist that no one else was in the office with him at the time and there are no video cameras in his office."

Brian's face was grim. "They were setting an example," he said.

"Who was setting an example?" Tyrell asked.

"Whoever doesn't want the information found," Brian replied, pushing his plate away and rising from his chair. "We'd better go."

"That's a hell of a way to die," Tyrell mumbled, standing and grabbing his backpack off the back of the chair.

"Isn't that the truth," Makayla replied, following the others.

***

It didn't take long for them to reach the Wishing Tree. Large wooden supports helped to stabilize the massive branches of the century old banyan tree. There were scars where previous branches had broken off. The tree was surrounded by a low, metal fence with signs posted in a variety of languages prohibiting the hanging of paper placards or other items from the tree.

"There is a wishing board," Makayla said, reading the information about the tree.

Helen parked the car a short distance down the road. Makayla released Brian's hand, opened the door, and slid out. She smiled at him when he exited the other door. It had been nice sitting with him in the back seat while Tyrell rode up front with Helen for a change.

"This way," Helen said with a nod.

Makayla felt Brian capture her hand again and they walked along the sidewalk, gazing up at the tree. There was something majestic about the ancient tree with some branches growing down to form additional supports. Several older women stood nearby. Each of them was holding a small piece of paper and whispering. Makayla watched in fascination while the women tied colorful ribbons to the papers before turning and walking over to a large building shaped in the form of a temple.

"That must be it," Tyrell muttered.

"Wow! There must be thousands of cards here!" Makayla exclaimed, glancing at all of them. "How are we going to find the one that Harrington left?"

"We split up," Brian replied with grim determination.

"Don't forget the message; the White Rabbit," Makayla added, slipping her hand from Brian's and walking to one side of the board.

Makayla drew in a deep breath. There were literally tens of thousands of tiny pieces of paper attached to the wall. She shook her head at the overwhelming task of searching through each one. She was about to comment on the fact when a shop's sign caught her attention.

She stepped closer to the board and tilted her head so that she could see between two of the branches of the banyan tree. On the other side was a row of several shops, including one with a display featuring an advertisement for White Rabbit candy. In the corner of the window display was a statue of a white rabbit.

"Helen," Makayla called out in a soft voice.

"Yes," Helen responded from where she was searching through the board.

"Where did the GPS say we were supposed to go?" Makayla asked, still staring past the Wishing Tree.

"Here," Helen replied, glancing up when she heard the note of curiosity in Makayla's tone. "Why?"

"Makayla, did you find something?" Brian asked, walking over to stand next to her.

"I think so," Makayla replied with a nod of her head. "What if Harrington marked this spot, but his note pointed to where he had hidden the information?"

"What…?" Brian started to say before he glanced at where she was staring. His eyes widened. "White Rabbit."

"White Rabbit candy," Helen murmured, shaking her head in disbelief. "Of course!"

"Isn't that some kind of candy that got a bad rap for killing a bunch of kids a few years ago?" Tyrell asked.

"Yes, but it is addictive. I can't eat just one piece," Helen admitted.

"You're a genius. Let's go," Brian said, brushing a kiss across Makayla's lips before he reached for her hand again.

***

Ren Lu straightened from where he was leaning against his car. His gaze narrowed when the small group turned to follow the path around the Wishing Tree instead of returning to their car. They were heading for the line of tourist shops on the other side. He could tell from the way they were moving and the excited expressions on their faces that they had finally discovered where the information was hidden.

Stepping away from his car, he strode around the opposite side of the path. He casually reached into his pocket and fingered the gun in it. He kept them in his sights, planning the best way to obtain what he had come for, and leaving with it. His gaze moved to the linked hands. Jacobs had an Achilles' heel, and that weakness was named Makayla.

Chapter 30

The delicious aroma of candy washed over Makayla the moment the door was opened. Her stomach growled and she self-consciously placed her hand over it. Despite the fact that she had eaten breakfast just a short time ago, her mouth watered to sample some of the tasty treats.

"Makayla and I will look around the statue while you two check out the rest of the store," Brian suggested, shooting a meaningful glance at the elderly clerk behind the counter.

"I'll go charm the old lady," Tyrell muttered with a mischievous grin. "That is one thing I'm good at."

Makayla's lips twitched when Tyrell turned a brilliant smile on the woman and began chatting. She highly doubted the woman understood a word of what Tyrell was saying, but he had captured her attention. Makayla walked beside Brian while Helen moved about the store like she was interested in the products on display.

The window display was open to the store's interior. The almost three foot high wooden rabbit was surrounded by fake grass and bags of sugary confections. Makayla reached out and ran her hand down along the back of the rabbit. She paused when she felt a small, round opening in its back. It looked like the display had been mounted elsewhere at one time.

"Can you feel anything inside?" Brian asked, glancing over his shoulder to check on Tyrell and the clerk.

Makayla slid a finger into the half-inch size hole. Her hand froze when she felt cool plastic. Stepping closer, she carefully worked her finger deeper into the hole so she could pull the item out. Triumph filled her when she saw the end of a flash drive. Pressing down, she slid it the rest of the way out.

"Bingo," she whispered, turning to Brian with a huge grin and holding out the flash drive.

Brian flashed her a pleased grin and reached for the flash drive. He turned and cleared his throat to let Helen and Tyrell know that they were done. Tyrell muttered something to the clerk and turned toward them. Makayla saw the grin on Tyrell's face fade and grow hard. She glanced toward the door to the shop when it opened and a tall man stepped in. The soft sound of her swiftly inhaled breath warned Brian and Helen of the danger that had entered the store.

"I wouldn't, Mr. Jacobs," Ren Lu stated, closing the door behind him and turning the lock. He reached up and flipped the sign from 'open' to 'closed'. "Keep your hands out and step toward the counter."

Makayla could feel Brian's body stiffen with fury. His body tensed even more when Ren Lu pointed the gun at her. She swallowed and gripped Brian's arm.

This was the cold blooded killer who had shot her the first time.

"How did you find us?" Brian asked, stepping toward the counter.

Ren Lu spoke in quiet Cantonese to the elderly clerk instead of answering Brian. She replied, her gaze flickering nervously between him and the gun he was holding. Ren Lu spoke again, this time in a curt tone.

"Everyone please follow Mrs. Chan to the back," Ren Lu ordered. "If you try anything, I will kill Makayla first."

Makayla bit her lip to keep from making a nasty retort. She started to step forward ahead of Brian, but Ren Lu shook his head and motioned for Brian to go first. Brian's soft curse echoed in the room.

Makayla jerked when Ren Lu gripped her arm and pressed the gun against her side. He squeezed it in warning when she tried to put some space between them. She scowled at him, but kept her mouth shut.

"I will kill him this time, Makayla," Ren Lu warned.

Makayla's throat tightened at the menacing promise. She understood what Ren Lu was telling her – resist and Brian dies. If Brian resists, she does. It was a lose-lose situation.

She followed the others through the beaded doorway into a long, but narrow back room. The room contained a small, round table with two chairs, a sink, and was filled with boxes of candy. To the side, there was a bathroom about the size of Mrs. Leu's utility closet.

"I'll take what you found," Ren Lu ordered.

Brian's lips tightened and his fingers curled around the flash drive. Makayla drew in a frightened breath when Ren Lu moved the gun he was holding and pressed the cold tip of the barrel to her temple. Her body began to shake and she had to lock her knees to keep from collapsing.

"Here," Brian said in a hoarse voice. "Please...," he started to say, his eyes wild with rage and fear.

"Take it from him and hand it to me," Ren Lu ordered Makayla.

Makayla reached out a trembling hand and took the flash drive from Brian. Her fingers caressed his hand when she did. Fear that it might be the last time that she ever touched him made her linger longer than she should have and she flinched when Ren Lu's fingers bit into the soft flesh of her arm.

"Here," Makayla whispered in a barely audible voice.

Ren Lu took the flash drive from her. She closed her eyes when he didn't remove the gun. Her lips parted and she fought the urge to scream at him to just get it over with if he was going to kill her. Her eyes popped open when he spoke.

"Get into the restroom," Ren Lu ordered.

"All of us?" Tyrell asked, glancing skeptically at the tiny room before he raised his hands when Ren Lu turned the gun on him. "I'm not arguing."

"Smart move, Mr. Richards," Ren Lu replied in a calm voice. "Go."

Makayla watched the others move into the cramped space. She wasn't sure they would all fit. Ren Lu kicked the door closed with his foot.

"Prop a chair up under the handle," he ordered.

"What… What are you going to do with me?" Makayla asked in a trembling voice, following his order.

"Sit down in the chair," Ren Lu instructed in a hard tone.

Makayla didn't need to be told twice. Her legs were shaking so badly, she was actually thankful for that one small order. She sat down in the chair, a little nervous when it wobbled.

"Put your hands behind your back," Ren Lu said, pulling several plastic ties from his pocket.

"You know this is déjà vu, don't you?" She muttered when he looped the strap around her wrists and pulled it tight.

Ren Lu's warm breath brushed against her cheek when he released an amused chuckle. She turned her head to glare at him. A swift gasp escaped her when she realized how close his face was to hers. She stared at him with wide, startled eyes.

"So beautiful," he whispered, running the knuckles of his right hand along her cheek.

Makayla closed her eyes when he leaned forward and pressed a soft kiss to her lips. She was surprised that his lips were warm. She blinked when he pulled back and stared at her for several long seconds.

"Such a shame," he murmured before rising. "Good luck, Makayla Summerlin. I hope our paths meet again."

Makayla knew her mouth was hanging open when Ren Lu quietly opened the back door of the shop and stepped out. She blinked, shocked not only by his tender kiss, but the fact that he hadn't killed any of them.

"Bri… Brian," Makayla called out.

"Makayla!" Brian's muffled voice echoed through the door.

"He's gone," she said in a voice loud enough to be heard. "I'm tied to a chair in front of the door. I think I can move it."

"Let me know when you are clear," Brian responded.

It took several tries before she could straighten the chair and bounce it far enough to the side. She was fortunate it didn't break. Once she was clear, she yelled out to Brian. Several minutes later, the door was opened and she was free.

"God, I was terrified he had taken you again – or worse," Brian muttered, his body trembling violently while he held her pressed against him. "I love you, Makayla."

Makayla's arms tightened around his waist. She was shivering with reaction and shock. Her gaze moved over to where Tyrell was talking to the elderly clerk while Helen made the woman a cup of hot tea on the ancient hot plate.

"The information...," Makayla started to say before Brian silenced her with a kiss.

"Fuck the information," Brian finally said, resting his forehead against hers. "Nothing is worth your life."

"I'm so sorry, Brian," Makayla whispered with regret.

"The governments will find another way to discover what they want to know," Brian assured her, straightening so he could glance at the others. "We need to get back."

"I'm good with getting back to normal," Tyrell muttered. "Oh, by the way, the government owes me a new lens. I busted my nice one saving your ass."

Epilogue

"What's wrong?" Makayla asked, glancing up at her grandfather two days later. "You look like you've either just won the lottery or been struck by lightning."

"That was the Royal Hong Kong Yacht club," Henry said with a shake of his head. He rubbed his broken arm before he scowled down at the cast. "This damn thing itches and I can't scratch it."

Makayla rolled her eyes at his complaining. "What did they say?" She asked.

"They said the *Defiance* is back in her berth," Henry grinned.

"What?!" Makayla exclaimed, sitting up from where she had been lounging on the back of Kevin's boat waiting for Brian to get back from the Consulate. "Are you serious?"

"Yep," Henry grinned. "Do you feel up to taking a drive?"

Makayla frowned. "I'm not about to learn to drive in this traffic," she muttered. "Did you call a taxi?"

"No, I asked Tyrell to take us. Brian is going to meet us there," Henry said.

"Oh! Cool. I'll go get my stuff," Makayla replied, rising from the lounge chair.

She slid past Henry, pausing to brush a quick kiss against his weathered cheek. It was good to see the healthy glow return to his face. The doctor Kevin had hired to check on Henry had assured her that all her grandfather needed was time and rest to recuperate.

Since they had returned two days ago, life had been busy. Helen had been reinstated at the police department and was investigating Sun Yung-Wing's mysterious suicide. She had also dropped by the previous night to have dinner with them, much to Kevin's delight. Kevin had volunteered to help Helen with her investigation. From the rosy glow on Helen's cheeks when Kevin made his offer, Makayla suspected that Helen had been very pleased – and not just from a professional interest.

Brian had returned to work at the Consulate and had been gone more than he had been there. Makayla was surprised at how much she missed him when he was gone. She had gotten used to being with him almost constantly over the past week. They still had the nights, though, she thought with a wave of warmth.

"I'm ready," she said, pulling her hair out from where it had gotten caught under the strap of her purse when she had slung it over her head. "Thank you, Kevin, for everything."

"Anytime. I enjoy the company," Kevin grinned. "All this espionage stuff sure beats sanding and polishing."

Makayla laughed and gave Kevin a hug before brushing a kiss across his cheek and stepping back. She suspected his enjoyment had more to do with a certain Hong Kong detective than it did the spy stuff. She knew the eccentric billionaire was still searching for Ren Lu. The man appeared to have disappeared off the face of the Earth.

A short time later, they were heading over the bridge back across to the yacht club. A smile curved Makayla's lips when she saw Brian and Helen standing near their cars when they pulled up. Makayla eagerly pushed open her car door the second Tyrell pulled to a stop.

"Hey," she said, her eyes glued to Brian's tall, lithe form.

"Hey yourself," Brian chuckled, brushing a kiss across her lips before he nodded to Henry and Tyrell.

"Have you been aboard her yet?" Henry asked, turning to the dock.

"No, we just arrived a few minutes before you did," Brian said.

"Is everything okay?" Makayla asked, following the others when they walked down the dock.

Brian released a deep sigh. "Yeah, they aren't happy that the information is gone, but shit happens," he said with a shrug.

"I'm so sorry," Makayla said, feeling his disappointment.

"Life goes on," he replied in a soft tone, squeezing her hand. "I'd much rather it be with you."

Makayla nodded. She knew he was thinking of Harrington. She had been shocked when he had shown her a picture of Harrington with his wife and son last night. The familiar, smiling face of a woman she had met a little over a week ago looked back at her along with that of a small boy – Hsu Lee-Harrington. Makayla realized that Hsu must have used her given name for protection. A wave of sadness swept through her at the pain and grief the woman was currently living through. Her heart ached for the little boy who would never know his father.

She and Brian had talked about it for hours last night. It had taken quite a bit of arguing before Makayla had finally accepted that Brian would be transferring to a less dangerous position in the United Kingdom. In the meantime, he would have a couple of months off before he transferred and would sail part of the trip back with them to Hawaii.

"I can't believe the *Defiance* is back," Makayla laughed, staring down at the sailboat. "It looks fabulous!"

"It doesn't look like anything was damaged," Henry replied, climbing down into the companionway.

"Did anyone see who returned it?" Helen asked, stepping onto the schooner.

"Not that I know of," Henry's gruff voice echoed from below. "Makayla, Brian, you two might want to come."

Makayla glanced at Brian with a confused frown. He jumped aboard before he turned to help her on to the stern of the *Defiance*. She released his hand and followed him down into the cabin.

Henry was standing near the table. He turned and held a white envelope with Makayla's name clearly printed on it. Makayla took the envelope. There was something in it besides the paper.

Tearing it open, Makayla dumped the contents out into the palm of her hand. It was a small flash drive – the same plastic and color of the one from The White Rabbit. She glanced up at Brian with a confused expression. She handed the flash drive to him and carefully unfolded the paper, reading the message neatly printed inside.

"What does it say?" Helen asked, scooting closer so she could look over Makayla's shoulder.

Makayla cleared her throat. "It says… It says 'Makayla, you were right. Being good is harder, but being bad is sometimes necessary if the greater good is to survive. Ren Lu'."

She glanced up at Brian. His face was taut with disbelief while his fingers turned the flash drive between them. He glanced back at her.

"Do you think it is…?" She asked in shock.

Brian nodded. "Yes. I think it is the information we were searching for. I don't know how or why, but if it is genuine, this could save thousands of innocent lives," he said. "I need to get this to my handlers."

Makayla nodded, turning to follow him. They climbed the steps. She gripped his hand when he helped her onto the dock.

"I'll see you later this evening," she whispered, hugging him tightly to her. "Be careful. If anyone knew you had this information...."

Her throat tightened. If the men who had killed Sun Yung-Wing knew that information was in Brian's hands, he would be a target again. She didn't know why Ren Lu had had a change of heart, but she was happy that he had. She couldn't help but wonder at his motives though.

"This doesn't change anything," Brian promised. "I'll see you this evening. Ask Helen to stay if she can. If not, I want all of you to return to Kevin's until I can go through the sailboat."

"I'll let you know where we'll be," she promised, brushing a kiss across his lips before deepening it. "I love you, Brian."

"Not half as much as I love you," Brian said before reluctantly stepping away.

Makayla watched Brian return to his car. She didn't return to the *Defiance* until he had disappeared from sight. Hugging her arms around her waist, she stared across the water. The sun was shining and the city of Hong Kong stood majestically bordered by the mountains in the distance. She turned and searched for the yacht that had been anchored in the bay, but it was gone. Overhead, a helicopter cast a shadow before it disappeared over the water and down along the bay. Makayla lifted a hand to shield her eyes when it passed over before turning and climbing back aboard the *Defiance*.

"Old man," she called out with a humorous grin. "Brian wants us to check the *Defiance* to see if Ren Lu left anything else."

..*

Overhead, Ren Lu held the binoculars steady until they passed over the figure below. He lowered them to his lap when he could no longer see the dark-haired girl watching from the dock. He calmly motioned for the pilot of the helicopter to continue to the yacht anchored offshore. He released a deep breath at the unexpected emotion burning through him.

He had completed his mission for the Chinese government with a few modifications. It would not hurt for other governments to have the information he had copied. In fact, it was a necessity if the world was to become a safer place. He pulled his cell phone from his pocket and quickly dialed the number he had programmed into it.

"Yes," the man on the other end said in greeting.

"Mr. Jacobs, I have information that might be of interest to you," Ren Lu stated, staring down at the roof of Brian's car crossing the Causeway.

"I'm listening," Brian stated in a voice filled with caution and interest.

To be continued…. **Freedom of the *Defiance*.**

When Tyrell Richards unwittingly photographs the brutal assassination of a major world leader, he finds himself on a hit list and must ask for help from some old friends who discover plans for another assassination – this time targeting the British Prime Minister.

Additional Books and Information

If you loved this story by me (S.E. Smith) please leave a review. You can also take a look at additional books and sign up for my newsletter at http://sesmithfl.com and **http://sesmithya.com** to hear about my latest releases or keep in touch using the following links:

Website: http://sesmithfl.com
Newsletter: http://sesmithfl.com/?s=newsletter
Facebook: https://www.facebook.com/se.smith.5
Twitter: https://twitter.com/sesmithfl
Pinterest: http://www.pinterest.com/sesmithfl/
Blog: http://sesmithfl.com/blog/
Forum: http://www.sesmithromance.com/forum/

Excerpts of S.E. Smith Books

If you would like to read more S.E. Smith stories, she recommends Touch of Frost, the first in her Magic, New Mexico series. Or if you prefer a Paranormal or Western with a twist, you can check out Lily's Cowboys or Indiana Wild…

Additional Books by S.E. Smith

Short Stories and Novellas

Dragon Lords of Valdier Novella
For the Love of Tia (Book 4.1)

Dragonlings of Valdier Novellas
A Dragonling's Easter (Book 1.1)
A Dragonling's Haunted Halloween (Book 1.2)
Night of the Demented Symbiots (Halloween 2)
A Dragonling's Magical Christmas (Book 1.3)

Pets in Space Anthology
A Mate for Matrix

Marastin Dow Warriors Short Story
A Warrior's Heart (Book 1.1)

Lords of Kassis Novella
Rescuing Mattie (Book 3.1)

The Fairy Tale Novella
The Beast Prince
*Free Audiobook of The Beast Prince is available:
https://soundcloud.com/sesmithfl/sets/the-beast-prince-the-fairy-tale-series

Boxsets / Bundles

Dragon Lords of Valdier Boxset Books 1-3
The Alliance Boxset Books 1-3

Science Fiction Romance / Paranormal Novels

Cosmos' Gateway Series
Tink's Neverland (Book 1)

Hannah's Warrior (Book 2)
Tansy's Titan (Book 3)
Cosmos' Promise (Book 4)
Merrick's Maiden (Book 5)

Curizan Warrior Series
Ha'ven's Song (Book 1)

Dragon Lords of Valdier Series
Abducting Abby (Book 1)
Capturing Cara (Book 2)
Tracking Trisha (Book 3)
Ambushing Ariel (Book 4)
Cornering Carmen (Book 5)
Paul's Pursuit (Book 6)
Twin Dragons (Book 7)
Jaguin's Love (Book 8)
The Old Dragon of the Mountain's Christmas (Book 9)

Lords of Kassis Series
River's Run (Book 1)
Star's Storm (Book 2)
Jo's Journey (Book 3)
Ristéard's Unwilling Empress (Book 4)

Magic, New Mexico Series
Touch of Frost (Book 1)
Taking on Tory (Book 2)

Sarafin Warriors Series
Choosing Riley (Book 1)

Viper's Defiant Mate (Book 2)

The Alliance Series
Hunter's Claim (Book 1)
Razor's Traitorous Heart (Book 2)
Dagger's Hope (Book 3)
Challenging Saber (Book 4)

Zion Warriors Series
Gracie's Touch (Book 1)
Krac's Firebrand (Book 2)

Paranormal / Time Travel Romance Novels

Spirit Pass Series
Indiana Wild (Book 1)
Spirit Warrior (Book 2)

Second Chance Series
Lily's Cowboys (Book 1)
Touching Rune (Book 2)

Paranormal Novels

More Than Human Series
Ella and the Beast (Book 1)

Science Fiction / Action Adventure Novels

Project Gliese 581G Series
Command Decision (Book 1)

Young Adult Novels

Breaking Free Series
Voyage of the Defiance (Book 1)
Capture of the Defiance (Book 2)

The Dust Series
Dust: Before and After (Book 1)

Recommended Reading Order Lists:

http://sesmithfl.com/reading-list-by-events/
http://sesmithfl.com/reading-list-by-series/

About the Author

S.E. Smith is a ***New York Times, USA TODAY, International, and Award-Winning*** Bestselling author of science fiction, romance, fantasy, paranormal, and contemporary works for adults, young adults, and children. She enjoys writing a wide variety of genres that pull her readers into worlds that take them away.

CPSIA information can be obtained
at www.ICGtesting.com
Printed in the USA
LVOW13s2315291216
519203LV00006B/86/P

9 781942 562856